313

Death Prone

Death Prone

CLARE CURZON

St. Martin's Press
New York

Library of Congress Cataloging-in-Publication Data

Curzon, Clare.
Death prone / Clare Curzon.
p.   cm.
"A Thomas Dunne Book."
ISBN 0-312-10453-7 (hardcover)
1. Yeadings, Mike (Fictitious character)—Fiction.   2. Police—England—Thames River Valley—Fiction.   3. Thames River Valley (England)—Fiction.   I. Title.
PR6053.U79D4   1994
823'.914—dc20   93-45246   CIP

First published in Great Britain by Little, Brown and Company.

First U.S. Edition: March 1994
10 9 8 7 6 5 4 3 2 1

ONE

Francine

OLD MATTIE TOOK MY COAT and showed me into the Hall of Mirrors, which in fact isn't a hall. That was a phrase I'd picked up as a child, taken on some early visit to a funfair most likely. But that's how it had first struck me, seeing myself repeated into infinity by the walls of glass, and the name lodged in my mind for ever.

It was really – had been, decades before I was born – a ballroom, but at that time had its furniture stacked and covered in dust-sheets. Later, in my adolescent imagination, I'd seen it in action, waltzed and polka-ed through its elegant assemblies, the crinoline hoops, the silken bustles, the powdered shoulders glittering with diamonds and emeralds, and the superb bewhiskered gentlemen. Even, in a splendid frenzy of imagination, I'd partnered a dark hero in full hunting fig, my chewed fingernails poised on shoulder of pink jacket. I remember still the delicious frisson occasioned by his baroque smile, the diagonal scar cutting his arched left eyebrow.

All that belonged to my lost years of torchlight scribblings under blankets. Since then I've dropped the lush prose. As a technical expert, I avoid clichés. The ballroom is itself a cliché, but it has significance, being also a part of my life, part of my family's history.

Maybe that was why Uncle Hadrian – Great-uncle to be precise, and when testamentary provisions are in the air it's wise to get things right – had chosen to have us all gather there. The customary dust-sheets were off, the floor waxed, crystal chandeliers ablaze, two dozen gilt and

1

brocade sitting-out chairs set round a central table with all its spare leaves inserted. Its vastness caused us to create our own social islands, with oceans of withdrawal in between.

Hadrian Bascombe had a more comfortable chair alone at its head, as befitted his status and poor health.

Perhaps status isn't the right word. He comes quite a long way down my list of worthwhile people. But he was the oldest dinosaur among us, and by a long chalk the richest. Therefore the most interesting prospect financially.

The rest of the family – by no means the twenty-four needed to fill the chairs provided – were distributed round the table according to personal preference. That is to say that Edith Halliday (Hadrian's second younger sister's only daughter) had gratefully lowered her tightly packaged bulk on to the chair nearest the door we entered by. Cousin Alastair, easily cowed as ever, had presumably been hallooed and roped in beside her, leaving the next trio to slip past and settle half-way between Edith's camp and that of our formidable host. Going by their previous track record I assumed they had met by appointment and steeled themselves to their social duty in some hotel bar.

Josh, my favourite of the family, and my mother's thin-thatched elder brother, had clearly done much the same with a round of golf and the nineteenth hole. There were still green smudges on the bottom edges of his beige slacks. I went across to where he lounged on the table's far side and took the chair he pulled out for me.

I should explain that Josh and I share our surname of Webster with the three then seated opposite; Josh, Morton and Mother having been the children of Hadrian's first younger sister. And Mother having neglected to marry before my birth. Perhaps my arrival had discouraged her, because despite two later marriages I remain her unique offspring.

There are three members of my generation. My cousin Dominic sat opposite, between his mother Marcia and father Morton. Hadrian's only other great-nephew, Edith Halliday's son Piers, was understandably excused attendance, being in North Africa with Voluntary Service Overseas. Which enables him to keep out of Edith's way until time relaxes her determination to force him into his late father's legal partnership in Oxford.

That explains all those present, I think. Except Alastair whom most of the family prefix with 'Cousin', his dead mother having been a much younger step-sister to the affluent dinosaur.

Hadrian's full sisters are dead too, and it was because he had announced his own imminent demise that we remnants had been called together. Mother alone had declined to put in an appearance and offered no excuses, but then our host would have expected no more and no less. He considered that Elinor Webster had always been a headstrong girl and was now a wilful middle-aged woman.

I eyed the family present, set apart in its three groups at the table with the old man at its head, and I observed that he was indeed very old and had shrunk into the carapace of his winged chair, an effect exaggerated by the way light fell only on the wrinkled backs of his horny hands and on the slightly shiny shoulders of his grey-green jacket. He looked like some ancient turtle up-ended, rolling its scaly head on a stringy neck, occasionally blinking its colourless eyes, and ready to withdraw if it found the external world not to its liking.

He caught my glance and gave a minimal nod in my direction. 'Last as ever, Francine,' he said drily, and the meeting was open.

Until then, except for the briefest of acknowledgements on entering, there had been no conversation. It was like being in church before service began. This was the way he chose to have it, had trained us to defer to him. And maybe, I thought, watching him carefully, it was a wise way of reserving what little energy he had left.

He spoke to us in his usual manner, which was mocking and disdainful, perhaps pausing more often and a little longer than on previous occasions. At the time I wondered if it was an affectation or a genuine indication of his failing strength. He had always been one to calculate his effect on others and modify the message accordingly. When he shifted slightly I caught the bright gleam of his eyes under their half-lowered lids. Whatever his health, he wasn't doped then. He gave the impression of having a special controlled tautness. It could be that he was in considerable pain.

For all that, he took his time, played his fish. Which was us. We'd all come for the same reasons: because no sane person offends a man who could alter the lifestyle of any of us with a flourish of the pen; and because – whatever we thought of him – we all wanted to know how soon the waiting would be over.

None of us, I think, came out of respect for the man himself. The most I could raise was a grain of rueful affection, because just now and then I saw in him something of Mother, and I'd a horrid suspicion that I'd never get him out of my genes. Perhaps I admire him a little for being able to glory in his own awfulness.

He knew what was in all our minds then. He spelled it out, grinning as he dwelt on our individual vulture ambitions: the Morton Websters' mania for ostentatious luxury, Edith's losing battle against nonentity, Cousin Alastair's incunabula-addiction, Josh's abstention from conventional efforts to gain the *dolce vita*, the youngest generation's eagerness to dazzle.

In my case he was perfectly right, so I assume he had equal intelligence of the others' needs and intentions. Perhaps he was a little less harsh on us young ones, but I winced just the same at the accurate assessment. Opposite me Dominic let out a wounded 'Honestly, that's hardly fair!' The absent Piers was unable to reply for himself but Edith bridled on his behalf, past coherent protest since she was already seething at Hadrian's more than adequate appreciation of herself.

The Morton Webster couple were stiff with chagrin and suppressed denials. This was during their own character assassination, after which Marcia turned a brightly eager gaze on the next victim, while Morton carefully assembled an expression of shocked disbelief.

Josh had taken it the best of us all, but then he *is* the best of us, at least in my opinion. He did his bloodhound thing, wrinkling his forehead, stared at the ceiling, his lips puckered in a silent whistle, and at the end nodded gravely in agreement.

'And so,' Hadrian continued, quavering ever so little, 'I find myself in a quandary . . . the sands running out so fast, the choices for me so few . . . those I leave to carry the torch . . . so miserably inadequate. Indeed, a poor lot . . . As you must know, I have always intended —' (wicked old man, that was his longest pause) '—that my fortune should . . . remain whole and undivided . . .'

Now there was an audible straining at the leash by at least half the contenders.

'. . . and nothing has persuaded me . . . of the widsom . . . of doing otherwise.'

He lay back in the wing chair and his face was hidden in shadow. His grey, mottled hands hung down as though all life had drained away. I thought it had been too much for him and I was on the point of rising to ring for his nurse when Josh kicked me smartly on the ankle.

'So I suppose,' the old voice quavered on again, 'that you are all curious . . . to know . . . my in . . . ten . . . tions.'

He raised both hands in mock helplessness. 'Well, I just don't know. But tonight . . . tonight I shall decide. Perhaps . . . on the fall of a coin . . . Who knows?' His sigh ended as a cough, and he gripped the table's edge while he fought for breath.

He stayed leaning forward, his turtle head outthrust, the dark eyes baleful as he surveyed us. 'But first I mean . . . to take my last farewell . . . of each of you . . . singly, as you are summoned. Until . . . I send for you . . . be so good as to gather . . . in the drawingroom . . . where you will find refresh . . . ments.'

As we stood he flicked a finger underneath the table and a distant electric bell sounded. Before we had all filed out to troop downstairs the rear double doors opened and the Asian male nurse entered in his white drill jacket and trousers. Josh closed the doors after us and we left the old man to be propped up for the next set of confrontations.

'Old age must be the worst disease of the lot,' Josh muttered as he followed me down.

'But don't pity him. He won't have that.'

He shook his head. 'I just feel sorry – and astonished – that the world must go on without him. It won't be the same.'

I stopped in my tracks. 'You're going to miss him?' But of course he would. In our own ways we all would. For myself – I knew suddenly I'd be upset, even shed the odd tear. Not for old Hadrian; just that sometimes life was sad, but the idea of leaving it even sadder. 'The end of an era,' I said aloud, but that wasn't quite what I had in my mind.

We all wondered what order he would take us in. Twenty minutes went by while we supped, courtesy of Fortnum and Mason, and then I was the first he called. The Parsee nurse came down and stood at the door. 'Miss Webster, please.'

'Miss or Mrs?' demanded Morton's Marcia sharply, ever a stickler for protocol.

'Miss Francine,' said the deep sing-song voice, and I put down my glass. 'Eliminating the impossibles first,' I assured them lightly and followed Mr Chadwala upstairs again, back to the Hall of Mirrors.

My great-uncle seemed to have recovered somewhat. He sat in the same chair but had Mr Chadwala pull out another for me round the table's corner so that by sitting slightly sideways we faced each other. The great crystal chandeliers had been turned off but a standard lamp shone full on me. Behind its glare he was a mere shadow. The surrounding walls of mirrors gleamed dully like pewter in half-darkness, mocking my remembered dreams of romance.

'You really are a wicked old man,' I told him, and he chuckled.

'Did you enjoy my little drama?'

'In a rather nasty way, yes.'

'You always did tell the truth.'

'*Nearly* always.'

'There you are, you see. Well, what shall I say to you now that we are private?'

'I think you said quite enough about me in front of the others. How about asking after Mother?'

'I don't need to ask. I know all about her. And about her new lover.'

'Then why don't we talk about you?'

And to my surprise we did. I asked questions and he

6

answered them, albeit briefly. His age was ninety-one, what he suffered from was emphysema and it bored him. If I didn't already know how he'd made a second fortune out of the one his mother had left him, he wasn't going to bother telling me. And I needn't think that showing all this interest in him personally was flattering. The sincerest form of flattery was imitation, and I couldn't escape that; it was born in me. 'When you're an old woman,' he threatened, 'you'll be just as awful as me! Worse, because you're a female.' He was still cackling when he rang for Mr Chadwala to see me out.

'Be so kind,' said the little Parsee, 'as to ask Master Dominic to come upstairs. And please to take your coat from Mrs Mattie and go home without speaking to the others.'

An odd request, but it was an odd evening altogether. I interpreted it literally, put my head round the drawing-room door and beckoned Dominic out. I told him I'd give him a lift back after he'd seen old Hadrian. There was nobody there I cared to say more to then, and I had Josh's phone number in my diary. So I just went out to the car and waited.

TWO

SUPERINTENDENT YEADINGS SIGHED AND TAPPED the pages which DI Mott had replaced on the desk. 'As requested, she didn't speak *to anyone else*, but she did to her cousin. She also took literally the message I sent, asking them all to write everything down as it happened, and to add their own impressions, so her florid verbiage is partly my fault, I guess.'

'She even took it literarily,' DS Beaumont said, grinning round at the rest of the team.

'M'm. Whatever she said about restraining her prose, it's hardly what you'd expect from a self-styled technical expert,' DI Mott agreed.

'What kind of . . .?'

'She graduated in Physics with Electronics, works for a West London conglomerate as technical writer, produces the nitty-grittyspeak that goes out with the hardware. Not advertising blurb.'

'Interesting. It makes this subjective account appear even weirder. Is she as candid as she sounds or just clever at pulling the wool?'

'That's what I'd like you to find out, particularly in view of our vehicle examiner's suspicions. I haven't met her myself. You're more her generation and she sounds a challenging young woman. The local sergeant was rather bowled over. See if she responds to you differently.' Yeadings handed the folder of papers to his DI.

'And the other accounts of Bascombe's clan gathering?'

'Factual for the most part, and censored concerning whatever disclosures the old man made about them personally. You might find Joshua Webster's diagrams useful. His family tree sketch and the seating plan for the meeting confirm what his niece Francine described.'

The Superintendent removed the reading-glasses he had recently admitted he needed for close work, and rubbed at the red mark on the bridge of his nose. He'd taken the damn things back to have the frames adjusted, but the man had only fiddled with the ear-pieces and the sore nose continued. At this rate he'd probably need to pad himself with cotton wool.

Mott grunted, running a finger over the family tree as he compared the sketch with Francine Webster's account.

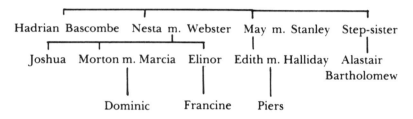

'Nothing fresh, except for Cousin Alastair's surname: Bartholomew. The old man's generation all dead. The seating plan agrees. Josh Webster isn't giving much away, is he?'

'Questioned on the lack of personal impressions, he said, "They're a dreary lot mostly, so all I really noticed was old Hadrian. It struck me he wasn't too well." A laid-back type, our Josh. Just before he left he mentioned he was the last one summoned for the tête-à-tête. At that point everyone else had left. He observed that the old man called them in precise order of age, youngest first, except that the real number one was absent – Piers Halliday, the lad who's abroad.'

'Leaving Francine to start the ball rolling. No sex discrimination in that, then. The family's a bit short on male heirs. The name Bascombe's disappeared, the old man being a bachelor who had only two sisters and a step-sister. His nearest male relatives are nephews Joshua and Morton Webster. Joshua appears to be unmarried without issue. Morton and Marcia have the one son, Dominic.'

'—who were the trio Francine was careful to avoid sitting with, preferring Uncle Josh. Dominic's twenty-seven, four years older than his girl cousin. The absent Halliday lad, Piers, is just twenty years and ten months.'

'Are we sure he's really where he's said to be?'

'Ethiopia? I'll have VSO check that. I'd like you to chat with his mother, before you see Francine. Meanwhile let's look again at that car business. Do we accept that Francine offered Dominic a lift at the time she says?'

'I don't see why not. She had the opportunity.'

'If she'd wanted to,' surmised WDC Rosemary Zyczynski, 'she could have claimed that Dominic scrounged the lift.'

'M'm, dodgy. Since he could later deny it.'

'When she wrote her statement nobody thought he'd survive. Just as well she didn't pretend it was his idea. We've complications enough.'

Rosemary was tracing routes on the ordnance survey map. 'It was a reasonable offer. See, the Morton Websters' house is at Beaconsfield, about eighteen miles south-south-east of the old man's. And Francine would have to pass through on her way to Stoke Poges, here. Another six miles or so. Near enough for her to keep in easy touch with the Websters.'

'But there didn't appear to be much contact.'

Mott nodded. 'You want us to sniff around, see what the locals have to say about family divisions?'

Yeadings grunted. 'We've little man-power for what could still prove to be pure accident. I can spare you twenty-four hours. Get them all talking about each other. There seems to be some deliberate distancing there. We might as well know why.'

'Not a very united family,' Mott agreed.

'Drawn together on a single string,' Yeadings reminded him. 'Great expectations. Enough to rally them to a very rich old man in his final days and then set them at each others' throats. That's all some people need as a motive for murder.'

'So Dominic Webster was the second one his great-uncle interviewed. Do we have a statement from him?' DCI Atkinson, paper-chaser to Yeadings, pursed his lips at the Superintendent, gloomily envisaging more shoals of ill-typed reports and print-outs.

'Fragments given us in his conscious moments, unsigned as yet. For the rest, it's a question of waiting, I'm afraid. However, I'll read you what we've put together.'

Yeadings cleared his throat and readjusted the near-sight glasses. ' "Francine went first. She was gone about fifteen minutes. Then she put her head round the door and beckoned me out. I thought she wanted to talk, but she just said, 'You're next. I'll wait outside and give you a lift back.' Mr Chadwala was waiting at the top of the stairs, so I didn't argue." '

'Did Dominic say what the old man talked about?'

'He hasn't touched on that yet. The essential was to find out what happened later. He had no recall of the accident or of the circumstances immediately leading up to it, but he remembers calling Cousin Alastair as number three to be interviewed. As he collected his coat from the housekeeper he left a message for his parents that he'd gone on ahead. Then he went out to join Francine.

'It was a crisp night, bright starlight with the beginnings of a ground frost. His cousin had the engine already running to keep warm. She moved across, expecting him to drive. He got in, remembers clipping on his seat belt and starting off. That's about his lot, and it leaves us dependent on the girl for her version of the accident, which we don't yet have in writing.'

'And this Francine didn't belt up?'

'Apparently not. Which is why she was thrown out when the car left the road.'

'Or she could have seen what was coming, unclipped and jumped clear in time.'

'As you say, she could have jumped. A cab driver coming up from Wendover saw the car go over the edge and a body thrown free. He did what he could, and

11

radioed back for help. A patrol car and ambulance were on the spot within twelve minutes. Fortunately the car didn't burn and firemen were able to cut the young man out. It was left on the hillside overnight, craned up and taken by loader to the Central Garage the following afternoon, probably an insurance write-off. In the meantime there'd been a sudden two-inch fall of snow there, and a slightly greater depth on Bascombe's driveway, which was cleared before anyone thought to look for traces of brake fluid.

'The preliminary breakdown report on the car said there had been no severing of the brake cables, but escape of brake fluid from the reservoir under the bonnet could have occurred prior to the accident. No great notice paid to that until this suspicion voiced by the injured man's mother that the car had been rendered defective. Which is when our own vehicle examiner took a look. You'll find his preliminary report attached.

'The brake system had certainly bled, whether where it was wrecked, on the girl's way up to Bascombe's, during the car's wait outside, or as young Dominic applied the brakes in negotiating sharp bends on the way down. So the crash could certainly be blamed on partial brake failure, probably compounded by panic reaction on the driver's part and the icy state of the road.'

'Had he driven the girl's car before?'

'We don't know, and he can't tell us yet. One interesting point: it looks as though the girl's aversion to his parents doesn't extend to Dominic himself. Or else she had some special reason for wanting to talk to him that night and to be free of handling the car while she did so.'

Atkinson considered this sombrely. 'Is Mrs Webster seriously implying the girl deliberately set up the accident? Risking her own car, let alone injury to herself?' He scratched his chin. 'Admittedly, with her practical background she'd surely be capable of arranging the brake failure.'

'She's also the only one with obvious prior access, the bonnet catch being operated from inside the glove compartment. And when she'd said goodbye, Mrs Mattie

Cooper waited at the house door to see Francine inside her car. She's certain the girl had to unlock it to get in.'

'Which doesn't guarantee that *all* the car's doors had been properly locked when she left it. Not to mention judicious fiddling of the windows with a wire coat-hanger.'

'Or someone else with access to her keys.'

'What do the experts say unofficially?'

'What you'd expect. It could have been accidental. On the other hand . . . So we have to look into it. Especially with the young man's mother shrieking like a steam valve under pressure.'

'With what precise accusation in mind? – GBH, or attempted murder? And what chance is there of her suspicions being founded on fact?' Atkinson challenged.

The Superintendent's eyebrows bristled just short of his hairline. 'That last is for the team to answer. And it'll have to be soon. Kidlington's rumbling on about known serious crimes already on our books. Nothing would please them more than to cross off one dubious murder attempt. But no short cuts. It has to be proved an accident, or else we collar some villain to stand trial.

'For twenty-four hours the team's off all other assignments. DI Mott's in charge with DC Silver, and Sergeant Beaumont paired with WDC Zyczynski. They've until noon tomorrow to get an answer. By which time Aldermaston could have come up with more detail on the car.'

'What's bitten the Boss?' Beaumont had mouthed as they reached the corridor after Yeadings' briefing.

'Hassle from on high,' Mott assured him. 'Live long enough and you may get some from me.' He grinned at the sour reception the others gave this.

'Right, you lot. First, Silver and I will see Morton Webster, while Beaumont and Z get Edith Halliday's statement. She lives in Headington. Then I want Z with me at the hospital when I pour honey on Mrs Morton Webster. She's screaming for action but won't leave her son's bedside. If she does have anything solid to go on we need it immediately, but I'll probably have to set up an appointment to interview.'

13

'How about the girl, Francine Webster?' Z asked. 'Is she still out of action?'

'Discharged herself twelve hours after being admitted. Attending Outpatients for dressings. Has two broken ribs, abrasions and considerable bruising. At present she's staying with her mother and stepfather near Henley. Under protest, it seems. Her solicitor phoned in a warning that her earlier statement was made while under the influence of prescribed drugs, and he insists on being present when we interview her again. And that will include questions on the actual crash. There's a lot we need to ask her, but for the moment we're letting her stew.'

'Get the others to dish the dirt on her first,' Beaumont said with grim relish.

Rosemary Zyczynski glanced sideways and decided that he was still in a mean mood, but at least he'd gone into forward gear. The mere hint of an attempted murder investigation had set his adrenalin surging, as for them all. Except perhaps the Superintendent this time. He'd seemed subdued. She wondered if there was anything wrong with his family. Not Beaumont's sort of trouble; that was unthinkable, Nan Yeadings being stability itself. But either of the children ill? It was hard on a man with his responsibilities to go home to a toddler's problems, as well as his Down's syndrome daughter.

Mike Yeadings dismissed the now compliant DCI Atkinson and took his reading-glasses off with both hands, the way the optician had demonstrated. He'd been doing everything scrupulously as instructed and the damn spectacles bit in worse by the minute. Now it wasn't just the bridge of his nose that hurt but the eye sockets themselves, with a dull, angry throbbing reaching up towards his temples and down into his back teeth. He refused to advertize his discomfort by roaring for aspirin. He would soldier on, get his desktop a little clearer and then make for home as circumstances permitted.

Angus Mott rang through for news of Dominic's progress and found that he had been transferred to Stoke Mandeville's spinal unit. The Sister on duty there would give no information by telephone, except to say that Mrs Webster was at her son's bedside. The husband had visited but been called away earlier that afternoon on business.

'Business,' Mott muttered and searched through his papers again. 'Do we know what the man does?'

'Gravel-digging and haulage,' Silver told him. 'You've seen those whacking great container trucks with Webster plastered all over them. Same Webster. He employs the men that run the plant that digs the holes that yield the gravel that fills the trucks to make the roads that carry the trucks that bring back the rubbish that refills the holes . . . to make the fortune that Jack built.'

Mott eyed him. Silver was the quiet one. That must have been his longest sentence yet since he joined the team. And it smacked of Beaumont's heavy humour. Maybe it was as well he'd split that partnership before Silver turned into a ventriloquist's doll.

'Big money,' the DC went on with unconcealed envy. 'He just sets the ball rolling and the chain gang gets on with turning it all into gold.'

'The enterprise society,' Mott said shortly. 'And we're supposedly a service industry, so let's not get political. Turn up his office number and I'll buzz him.'

But Morton Webster was not at work. His secretary hedged and then, reminded that the police inquiry concerned his son's serious injuries, admitted that she had phoned him at the hospital about a fictitious conference, and so released him from the boy's bedside. On her boss's orders, yes.

'So we should find him at home?' Mott inquired.

'That's where he said he'd be going.'

Mott thanked her, rang off and pointed Silver towards his coat. 'Let's catch the man right now. The secretary bird could make another call to warn him, and he sounds the slippery sort.'

Webster's gravel had to be extracted from a limitless source at the end of a rainbow, Mott considered as the two detectives drove between handsome brick pillars topped by stone gryphons, and followed a winding drive through landscaped gardens. An eight- or ten-bedroomed modern house built like a Spanish villa – white stucco, Moorish arches and all – set south-facing in four or five scenic acres was a long cry from the agricultural cottages facing the blown grit and stench of his filling-in dumps. But then, Mott mused, life was like that: architects didn't live in the tower blocks they perpetrated, any more than Members of Parliament were obliged to walk the streets enforcing the laws they fabricated. We all shove the consequences of our actions on to the next guy. Somewhere in between, democratic consensus is supposed to reconcile things, but only after considerable irritation and waste of energy.

Webster wasn't to be faced in his tycoon rôle today, however, but as the distressed parent of a young man possibly paralysed for life as result of an RTA. Mott had time to make the mental gear-change between envying the man's success and recalling his cause for grief. And, he asked himself ruefully, since those who rise to the top of the pile take disaster all the harder, who will he be shifting the blame to?

Surprisingly Webster hadn't been drinking, or nothing more stimulating than tea. The two policemen were shown into a chintzy sitting-room with a log-burning fire. The gravel and haulage master sat deep in an armchair with a low table before him. His discarded tray of tea things was on the floor beside his feet and he had been turning the pages of glossy country magazines. Blindly for solace, or to spot future rich pickings on the land market? Mott wondered as he took the chair which the man indicated.

'A bad business, sir. Is there any news of your son's progress?'

Webster glared at him from bloodshot eyes tucked too closely under the shadow of a bill-hook nose. He was long and thin, the almost translucent flesh of his face netted with broken blood vessels so that at a distance his floridity gave him a deceptively healthy appearance. But not a happy man from habit, the DI thought. The downturned mouth between deep calliper grooves had set that way decades before this recent blow. Seated higher opposite him, Mott looked down on the angular, mottled face

16

framed by a pair of sharp knees on which the long-fingered hands spread limp and pale.

'They say there's some hope of partial recovery. But then they would. I don't suppose they know much themselves yet.'

'Waiting's not easy.'

'Indeed it's not. My wife . . . my wife believes . . . Oh, I don't know what she believes. But she has to hang over him, willing it to come all right. She's . . . a very determined woman, but I can't help thinking . . . Still, it does no harm, I suppose.'

His voice was unexpectedly deep but the words were spoken with a finicky precision that was almost old-maidish.

'We have your statement here about the meeting at Mr Bascombe's house last week, sir, and wondered if you would care to alter or add to it in any way.'

'I doubt it. I can't say I remember very clearly just what I wrote. No, no point in showing it to me. I've just smashed my spectacles.'

He pointed pettishly to the floor where Mott made out the mangled shape of gold rims and the glint of scattered glass against the pale Chinese carpet. Surely no accident, this. He must have heeled the lenses thoroughly. So, under pressure, Webster was subject to childish tantrums.

'I have a copy with me. I'll read it through, sir, if you wish.'

'Do that, then.'

' "On Friday January seventh I received an invitation to visit my uncle Hadrian Bascombe at his home, Lynalls, above Halton, near Wendover, Bucks. The invitation was for two days later. It was in the nature of a family gathering and my uncle implied that due to his great age and failing health he wished to make clear his testamentary provisions for us.

' "It appeared, however, that he had drawn up no precise plans, but intended to interview each of us in turn after addressing a welcome to the family in general. Everyone invited attended, with the exception of my sister Elinor Godden and her husband, and young Piers, son of

17

my cousin Edith Halliday. I understood that he was excused due to Voluntary Service Overseas.

' "We all met together with my uncle first, then while awaiting our turns to speak with him individually we took refreshments in the downstairs drawingroom where the housekeeper Mrs Cooper had set out a cold buffet.

' "For some reason my uncle chose to interview the young people first, starting with my niece Francine, the absent Elinor's daughter. Some half-hour later I observed that my son was no longer with us. Cousin Alastair was also missing but came in shortly afterwards. I assumed that Dominic had followed Francine to see my uncle, and on referring to Mrs Cooper I was assured that this was so. Francine had left without taking her leave of us.

' "I continued my conversation with Edith and Cousin Alastair until he was summoned by my uncle's nurse. Mrs Cooper then came in and said that Dominic had already left. 'Gone on ahead,' were the actual words. I couldn't see quite how he had done so unless he had rung for a taxi, since we all three arrived together. He has his own car but had left it at home.

' "I was the last but one of the family to see my uncle. Consequently when my wife and I left, there remained only my elder brother Joshua's Ford Sierra in the courtyard. I drove by back lanes down to the main Amersham road, avoiding Wendover. There was little traffic about and on arriving home my wife and I retired to our bedrooms where the maid had left thermos flasks with our customary drinks. We assumed Dominic had gone socializing with friends. I was a little overexcited by the events of the evening and took two sleeping tablets to ensure that I didn't lie awake. It was therefore my wife who was awakened with the news of the accident, by a visit from the local police. It was quite difficult to rouse me. I was in no condition to drive, and we were taken by police car to the hospital at Aylesbury.

' "This was the first we knew of Dominic's having shared his cousin Francine's car. The accident had occurred at one of those bends on the way down to Wendover. Due to icy road conditions and unfamiliarity with the much

18

lighter car, Dominic, who was apparently driving, had lost control and the car went off the road, rolling sideways down the hillside. Both Dominic and his cousin were injured, but to what extent it is not known." '

There was a short silence as Mott put the papers together again, then Webster groaned, knotting his hands together and covering his eyes. 'Well, we know more now. He's paralysed. Could stay that way for the rest of his life.'

'He's in the very best place, sir. They pull off near-miracles at Stoke Mandeville.'

'Maybe, maybe.' He faced Mott impatiently. 'Well, that statement stands, I think. There's nothing to add.'

'Perhaps you'd be good enough to answer one or two questions arising from it, sir.'

The man looked away, his face sagging. Even the broken veins seemed to have drained of blood. 'Ask on, then.'

'You explained your nephew's absence but not your sister's. Was she also abroad at the time?'

Webster frowned. 'No, of course not. She turned up at the hospital about two hours after us. Didn't they tell you? She came to see Francine.'

'It's probably in another of the statements, sir. But why didn't she come to the family gathering when her daughter did?'

'I've no idea why Elinor does anything. She's totally unpredictable. Except that . . . yes, I should have guessed she wouldn't turn up. She wouldn't be bothered about what Uncle Hadrian had to say. And perhaps she'd expect to find out everything from Francine at some later date when they met up.'

'She wasn't interested whether he would make her a beneficiary in his will?'

'Not *a* beneficiary, Inspector. It was *the* beneficiary. That was the stupid idea he had: to keep the entire fortune in one piece, instead of sharing it sensibly around. We were all family after all. Every one of us had a right, and a need, to some consideration. But he decided to do just what his mother had done. Causing just as much unnecessary bitterness, it goes without saying. He inherited everything,

19

because he was the only son. God knows what yardstick Hadrian in his turn was using to make his choice, but you can be sure it was intended to cause the maximum discord.'

Colour had come back into his face, but now he looked blue. As Silver was to remark after they left, 'Went all colours of the Union Jack, and in the right order, didn't he?'

Mott watched the DC make a note of the answer, then went on. 'Did your wife notice that Dominic had disappeared from the supper room, sir?'

'Saw him called out by Francine, apparently. Didn't she put that in her statement?'

'We don't yet have a full one from her. But later, when Alastair Bartholomew was called away from talking with you, didn't she expect her son to return? She would surely have been anxious to know what the boy's great-uncle had said to him.'

'Like a cat on hot bricks,' the man said bitterly. 'She had great hopes that Dominic would be chosen heir, being the eldest grandchild of Hadrian's generation, and male into the bargain.'

'But she made no attempt to find out where he had gone?'

'She had no reason to suppose he'd left the house. There were several things he might have been occupied with inside it. He was always interested in the library there, or he could have gone to a bathroom. Eventually when Mrs Cooper came to inform me he'd 'gone on ahead', naturally I went across and told my wife.'

'I see. And did she then show any concern about his having left with his cousin?'

'She didn't know, how could she? Like myself she assumed he'd rung for a taxi. I think I may even have said as much. "The boy's taken a cab home. Wouldn't wait for us." Something of the sort.'

'And your wife's reaction?'

'Eh? Oh, speculative, I suppose you'd call it. She calmed down a bit, said she suspected the old feller would have given instructions that no one was to return to the others after he'd seen them. Sort of trick interview such as you give high-flier candidates, where surprise is the necessary element. She rather purred over that, thinking Dominic might stand a good chance at that sort of thing.'

'And I understand that your own interview with Mr Bascombe was the last but one.'

'That's right, before my brother Joshua. We went in after Edith.'

'*We?* Your wife accompanied you?'

'Yes. We were the only married couple there. My uncle . . . er, chose to consider us as a single unit.'

His voice had become tighter and a spot of red flamed suddenly in each cheek.

Hadrian sarcastic about Morton's inability to rise above Marcia's domination? Mott asked himself. If Francine's description of the old man had been anywhere near correct, certainly there would have been some kind of taunting, and even before their interview it seemed that neither of them had excessive expectations for themselves, only for their boy. So they considered themselves out of favour. The old man had been having malicious fun at the expense of them all. Which left one almighty question unanswered.

'So at the end of this series of private discussions,' Mott ventured, 'what conclusion had Mr Bascombe reached?'

'How the hell would I know?' roared Webster, rising in exasperation to his feet. 'The future's left in limbo, isn't it? Just like my son!'

THREE

WDC ROSEMARY ZYCZYNSKI CRUISED ALONG Ashbourne Avenue, scanning gateposts and fanlights. Some had numbers, but the majority boasted only names: Fairview, Lyndon, The Limes, Eversfield. A middle-income district with middle-class pretensions and middle-brow tastes. The house they were seeking was on the near side: Medlow, a between-wars semi-detached, and if not mock Tudor that was only because its architect lacked any talent for satire.

The blue Ford Escort rolled to a stop just past it, then reversed to be opposite the privet hedge of its small front garden. DS Beaumont leaned forward from the passenger seat and grunted. Dull and respectable, was his mental comment. He turned to his companion. 'Go on, then. Give the lady a buzz.'

'I thought that since I'd done the driving . . .'

'Don't get bolshie, Z. I stay in radio touch. You do the running.'

Rosemary unclipped her seat belt, suppressing the irritation which had risen slowly like boiling jam throughout the sergeant's prolonged listing of women's less favourable aspects, a muttered cadenza beginning when she'd picked him up from his home and broken only by the necessity to be quiet in the Boss's presence. She wondered if he meant her ears to stand proxy for those of the once rebellious, now unwelcomely returned, wife Cathy. Or perhaps familiarity had made Beaumont forget that she was the token female of the team, accustomed as he now was to taking her as a decent enough chap.

A searing wind tore at her nylon-clad legs as she swung them out. She snuggled deeper into the sheepskin car coat she had bought in the sales with Auntie's Christmas cheque. She had intended reserving its silver-grey elegance for best occasions, but the weather had demanded otherwise. Sooner or later a proper attention to the job was going to require sudden sacrifice of its pristine beauty. She admitted it was a mistaken self-indulgence succumbed to in the aftermath of coloured lights and Christmas carols, but at present a consolingly comfortable one.

Dead oak leaves ticked in a flurry round her ankles, interspersed with the occasional snowflake. She walked up the short flagged path and pressed the doorbell. Silence built up for a moment before she rang again and stepped back to survey the blank windows. A third attempt still brought no reply. Rosemary went back and bent to the misted car window. Beaumont cleared a patch.

'Shall I try the neighbours?' she mouthed.

The DS gestured for her to go round and get back in. 'We'll take a break, see what comes up.' He had found her supply of butterscotch (for emergencies only) and could barely speak. As she settled in beside him he generously offered her one. They sucked in silence but for the background messages from control.

Nine-fifteen on a Monday morning. The early business and school traffic was clearing at the road's end. Only three cars had pulled away from houses in this street since their arrival. There should be a lull before the next rush for ten a.m. clocking-on; though maybe the locals – executive and managerial to a man – were way above signifying their arrival at work. And home by five, Beaumont thought sourly. With nerves untaxed and all their energies conserved for the diversions of the evening; clubs and pubs and birds you kissed goodbye when replacements hove in sight. Wives, maybe, in the background, beavering away at committees and evening classes; children grown up and away. Some have all the luck.

Ahead, on the far side, a stoutly bundled female figure was fiercely pedalling towards them on a too-small bicycle, knees pistoning under chin, grey hair escaping from under a close dark hat. She swerved across the road to pull up before their windscreen, lugged the bike on to the pavement, propped it against the privet hedge and came to rap sharply on Beaumont's window. 'You can't park here, young man!'

Slowly the DS wound down the glass, flicked the butterscotch, now mercifully small, into one cheek, and regarded the woman levelly. 'Mrs Halliday?'

She hadn't expected to be addressed by name, smote her breast as if winded, and demanded, 'If I were, who would you be?'

He had his warrant card ready, having recognized the type. She took it from him, held it at arm's length and attempted to read without her glasses while he enlightened her. Finally she darted several piercing glances between the photograph and the man it unflatteringly portrayed.

'This is my colleague, Detective-Constable Zyczynski. We should like a word with you, Mrs Halliday.'

'I really can't imagine why.'

'There's no reason why you should,' the man said flatly.

She frowned. 'Why I should what?'

'Exert your imagination. If you will give us a few moments of your time we will tell you exactly what we wish to find out.'

'Oh.' She beat her breast again, took a deep breath and suggested, 'You'd better come in, then. We can't converse out here in this frightful wind.'

But there was no offer of tea or coffee when she had unlocked the front door, using a key-ring on a long chain which she groped for in some inner layer of clothing. She dumped on a hall table the newspaper for which she had made her sortie, showed her two visitors into a severely furnished sitting-room on the right of the entrance hall and grudgingly turned on a gas fire in the hearth to supplement the feeble background heating.

She waved them to seats, perched, still in her outer clothing, on the edge of a lattice-backed chair, and demanded, 'You have some questions for me? You are at liberty to ask them, but I must warn you that my late husband was a solicitor and I know you have no legal right to force me to a reply.'

Beaumont had by now decided he wouldn't care to force her even through a cheese shredder, but with the promise of some degree of opposition on her part he was warming to his task.

'Quite,' he agreed. 'And in any case it's likely that you won't be able to remember. With a lapse of over a week most people . . .'

Edith Halliday bridled visibly at being classed with the majority. 'I assure you there is nothing amiss with my memory, young man.'

'Sergeant,' he reminded her helpfully.

If she sniffed, it might have been due to the change of temperature from outdoors. In any case she took a moment to search her person, produced a handkerchief and trumpeted into it. 'A week, you say. Then doubtless this is some inquiry arising from that unfortunate accident of young Dominic's. Well, of course, I shall say nothing that might in any way prejudice his case. I trust you are not expecting . . .'

'His case, Mrs Halliday? What case would that be?' The Pinocchio face was all innocence, the eyes quite circular.

'Well, his insurance, I assume. Or the girl Francine's, since I am informed it was her car, though I can't understand why they . . .' Her voice tailed off.

'Yes?'

'I can't – er, see how I can help you.'

'Mrs Halliday, you said "I can't understand why *they* . . ." Perhaps you were going to speculate on why Dominic Webster shared his cousin's car on leaving when he'd arrived in his parents' Rolls.'

'Yes, the *Rolls!* Naturally Morton would turn up in that, wouldn't he? Wanted to demonstrate to Old Hadrian how well the trappings of wealth sit on him. Some of us aren't so fortunate. And Marcia with her pastel mink and French perfume! You'd think the message would have reached her by now that no thinking woman hangs dead animals on her body any more or uses preparations that have been tested on poor dumb beasts!'

25

For an instant Beaumont pondered whether dumb beasts were rendered speechless by the sheer verbosity of their defenders. 'So why didn't Dominic choose to return in equal comfort?' he suggested to her, to stem the flow.

'Obviously they were up to something.'

'The cousins.'

'Yes. Oh, I don't suggest they were romantically involved – though I wouldn't put it past either of them to make a show of some such in order to double their chances with their great-uncle. It's all a question of money, you know. Some people will do anything for it. The more they have the more they want. They're in its power. It's a drug!'

Unoriginal, Beaumont considered, yet true. But the implied obverse – that those without money were free of its lure – was a damn lie. He sighed and decided to put on some pace. 'You came about half way through those Mr Bascombe saw individually, I believe.'

'The fourth. After Francine, Dominic and Cousin Alastair. Though why *he* should have precedence over me I can't imagine. He's not a blood relation at all.'

Imagination again confessedly beyond her. Yes, that might well be so, the DS reckoned. He gave in to the imp tempting him to lead the lady on. 'I understand that Mr Bascombe asked for the family in order of age, youngest first,' he offered.

Her eyes narrowed as she considered this. 'Well, of course, I'm considerably younger than Marcia,' she agreed with some satisfaction. Her cousin's wife was clearly her personal yardstick, even a yard broom with which she'd beat herself.

A new thought struck her. 'In that case, if my son had been present, he would have been called first of them all.'

'It would seem so. Did he know about the family meeting?'

'I cabled him,' Edith Halliday said tightly, 'but apparently it didn't reach him in time. They're very dilatory out there about sending messages on. I explained as much to Hadrian but he can be very obtuse. He always took a delight in misunderstanding one's meaning.'

'Awkward,' Beaumont allowed. 'What did he say?'

26

'Oh, something about Piers wisely opting for a life of poverty among the world's deprived. He knows very well it's nothing like that. The boy merely feels, quite rightly, that he should make some effort to serve his fellow men before taking on the responsibilities of . . .'

'Of possible wealth later. Quite.' He was beginning to feel ever so slightly sorry for the woman floundering between her limited postures. To allow her breathing space he nodded towards Rosemary Z, inviting her to take over.

'Did your uncle have much to talk about when you spoke with him alone?' the WDC asked.

'Hadrian? Oh well – er, he's never short of things to say. He was – uh, reminiscing a little. About times when we were all younger. My late mother was his second sister and there were big gaps in his generation, so when Grandmama called the family all together I was the baby and he was already quite an age. We were never close.'

Got up each other's noses, Beaumont translated for his own use. He could imagine the scene: the caterwauling infant grandchild, and then the tetchy, middle-aged heir apparent kept waiting in the wings for his heritage just as he now made his juniors do. That's where he'd learnt how far to turn the screw, adding his own refinements.

But Rosemary Zyczynski's train of thought had chugged off on another line. 'Perhaps,' she suggested, 'Dominic Webster knew it was a case of youngest first, and realized his father wouldn't be free to drive back for some time. So he preferred to accept the earlier lift with his cousin.'

Edith Halliday seized readily on the change of subject. 'Well, either they'd arranged it in advance, or when she called him for his interview. There's collusion there of some kind, I'm certain. Those two are up to something.'

'It was unfortunate for him in the long run,' said Rosemary thoughtfully.

'That's what comes of flashy show-offs,' Edith asserted, closing her lips and breathing heavily. 'Once young people get behind the wheel they seem to forget there's anyone else on the roads.'

'So what do you think happened?' Rosemary asked simply.

'Surely that's obvious. No other car seems to have been involved. He skidded on black ice going too fast at one of those treacherous corners and went over the edge. It could have happened to me if I hadn't taken the greatest care. I saw all the activity with police cars and an ambulance when I passed, but of course I'd no idea ... It was the boy driving, or so I read in the newspaper. But it could equally well have happened with Francine. She's as harebrained and impetuous as her mother.'

'Her mother wasn't present that evening, I believe,' Beaumont tempted.

'She wasn't. There's no love lost between Hadrian and Elinor. And that's not surprising if some of the stories I've heard are true.'

'Oh really?'

But Edith was not revealing more. Perhaps truth was shorter in supply than imagination at that point. Or it might be that she had a late thought for not washing the family's dirty linen in public until the main soiler was irrevocably off the stage. Whatever, she clammed up at that point and switched to fussing about her person, unzipping the clumsy boots she'd worn for cycling, pulling off the close hat and tossing her spikes of grey hair about her shoulders like a girl in a shampoo advert but with less attractive effect. She rose to her dumpy five feet two inches and slid the rabbit-lined raincoat off her shoulders. Underneath she was wearing the navy blue uniform and trappings of a Guide captain.

'That could explain,' Beaumont was to remark later when they discussed it on the way back, 'why she was out for a wobble on her bike. She must be setting the girls a green example, not polluting the earth's heritage with foul petroleum fumes.'

'It could be for economy too,' Z warned. 'That house is too big for one person, and the heating was set very low considering the outdoor temperature. The room's underfurnished and beginning to look shabby. I think Mrs Halliday has seen better days. Her son's school fees aren't far past and he can't be contributing any income yet. She probably wouldn't admit how much of a struggle it is to keep her head above water, especially in the face of her cousin Morton's apparent affluence. It seems a permanent thorn in her flesh.'

However, having shed her chrysalis, the emergent Guider had become instantly brisk, bright and charitable. She stirred the contents of an ornamental Toby jug on the mantelpiece with a questioning finger, extracted an elastic band and, twisting her hair in one hand at neck level, slid the band over to produce a tuft jutting stiffly out behind like a bottle brush. 'There, that's better. Now perhaps you would like a nice . . .'

The phone's shrilling cut through her intended offer of tea. An old-fashioned instrument, not the modified cooing kind. Edith Halliday put a hand to her forehead. 'Never a moment to oneself. Do excuse me.' She bustled out to the hall, closing the door behind her.

'Silly old trout,' commented Beaumont and padded across to open it a crack. He laid his head against the panels.

She identified herself by the telephone number, a little breathless and eager. 'Oh, Alastair, it's you. What an . . . Yes, of course. Well, actually I have someone here. The *police!*' She barely hissed the last word, as if it were a dread disease communicable by word of mouth.

'*You've* had them too? About Dominic's accident, yes. They're talking to the younger ones first, it seems; the way Hadrian did. Of course, I haven't breathed a word about Dominic's *drinking!*'

There followed a short pause while Alastair Bartholomew passed on his news.

'Oh surely not! How appalling! You mean it was Marcia who started all this fuss? How vindictive, but then I've always thought . . . No, I'd assumed it was something to do with the insurance, and they wouldn't have breathalysed him in hospital in that state, would they? I thought medical staff kept the police away to protect the patients. Of course a blood sample would have been taken if he needed transfusions – which he must have done. Do you suppose they . . .?

'*What?* She actually . . .? Deliberately damaged? It's

beyond belief.' Edith drew a long breath. 'Well, naturally she'd be trying to divert all the blame on to Francine,' she declared with authority.

To the eavesdropper it seemed that the woman's dormant imagination had sprung instantly to wild life. He grinned happily at Z and gave her the thumbs-up sign.

Edith gabbled on. 'Of course it's Francine Marcia's getting at. Who else would have had the opportunity? . . . Yes, I know it was her own car, but it can't have been a very expensive one, and if she thought she stood to gain a fortune . . . Oh no, not really on purpose . . . But if Hadrian had given her any inkling that he favoured Dominic and she was second choice, well, the wish is often father to the thought, if not the act. Oh dear, this is all most distasteful. Listen, my dear, I'll ring you back. It isn't at all convenient now . . .'

Beaumont eased the door shut and stole back to his chair where he took up a somnolent posture.

Mrs Halliday appeared briefly in the doorway slightly flustered. 'I'm just putting on the kettle,' she claimed and departed.

Quickly the DS relayed to Rosemary the gist of the phone conversation. 'Get it all down,' he ordered. 'I'm going out to show the lady how helpful a man can be in the kitchen. If she's got any decent china that'll keep her mind off mulling over what she's just learnt.'

Wrong-footed by Beaumont's invasion of her domestic zone, Edith Halliday guided him towards kettle and tea caddy while she guarded the crockery and retrieved an iced ginger cake from a green and white Habitat tin. She refused his offer to carry the laden tray but nodded him ahead to open the doors for her. Behind her back he pulled an obsequious forelock.

In the interval between questions Edith had persuaded herself that discretion was the safest option. Seeing that she had no intention of confiding the content of her phone call, Beaumont proceeded to break to her, as if for the first time, the direction in which Dominic's mother had pointed the investigation.

Mrs Halliday met each fact with little monosyllabic

sounds of amazement, shock or disbelief as she felt proper. To the news of Dominic's transfer to Stoke Mandeville's spinal unit she reacted with a quite genuine horror.

'Oh no! The local newspaper said nothing about his injuries being so serious. Just that both of them were being kept in hospital overnight. I'd no idea. Oh poor boy! How really dreadful.'

'It is,' Rosemary agreed, recognizing her real distress. 'So you see why it is necessary for us to follow up any suspicions that the car could have been tampered with.'

'But who would have done a thing like that?' the woman wailed. 'There was only the family there, and old Mattie Cooper and that little Indian who looks after Hadrian. Of course, while we were all talking to Uncle, the nurse *could* have slipped out and damaged the car.'

'But why should he?' Beaumont asked. 'Any member of your family present could have chosen their moment and done the same while Francine was called away. With possibly a valid financial motive, if it was assumed that the first one called would be the most likely sole beneficiary.'

'Let's suppose that while the family took refreshments downstairs he did actually make up his mind – as he'd said he intended to do that evening – and he opted for Francine. With the supposed heir's removal, he would subsequently have to rethink, choose another. And if he showed his preference in the order he called you all to his tête-à-têtes, then a fatal accident to Francine would have been primarily to Dominic's advantage, don't you agree, Mrs Halliday?'

'But that would be—'

'Attempted murder, Mrs Halliday.'

'No, oh no! Nothing so . . . deliberate. Dominic would never . . . Anyway he wouldn't have accepted a lift in that case. Far too risky.'

'So someone close to him, ignorant that he'd be in the car, and who would benefit from his inheriting . . .'

'Surely not! She would have to be out of her mind to . . .'

'And then, ironically, it wasn't Francine who was seriously injured but Dominic himself.'

31

Beaumont watched the woman, his round eyes narrowed to near-slits. This was the second time she'd seized on her sister-in-law as villain of the piece, but on the phone to Alastair there had been a gossipy relish in her lesser speculations. Now, unless she was a consummate actress, the real significance of criminal intentions had struck her and she was appalled.

'A terrible accusation,' the DS said sombrely. 'And if it can be proved, then a dreadful action, whoever the intended victim was. So we need to know first who, if anyone, knew that Dominic was to be in the car with his cousin.'

The stunned look faded as Edith Halliday tried to follow his meaning. 'But none of us knew. How could we? Neither of them came back after they'd seen Hadrian. Either Francine invited him or Dominic asked for a lift on the spur of the moment, if indeed he knew Francine had come in a car of her own. I, for one, didn't know she had one, and as Hadrian actually remarked, she'd been the last to arrive, so we never saw it.'

'You have a point there. We believe it was Francine who invited her cousin. So, in view of all this and supposing that someone did know of the girl's car, do you consider Francine was the real target of the attempt?'

'There was no attempt. It's preposterous to think . . .'

'Yes, Mrs Halliday?'

'Unless . . . as you pointed out, being the first one Hadrian called, so perhaps his most likely heir . . . Or so someone could have thought. And Dominic his second choice. So removing Francine . . . yes, that might have meant Dominic inheriting.'

'So *cui bono*, Mrs Halliday? Who's to benefit, apart from the young man himself? We seem to have come in a circle, don't we? And yet it's his parents who are insisting we look into the matter.'

'I suppose they might, in order to avoid suspicion.' Edith Halliday put a hand to her throat and made a low moaning sound. There was only one member of the family she could even wildly suppose capable, and she was already ashamed of how far she had allowed herself to believe such ill. 'Her own son!' she murmured. 'To have it rebound so . . . and know oneself responsible. It's enough to send her right out of her mind.'

'It's a great pity,' Beaumont said as Z let in the clutch and they pulled away from the house, 'that with such a promising motive, Marcia Webster didn't have the means or opportunity. Can you actually see her risking her pastel mink while she fiddled under a greasy bonnet? I doubt if she even knows there's an engine there. And according to what the others have said so far she was dominating the drawingroom for the entire waiting period.'

'Which still leaves Dominic's father,' said Rosemary, swinging the Ford away from the kerb. 'Let's hope DI Mott got something incriminating out of him.'

FOUR

MARCIA WEBSTER FROWNED AT THE nurse bringing a tray with cup and saucer. There was even a stupid little pink-iced cake in a paper frill. As if she had time or stomach for eating now.

'Can I go back and sit with him?'

'Doctor's still making his examination. I'll call you the minute he's gone and we've straightened things.'

Marcia shrugged. Straightened what? She supposed the woman meant emptying that disgusting little plastic sack of yellow fluid under the bed. *Dominic* catheterized, like some senile bed-wetting dodderer! He would hate that if he knew.

As it was, they kept him barely conscious most of the time. At least, she supposed that was the result of drugs. He couldn't really be so weak, could he? There had been an awful moment back at the other hospital when she'd been thrust out of the way and they'd called urgently for the emergency trolley. The houseman on Casualty had shouted for atropine and adrenalin. She'd remembered cardiac arrest in a hospital series she'd followed on TV where they clamped two sort of pan lids with wires on the patient's chest which made him rear in convulsions. She had screamed and beaten at the white-coated back that stood between her and the bed. Didn't they know Dominic had broken his back?

Someone had taken her wrists and pulled her away. A big black in porter's uniform. He shut her in Sister's room, knelt down and talked endlessly at her until she agreed to stay there. She was useless, in their way; that was what he really meant, but she didn't think that was what he actually said.

Not that it seemed likely then that they could do much more themselves. Segregation and cups of tea, that was all. And Dominic wired up to a lot of machines, like a malfunctioning robot. Leaving it to time to decide whether he lived or not.

And still at this second hospital there was the same waiting and the eternal cups of tea following each other. She stared with hostility at the little tray beside her, and found she had already emptied it, eaten and drunk. And felt dried out again.

The door opened and the Surgical Registrar came in. Tall like Dominic himself but not so good-looking. His voice was soothing, so that she had to tear her mind from the sound to concentrate on his words.

There had been some response in the fingers of Dominic's left hand, and hopes were roused for eventual recovery of the use of his arms. Below that area he couldn't say. It was early days yet. Why didn't she just slip in to see her son for a moment and then go home for a few hours, get some sleep in her own bed? It was unlikely there could be any significant change in his condition for a matter of days. He would be maintained in a restful state to keep movement to a minimum.

Like an automaton she rose and followed him out, turned left towards the small white cell Dominic was housed in. With brief anger she passed a uniformed constable coming out. He was tucking away a notebook in his breast pocket. The police having priority over her, his mother!

But they had to find out exactly what happened at the crash, how Francine had contrived nearly to kill her cousin and escape real injury herself.

Yes, this was something she could help with herself. She would go away for a few hours, just as the doctor said. But she wouldn't be resting. She would insist on seeing that Superintendent who had wanted a statement from her. Whatever else was in doubt, one thing was certain: any statement she made on Francine would hold nothing back!

35

*

Superintendent Yeadings was at home being offered tea, sympathy, and a strong dose of Paracetamol. The degree of sympathy was modest because Nan, sometime Casualty and Theatre Sister at the Westminster Hospital, had little faith in the male reaction to minor infirmities.

Nevertheless, while briskly handing out a remedy and the advice to sleep it off, she didn't at all care for the way poor old Mike's face had suffered a seismic change. The valley between nose and cheek on one side had disappeared. In its place a florid angled plateau extended to an as yet unexploded Etna of impressive proportions. She had met some boils in her time but this was a medal-taker. And had gathered so fast; although when she came to think, really think about it, she had encountered Mike at breakfast this morning without actually seeing him. If he'd gone to work in his pyjamas she would have noticed, but what with Sally's pick-up coming early and Luke's spilt porridge, Mike's face had been familiar wallpaper, no more. She seemed to remember him grunting or something when she busily planted her send-off kiss. And still she hadn't taken account of the dear old thing's sore hooter.

'You'd better see Dr Harris tomorrow for a check-up,' she said as he blundered bedwards. 'I'll ring and get you an appointment.'

Mike waved a dismissive hand but didn't forbid it. Which was a bad sign in itself. Nan clucked, annoyed with herself that she should let any of her clutch get in so low a condition. It smacked of neglect; even of implied indifference. Giving too much attention to the little ones and overlooking man-mountain. But she would make it up to him, once she could get close without causing excruciating tremors.

The phone call from DI Atkinson was the utter limit but she managed to hold back a flood of recrimination against Thames Valley force in general and Mike's paper-chaser in particular. Even so he was aware of an unusual terseness in her response.

'Well, I'm sorry Mrs Yeadings. He didn't look too good

when he left here, it's true. I just rang because this woman who's announced she's coming in was one he's specially interested in.'

'And he's a man *I'm* specially interested in, Acky. Can't Angus see her instead?'

'He was tasked for it later. Trouble is we can't get a reply from his car. He's not back yet from interviewing the woman's husband and we'd like to get her talking before they get a chance to exchange notes. I've called in the other pair and they're on their way. We'll manage somehow. Don't tell the Boss I bothered you, ma'am, or he'll skin me.'

'*Pax sit* and all that, Acky. Sorry if I jumped down your throat. Incidentally, what's the lady's name? . . . Webster, I see. No, it rings no bell. I'll tell Mike when he wakes up. Thanks Acky, goodbye.'

Shown into a small interview room with off-white slatted sunblinds, Marcia Webster felt caught up in the replay of a familiar nightmare. The uncluttered, washable surfaces, the sense of suspended time within, while a confused rush of movement and official voices reached her dimly from outside: all this was still hospital, hospital, hospital. The same demand on her to wait and – as a last straw – the repeated offer of tea, pushed her almost to the brink of hysteria. Only a sudden weariness saved her from losing control. Left alone, she chose a chair against the light, under the high reinforced window, leaned gratefully back and closed her eyes.

Angus Mott came into the yard like a cyclone, contacted by car radio on his way back from Beaconsfield. Rosemary Zyczynski was waiting for him in the corridor. 'So after spreading hints, Mrs W's finally got round to lodging an official complaint? Sounds a pretty ferocious lady. Is she tearing the place apart?' he demanded of her.

'Actually I think she's asleep. Hasn't moved for the last fifteen minutes, so I didn't go in. You've time to draw breath.'

He didn't miss the warning in that, went to toss off his car coat, wash, and comb his hair before he returned with a surface calm to match the WDC's.

Z opened the door, gave a quick glance at the seated woman, and turned back to address the DI loudly while she held it ajar.

By the time Mott entered, the visitor was sitting stiffly erect, her grey eyes boring into his.

'Mrs Marcia Webster? My name is Mott. Detective-Inspector Mott. I'm sorry you've been kept waiting.'

Vertical muscles drew taut below her prominent cheekbones. 'I want to speak with Superintendent Yeadings. He sent me a message yesterday that he would see me as soon as I could get free. Now they tell me he isn't here. Where is the wretched man?'

'In our work , Mrs Webster, emergencies come without warning. Mr Yeadings is a very busy officer . . .'

'But I need someone senior.'

'Inspector Mott is the most senior CID member available,' Rosemary said quickly. 'And one with legal qualifications.'

Marcia Webster flicked a disdainful glance at her and returned to her survey of Mott. Perhaps he was older than he at first appeared. The handsome-sportsman features topped by crisp blond hair could have caused her to categorize him wrongly. There was a levelness of gaze and a tilt to the jaw that indicated confident authority. She recrossed her legs, pursed her lips, reminded herself she was a woman and of some standing herself.

'Very well then. But I expect the Superintendent to be informed of everything I say to you.'

'I can assure you he will be. Detective-Constable Zyczynski here will make full notes of your statement.'

'Less a statement than an accusation, Inspector. I want the girl who . . . wrecked my son's life to pay for it!'

Mott moved forward, lifted a chair for Rosemary and settled it back near the door. Then he drew another towards Mrs Webster and sat down squarely in front of her. 'We have to do this in a set order, as I'm sure you appreciate. Name first, then address, then reference to the alleged offence and its date.'

His tone was polite, in no way concessionary. Scrutinizing him, she pulled herself up short. In such a vital matter she couldn't afford to be gauche. With this man she carried no weight as yet; it would take all her persuasion, all her charm to convince him of the right of her case against Francine. 'Have you met my niece?' she demanded abruptly.

He realized that she hadn't heard what he said, so intense was her need to put her own message across. He waited a moment then quietly told her he hadn't seen Miss Webster, just read her preliminary statement about the meeting at her great-uncle's. Nothing yet about the accident itself, although there were notes of her answers to some early questions at the hospital.

'Nothing about how it happened? Isn't that rather remiss?' she countered. 'After all, she's the one most involved. It was her car, her insistence my son should accompany her. She it was who – miraculously – managed to survive almost unscathed. I hope you aren't nursing any illusions of her exaggerated sensibility. She is a modern young woman with a quite embarrassingly frank manner, but she can be very devious. It's a family trait she inherits from old Hadrian's side. You'd do well to be on your guard when you meet her. I should have thought perhaps someone older, less susceptible to a young girl's attempts to ingrati . . .'

'So we will start with your full name, Mrs Webster. Then your address, date and nature of the incident you wish to make a statement about.' This time he spoke more insistently, overriding her protests.

Then, over his shoulder to Rosemary, 'There's a fresh cassette beside the machine. Slip it in. I want a recording of this.'

At the outer door Rosemary said goodbye to the woman but received no answer. Returning, she passed the desk sergeant's raised eyebrows without comment. In the interview room Mott was hearing the tape through. At its end he asked, 'Want a repeat of the bit you missed?'

'I've got a shorthand note, thanks. What's it worth, do you think?'

'Accusation without any material back-up.' He

shrugged. 'We can't discount it being an accident merely because she's convinced of a deliberate murder attempt.'

'Believing what she wants to believe,' Rosemary murmured. 'We all do it to some extent, I suppose, and she's one of fate's pampered darlings. It must go hard with her when the wheels start falling off. Did you get anything to back it up from Dominic's father?'

'He's shaken, but not vindictive. I guess he'll push the insurance for all his son can get. Dominic was covered for driving any vehicle. The girl had only third party cover so she's lost out badly unless she claims against her cousin for his careless driving resulting in a write-off.'

'Which makes it just another traffic incident and not our concern. With more bad blood created between members of the family, and there seems to have been no scarcity of that. Edith Halliday was clued up on the cross-currents, but had some late misgivings about telling all she knew. If you don't need me at present, Guv, I'd like to type up my notes on her for you to read.'

'Best do that. But leave this last material for the moment. As soon as I've caught up with hunger pangs I'll want you to go with me down to Henley. As Mrs Webster pointed out, it's more than time we had a signed statement about the accident from Francine herself.'

But even here Mott was to be frustrated. By the time he had followed up a microwaved portion of cod, chips and peas with synthetic lemon meringue pie, new instructions had been issued from the Yeadings sick-bed. Miss Francine Webster and her solicitor had booked an appointment for 11.15 a.m. tomorrow. The Superintendent would see them himself in Interview Room 2 with DI Mott in attendance.

So, as he couldn't claim the message had missed him, he put the Francine interview on hold. It was good to know that old Mike would be immediately back in harness, but he felt some regret for himself, if she proved as disturbing as her vindictive Aunt Marcia had implied. He might have enjoyed being left to tackle a girl he'd been so specifically warned against.

At that moment Francine was heatedly facing up to her

stepfather. 'I think it's stinkingly high-handed of you,' she accused him. 'I'm quite capable of making my own arrangements. And as for saddling me with that frosty-faced prude Andrews . . . God, why him? We don't even speak the same language.'

'That's why it's essential you take someone along to restrain yours.' Frank Godden gave her his pale rabbit stare. 'If you don't exercise the utmost caution you'll have all manner of accusations levelled against you, quite apart from suggestions that you were driving a vehicle that wasn't roadworthy. Morton and his wife could make claims running into hundreds of thousands because of Dominic's injuries.'

His moist, prominent eyes had an almost nudging suggestiveness. She drew breath and instinctively moved away. 'Let's get this straight. I'm damn sorry about Dominic's bad luck, but the car was in good shape. I wasn't driving and he was. So whose pilot error is it in that case?'

It needled him. 'You're like your mother. You think you can always get your own way with a mixture of shouting and wheedling. Well, take it from me, it doesn't cut any ice with policemen. They'll enjoy every minute of it and when the fireworks are finished they'll start plodding all over you with their great boots, pick up some unconsidered remark you've let slip and inflate it into something quite damning. You need Andrews there to say, "Don't answer that," when their questions get too close. And you'll do well to follow what he says.'

'You have no confidence in me, have you? How come you know so much about police procedure? Did you once park on a double yellow line in your debauched youth? And you're right: I *am* like Mother, therefore perfectly capable of getting my message across if there's nobody there to misinterpret it. If you doubt that, ask yourself who comes off best whenever she starts disagreeing.'

The girl started to walk away, then turned again defiantly. 'I should never have agreed to come and stay here. It seemed a good idea when I was feeling shaken up, but I'm not an invalid and I'm damn well not an idiot. So lay off, Frank. I'm not your daughter and would never have wanted to be.'

His gaze fell in the face of her anger. A phrase reverberated from the past and he knew it was in her mind too just then, unspoken. 'I prefer to be known as a bastard!' She had been only thirteen when she'd flung that at him. Nothing that he'd done in the years since – and he'd made such efforts to understand and be kind to her – had changed her in that. Francine was unyielding in her resentment of him, constant in her rebuffing.

'I suppose that means you'll flounce out?'

She looked back at him, smiling. If she said yes, that would be to agree with him. And she wouldn't say no, which was what he'd tried pushing her into. So she stayed silent, smiled her mother's mocking smile and left him baffled.

Alone in her room she laid plans for the next day. She would phone Andrews early at his chambers pleading sickness. He should re-book their police interview together for late that afternoon. Meanwhile she would fix up for a hire car and keep the original appointment with the man Yeadings on her own.

When Nan Yeadings took in a tray with toasted sandwiches and coffee to share with Mike, having sent the children to bed, he was just reaching again for the phone.

'Oh no. Over my dead body, darling. The thing must be white-hot anyway. Can't trust the rest of Thames Valley to manage alone, can you?'

'It's important, Nan. If Acky forgets to let Angus know . . .'

'Don't insult him, Mike. He has all his marbles and he's a long way over twenty-one. I'm taking that phone downstairs when I go. One more squeak from you and it goes right to the bottom of the garden.'

'You're a nag, Nan. D'you know that?'

'That's no more than you need. Any vital messages you have to send, just write them down and I'll pass them on, but for heaven's sake switch off. You've an appointment with Dr Harris for eight-forty tomorrow morning and I'll drive you there on my way to school with Sally.'

'End of message?' He sounded chastened but she wasn't deceived.

'Momentarily, yes. Eat up and you can take some more pain-killers with your last drink.'

He meekly did as bidden and settled down for an early but disturbed night. By Tuesday morning his whole face was a burning, throbbing mass, one eye half closed. Nevertheless, on being dropped at the doctor's surgery he commandeered the phone and demanded to be picked up by patrol car. Twenty minutes later, having received a hefty antibiotic injection in one buttock and with his prescription for tablets entrusted to the driver, he was on his way to work. It was left to Dr Harris's receptionist to explain his defection when Nan arrived back to pick him up.

The earlier appointment with Francine and her solicitor having been shifted to the afternoon, he felt free to immerse himself in paperwork from a previous case of aggravated burglary. A call from Reception to announce the young lady's actual arrival set him wondering. 'Alone?' he queried.

'Yessir, grinning like a Cheshire cat when I asked after Mr Andrews. Said she'd managed to throw him off, sir.'

'Well, I'd better see her. Get Z to bring her along.'

He had time to stand, stretch and rub at his sore buttock before the two young women arrived. Rosemary knocked and at his roared answer held the door wide for the other to enter. He saw at once the reason for this as his visitor lurched in, the misshapen hip swinging her long, gipsy-patterned skirt just clear of a thick-soled boot. Why had nobody thought to tell him she was disabled?

'Miss Webster?' he asked, indicating a chair.

'Francine,' she said shortly and gave him a hard stare from dark eyes under short, straight brows. She had beautiful ivory flesh and a clearcut jawline which extended into the curve of her upswept, softly bleached hair. A challenging face, the eyes dominant against the creamy whole. It was at the same time startling and yet gave the clue to much he had already wondered about her.

She was frankly staring. 'Sorry about my appearance,' he found himself apologizing.

'What is it with you people?' the girl demanded, looking from him to Rosemary Z.

'Bit of infection in my case,' he admitted, 'but WDC Zyczynski's are honourable scars gained in the line of duty. Have a seat.'

She managed to sit gracefully, gathering in her long skirt and spreading it about her ankles. Again he was aware of a contradiction in her, this time between her modern direct-ness and the old-fashioned, elegant movements.

'I thought,' she said forthrightly, 'that most skin prob-lems were psychosomatic. Nerves, you know.' She was staring pointedly at the ruby excrescence that dominated one side of the Superintendent's face.

He stared unwinkingly back from his good eye, leering from the one overshadowed by the boil. 'There are other options. Bubonic plague, for one. Highly contagious, of course.' He offered his hand across the desk and she took it, a brief glint of humour passing between them.

Francine smiled, suddenly quite beautiful. 'My step-father's a dermatologist. I've picked up some of his jargon.' She turned to consider the livid scar running from the policewoman's eyebrow into her hairline. It had to be fairly recent. Under a gleam of grease there was dry flaking to either side of the puckering. 'Were you attacked?'

Z waited for Yeadings to nod before she answered. 'Sort of. Pushed down some stairs.'

'It was a murder case*,' the Superintendent put in. 'Z happened to recognize a face from the past.'

'I'd have been scared half to death,' said Francine.

Z smiled. 'I was, when I came round.'

'So,' he plunged in, totally insensitive Plod, (yet hadn't Francine started this herself?) – 'how about you?'

They saw her recoil, but she had herself in hand. Just a flicker of the eyes away and then she was facing up to him, chin high. 'I was born like this,' she claimed.

'So you've had time to get used to it.'

'You could say that, yes. Not that I care exactly to be this way.'

* *First Wife, Twice Removed.*

44

She really was something. He sat slumped opposite and let his eyes tell her what would almost surely have embarrassed her in words. Behind her, Rosemary Z looked frankly incredulous at the turn of the conversation.

'Well now,' Yeadings invited, 'shall we get down to business?'

FIVE

SHE DICTATED HER USUAL ADDRESS which was a flat shared with an ex-schoolfriend at Stoke Poges, roughly between Beaconsfield and Slough where she worked. Her flatmate was at present visiting a brother in Zimbabwe and wouldn't be back for two months. Which was why, feeling rather groggy after the accident, she'd foolishly been prevailed upon to stay with her mother and stepfather near Henley.

'The aforementioned skin specialist,' Yeadings prompted. 'Why foolishly?'

'Oh, Mother's fine, in small doses. I can't stand Frank, though.'

'Glad to break away? Did you find it difficult when you were younger and obliged to put up with him at close quarters?'

'You mean the wicked stepfather syndrome? God, nothing like that: I was never abused. Better perhaps if he had been that way. At least there would have been intervals between his gropings. No; the man's tedious, an ingratiating foot-in-the-mouth bore one's never rid of.'

'I've heard more flattering accounts of him,' said Yeadings mildly.

'Oh, as a professional, no doubt.' Her voice was heavy with disdain. 'I'm sure he goes through the actions very well in his surgery. Patients actually like him because he's polite, doesn't openly disbelieve their list of symptoms. He butters them up and hands out a prescription or performs some finicky surgery. But as a real person, there's just nothing there. He presumes on our relationship, and my

46

name being Francine – from a period long before Mother had come across him – he delights in thinking people take him for my natural father, since he's called Frank.'

Yes, Yeadings could see the man wouldn't score highly with her over a gaffe like that. 'And your mother?'

This flustered her. 'D'you mean what is she like? Or how does he react to her?'

'Where does she fit in with all this?'

'She's the chessboard queen, has all the best moves, dominates the other pieces, is the vulnerable king's ultimate protection.' Her mobile face flickered ruefully. 'You could extend the imagery to say I was the queen's pawn. But strictly off the board. I got knocked out in the early stages of the game.'

Yeadings smiled. 'You have quite a sense of the dramatic. I understand you're a member of the Stoke Amateur Players. I must bring my wife along some time when you've a plum part.'

'You could wait a long time. I occasionally hobble on with a tea tray; lift the phone and – big moment – actually speak: "Madam, it's for you." No, I'm happier as stage manager. My technical skills come in handy, and I can get audio gear and props cheaply through contacts at work.'

Yeadings nodded. She had been talking faster and faster, as if desperate to distract him from some other topic. Now he withdrew from the conversation and sat with his eyes flatly fixed on her. She came to a sudden stop, short of anything to say.

'We seem to be avoiding the obvious,' he suggested eventually. 'I imagine you want to know what progress we've made, one way or the other, checking on reported suspicions. Not much, I'm afraid. Plenty of paperwork, but as yet no conclusions.'

'Yes, well, actually – about the paperwork. You know that statement I made, on the family get-together?' she asked in a small voice. 'Do you think I could see it? I was a bit woozy at the time. I don't remember now what I wrote; may have got something wrong.'

He considered her. 'I can probably find you a photocopy.'

'Thanks.' A flicker of doubt crossed her face. 'Just a photocopy?'

'The original is a listed document, in case there has to be a criminal investigation.'

'And I might want to alter it, destroy it, something like that? God, was it so damning?'

Not damning, he thought. Revealing, certainly; not the purely factual information the police had been after. Something more emotional, a personal reaction.

But on further examination, hadn't it seemed suspiciously like an attempt to put across the writer as warm, impulsive, wittily alive to the varied characters present and their shared expectations? And yet subtly casting veiled aspersions. Written so soon after the accident that followed the meeting, with Francine supposedly still in shock, wasn't it improbably guileless? Was she playing him cleverly even now?

The solicitor foisted on her by her stepfather had put foward a claim that she'd made that statement while under sedation. So had she come here to strengthen the suggestion, in case there was some unconsidered matter included which could later prove embarrassing to her? She wasn't looking particularly clever at present. More apprehensive. How much of that was assumed?

'Don't you trust your accuracy?' he asked.

She closed her eyes and he waited. At length she admitted, 'I . . . I have a lot of strong opinions, about people and things, which I prefer not to air. Normally, that is.'

'And the circumstances weren't normal then.'

'That's what I mean. I may have exaggerated . . . It could prejudice you.'

He felt himself smiling and covered it with a cough. 'We read a lot of statements here, Miss Webster. I think you can trust us to separate the chaff from the grain.'

'So I did go to town on the others.' Her groan had only a slight theatricality, but it showed she was regaining confidence. 'If you'd let me see a copy, then?'

He nodded across to Rosemary Zyczynski who picked up a clipboard from the floor near her chair and withdrew some typed sheets. She handed them to Yeadings who laid them on the desk in front of his interviewee. Francine leaned forward, hands clenched in her lap, to read the statement through. Not touching it, Yeadings observed. As though the paper carried infection. Or as if it physically represented some kind of trap.

After her second reading she sighed and sat back. Her eyes, meeting his, were cockily defiant. 'I went over the top a bit. So what?' But the flush that now stained her neck told him more.

'As you see, quite harmless,' he said gently. 'A personal account by someone with a perceptive eye, someone vulnerable who protects herself with a cover of wry humour.

'But also a detailed account of a family gathering totally unconnected with the traumatic experience which immediately followed. And that is what I find curious. You might ask yourself why the story breaks off just there, as you left the house.'

'It's what I was asked for. The policeman wanted to know who of the family was there, and what the meeting was about. Well, I listed them all. And it was about money, which is what we're all hooked on.'

With her gaze fixed on the floor she launched suddenly on an account of the accident itself. Again it was subjective, glossing over nothing she had experienced, and yet the voice was impersonal, the delivery rapid as if she quoted some reading matter so familiar as to have become of little interest.

Abruptly it ended and she stood, glaring down at his watchful eyes. 'Make of it whatever you wish. You will anyway.' She shrugged, gave Rosemary an almost contemptuous glance and made for the door. There she turned to face Yeadings.

'If you want me to put in writing what I remember of the accident, I'll do that myself at home, a second statement from where the first one ends. But I won't sign anything one of you has written. And I still don't understand what all the fuss is about. Just a simple skid on an icy road. Hard luck on Dominic to be hurt so badly, but

49

nothing sinister about it. I know nothing could have been done deliberately to make the car unsafe, because nobody would want to hurt me.'

And she went, leaving the door wide open behind her.

'M'm,' said Yeadings, while Rosemary closed it. 'However true the rest of what she said, that last was a thumping lie. Francine Webster is one very disturbed young lady. She could share a feeling I have that there's more to come.'

The duty constable on the door watched through his square of glass as the girl came limping down the corridor, passed without acknowledging him and continued out to the car park. Hers was the hire car at the far side among the slots marked 'Chief Inspectors'.

Cheeky little bit of skirt, couldn't be bothered to follow the arrow round marked 'Visitors'. He'd been busy on the phone when she'd parked or he'd have sorted her out then. Left in a paddy, so maybe whoever had seen her had done his work for him.

He looked down the list of entries and saw she'd been booked in for Detective-Superintendent Mike Yeadings. Something serious, then. If so, one thing was sure: someday she'd get her come-uppance.

Francine revved the unfamiliar engine, circled the car park and, meeting the main road, turned left for the M40. Lazily falling flakes of snow began to build up on the windscreen. She switched on the wipers. She would drive for an hour or so to settle her mind, then work back towards Turville Heath. With any luck she'd find Josh at home, pottering in his heated greenhouses. She had to let off steam to someone, and he was the only person she could trust.

Contrary to expectations, Josh was indoors watching television. The woman who came in twice weekly to fill his fridge and dust and polish what he himself kept scrupulously tidy let her in.

'There's decadent,' Francine taunted him in a mock-Welsh accent. 'Lovely winter day like this, barely below freezing, and you're cowering by the fy-yer.' She blew a few snowflakes off the sleeve of her leather jacket in his direction.

'Fran, this is nice. Had your lunch? Actually I'm waiting to hear if the racing's been cancelled for the afternoon. The going's pretty hard everywhere, and there's quite a bit of snow in the north.'

'I've been encountering some frosty conditions myself,' she claimed, dropping her jacket and gloves on the floor, then smiling forbearingly as Josh retrieved them and carried them out of the room. 'Lunch,' she called after him, 'would be nice if it doesn't require you to start cooking and all that fuss.'

'I'm sure Mrs Todd will conjure up something to suit you. Make yourself cosy while I go and ask.'

He returned to find her watching horses parading in a saddling enclosure. 'Chepstow's off, but Lingfield Park's on. What are you putting your money on?'

He leaned over and removed the control from her hand, snapping off the programme. 'You're more important. How are things?'

'I wish I knew. There's this odd feeling I've got – not exactly physical – that's someone's coming after me.'

'You've had a nasty experience. It takes times to rebuild self-confidence. Did you drive yourself here?'

'That doesn't bother me. Except having to hire a car. I miss my little Panda.'

'So what exactly is the trouble?'

As she made no reply, hunched forward to stare at the ground beyond her feet, he came to sit on the arm of her chair. 'Let me guess. A shade of guilt, because it was Dominic and not you who took the main brunt of the accident? A residual uneasiness about the family animosities stirred up by old Hadrian last week? A vague suspicion that somebody might go so far as to act on those feelings, with you as recipient? And an undercover shame that you should find room for such doubts about your nearest, if not necessarily dearest?'

She turned on him impatiently. 'Since the police think there might have been dirty work, they must have some reason for it. If they're right, it must have to do with money, musn't it? One of the family pretty sore over the way old Hadrian meant to make out his will. He said he would make up his mind that evening; choose one person.

'Well, when I saw him he hadn't decided, and there was nothing about our interview that could have swayed him in my favour. Just the reverse. I know I couldn't have been his choice. If anyone thinks I was, that must be based solely on my being the first one he called in to talk with.'

She faced him frowning, almost scowling. Her outthrust lower lip momentarily gave her pretty face a blunt, puppyish look. 'You say you were the last in, Josh. If he'd given any clue to this thoughts, you'd have been the one most likely to pick it up. So did he say anything, anything at all, to indicate . . .'

Josh had moved back to his own chair and lay sprawled at rest. He could have been asleep with his eyes open. His face had no animation. 'You don't need to know,' he said. 'What good would it do?'

'For God's sake, Josh, do you think *I've* got murderous intentions? Over *money*? It's just that I feel so helpless not knowing, perhaps being the target for someone vicious. Someone familiar I ought to be able to trust. I'm scared, Josh. I just want to know there's someone with a better right than me to be crept up on and killed!'

Her voice broke in a half-laugh, but he knew her fear was genuine.

'If I had any inkling, it wouldn't help to tell you. Suppose I said a name – any name I thought up – would that make it more bearable?'

'Maybe not. But at least I would have some point to start thinking from. I wouldn't be entirely in the dark.'

He regarded her sombrely. Francine the carefree waking at night to feel hounded, lying wide-eyed, sleepless, wondering which direction the danger would come from, mistrusting everyone? He shook his head.

'Fran, I wasn't with him two minutes. He was very tired by the time he reached me at the bottom of the list. Almost at the last gasp, as it struck me. Mr Chadwala was hovering throughout. He put a cash-box on the table between us, and Hadrian nodded for him to count me out the notes. One thousand pounds in new twenties.

'I thought he was paying me off, but it wasn't that. He said, "You're a gambling man, Joshua. I want you to place this on a horse. I don't know where it's running next or when, but I just fancy it. Do that, will you?"

'I felt unsure of him then. What he was up to, I mean. As if it was some subtle trick to get at me. I asked if he wanted it staked for a win or each way. His eyes lit up. He looked positively wicked. "Oh, to win," he said. "Definitely to win. Let us not fudge the issue." '

'And did you do what he said?'

'Two days later, at Windsor. They were offering twenty to one. I put all the thousand on.'

'And did it win?'

'It came in third.'

'I see. He'd lost out.'

'Not exactly.' Josh sighed and the bloodhound wrinkles came back between his eyebrows. 'I backed it each way.'

'Although he'd said . . .? Why, Josh?'

'I don't know. I keep asking myself that. Did I want to think I knew better than him? Was it to cut him down to size in some way, as a petulant gesture of independence? Anyway, right at the last moment there was this overwhelming – *urge to caution*.'

'So you actually made money where he would have lost it. What did you do then? How did he take it?'

'I thought about it for a while. Then the day before yesterday – Sunday morning – I rang to tell him. Mr Chadwala answered the phone. He was near to tears. He told me that Uncle Hadrian had had a stroke. So I just said I was sorry and left it at that. His money's safe. I opened a special account at the Woolwich Building Society in my own name as trustee. It might just as well accumulate interest while I think what to do.'

The silence built up as his words died away. Francine stared at him, unsure how to comment. There was something about Josh then that didn't seem quite right. As though even while being frank he was somehow deceiving her. She waited until his gaze flicked up, met her own, darted away and then reluctantly returned. 'There's something else, isn't there?'

He shrugged. 'That's all there was between us. No questions, no advice, no recriminations. He simply asked me to place a bet. I did it my way.'

A corner of his mouth twitched. 'Not my usual way. Normally I too go for winners. However, this time I went for cover, and it paid off.'

Her dark eyes continued to fix his. So like the old man's. Josh felt skewered by the intensive stare. It took her a little while to work out what he was holding back, but at last she got there.

'So what was the horse called?'

'Does it matter?'

'I think it probably does.'

'Because you want to try your own luck on it?' he suggested with false lightness.

But she wasn't to be diverted. 'It's name, Josh.'

He ran a bony hand over his thinning hair, let it drop back on the coffee table beside him, and the signet ring on his fourth finger rang dully against the wood. 'A roan gelding. Three-year-old. Called Tontine.'

'Tontine.' Francine went on staring at him. The word meant nothing, and yet from somewhere she seemed to remember hearing it before. Or reading it. Its sound reverberated like a bell, or like a damp finger rubbed round the rim of a wine glass. *Tontine.*

'It means something, doesn't it? What does it mean, Josh?'

Eventually, he thought, Francine gets what she wants. Almost always. So why not now? 'Tontine,' he echoed regretfully, and explained.

Mrs Todd came in with a tray of ham omelette and salad. Josh settled it on Francine's knee. 'I'll see to the coffe myself. I know you like it strong. Give a shout when you're through.'

She sat thinking for a while before she started on the meal, but at the first taste discovered she was ravenous. Eating was so much less complicated than puzzling out just what old Hadrian had intended. Malice of some kind, certainly, but how far had he intended Josh to spread the story? And had it been a clue to his real intentions or merely another wicked joke at everyone's expense? She was glad Josh had left her alone at that point. Too much was uncertain, and she would need time to decide whether the new knowledge left her feeling safer or not.

When Josh came back with the freshly brewed coffee she asked if he had the latests news of Dominic. 'I tried once going into to see him but Marcia was sitting there like a dragon guarding a magic cave. Mother rings the hospital each morning, but I missed seeing her today before I left.'

'They seem a bit happier about his chances. The crack is in one of the lower vertebrae and the nerve may not be too badly affected. They're considering an operation to free it from pressure. Apparently Dominic asked after you and was relieved to hear you were back on your feet.'

'No more ungainly than usual.'

'If you wish to put it that way. I had the police here, of course. They wanted to know about the family gathering and what conversation I had with you before Hadrian sent for you.'

'I suppose we must have been chatting about something while we pecked at the food. Your orchids and the New Year party where I did a Cinderella act, wasn't it?'

'That and useless Christmas presents, so thank God for the Oxfam shop.'

'What use can our wonderful policemen make of that, I ask myself.'

'Sherlock Holmes himself would have found little to work on. Francine, this tontine business . . .'

'I don't want to talk about it, Josh. I have to think first. How about treating me to a tour of the hothouses? I've deprived you of the sight of glossy horseflesh; maybe your little green pets will help make up for it.'

He relieved her of her cup and they went out by way of the kitchen, where Mrs Todd had just put on her outdoor clothes preparatory to leaving. 'I've took me money, Mr Webster,' she said, 'and I'll be in Friday same as usual. Nice to see you looking well, miss. We was ever so sorry to hear of your accident. Glad it wasn't worse.'

'I really believe she meant it,' marvelled Francine, watching the ample spread of Mrs Todd's back diminishing in the distance.

'Of course she did, dunderhead. We all mean it. Leave those things in the sink and come and see my rooted hibiscus cuttings. I'll pot you one up if you promise not to overwater it.'

They went the length of the first glasshouse, which had a central partition separating the two temperature zones. At the far end, in a steamy rain-forest atmosphere sustained by a timed sprinkler system, were his exotic blooms. A tripod fixed with his professional camera was aimed at a curtain of orchids hanging over a stone-edged pool. 'Just waiting for the critical moment,' Josh explained. 'Another hour and they'll reach perfection.'

'To me they look perfect already.'

'Wait and see the finished picture. Which reminds me, I want you to sit for me again. There's a portrait competition coming up in April and I've an idea for a study. Will you come over one day before you go back to work?'

'I'm going back tomorrow. I've just decided. Nothing to do with the threatened photograph. Simply that I've had all I can take of Mother and Frank's cosseting. It's time things settled to normality again. I shall pack up tonight and go back to the flat.'

'And be on your own there?'

'No, actually we've a temporary lodger. A sort of forty-second cousin of Sarah's. You ought to meet him. He makes videos and he's come to work at Pinewood on TV ads.'

Josh raised an eyebrow. 'Like him?'

'He's quite dishy in a rough diamond sort of way. A New Zealander. We get on pretty well. It'll be a relief to be back with someone who's never met the more awful members of my family.'

'I hope that leaves me out.'

Francine followed her uncle from the glasshouse and waited while he locked its outer door. Although she now shrugged her leather jacket back on, the drop in temperature was cutting.

'Come indoors for a snifter?' he asked. He brushed loose

snowflakes and a single red petal from his jacket sleeve, avoiding her mocking eyes.

'Not as I'm driving, and I'd best get back before it comes on too badly. Thanks anyway.'

He saw her to the car, wedging the plant pot carefully between two cartons on the floor while she clipped herself in, still carrying with her the green scent of pelargoniums and the sweetness of freesias.

'Try not to worry,' he said hopefully.

'More a case of wondering. What old Hadrian intended; just who he meant you to share your story with; how far he intended us to speculate on its implications. Is it bluff or even double-bluff? I almost wish I hadn't asked you the horse's name.'

'Well, you did. Fortunately the constable who questioned me about my interview with Hadrian didn't go so far. I just said I'd backed one for the old man and it had come up. A sanctimonious copper; probably thought betting the root of all evil. Anyway he left it at that.'

He stood back. 'Well, safe journey home, Fran dear.'

His niece nodded, switched on the engine and lights. Her wipers cleared the windscreen outside. Inside she used a sponge and hoped the car would warm quickly. Hiring it for a week had cost more than she'd intended, and her insurance hadn't covered a temporary replacement.

Still, she'd had to see the Superintendent and get a copy of her earlier statement. Not that it was much help after all. She had an uneasy feeling that instead of covering up she'd given him more to work on.

Damn him, she thought, turning towards the motorway. Damn Mr Prying-eyes Cyrano-nose Yeadings!

SIX

YEADINGS HAD GIVEN THE TEAM until midday to look into the Webster question, and it was past one when Francine left him, still with no positive indication that the incident above Wendover had been more than a routine case for Traffic Division.

Whatever written account the girl might submit later, his immediate questions had now been answered. She had confirmed the statement written while under sedation: yes, she had offered Dominic the lift, handing him the keys to drive. And because she had already taken the passenger seat he hadn't demurred.

No, she hadn't noticed anything unusual in the car's performance on the way up to her great-uncle's, but due to the icy roads she had avoided use of the brakes, changing to low gear early before turnings and roundabouts.

'Another thing,' she'd claimed, lifting her chin and meeting his eyes defiantly, 'there's no extension added to the Panda's pedals for my shorter right leg because normally my shoes have inbuilt compensation. That night was specially cold and I was wearing some new fleece-lined boots which haven't been modified. When I finally pulled up at Hadrian's, any long action in the brake pedal would have seemed due to that. I felt nothing odd.'

And the question of the courtyard light: on arrival she hadn't noticed whether it was functioning or not. By the time she cut the car's headlights Mattie had opened the double front doors, so the corner would have been well enough lit. She'd locked her driving door and checked the other three. The bonnet lid had not been unlatched or she

58

would have heard it vibrating as she drove.

On leaving, it was the first time Dominic had been in the car. Used to more powerful models, he'd probably noticed nothing amiss in any long drive of the pedal. The first quarter mile from the house was fairly level. It was on the steep descent, at the second bend, that he'd cried out, 'God, I've no brakes!'

They had both reached for the handbrake, and the car spun violently, skidding across the far side. Dominic tried to steer out of it but there must have been ice. Francine didn't recall the car door opening but felt a rush of chill wind and she was falling through dark space, landing hard, rolling over and over on rough grass.

The car had bounced on down the hillside with a tearing and crunching of metal, twin shafts of light lunging and veering to cut off as it struck the trees.

She hadn't lost consciousness but was temporarily incapable of movement. She'd heard a car labouring uphill somewhere on the road above. When a man's voice called she'd made some sort of answer. Then hands were touching her; something soft was pushed under her head, with an answering agony through her shoulder and side; a promise that help would come soon.

Nothing in her account had disagreed with any other statement taken. Mattie Cooper had already said that the courtyard light had failed during that evening and a bulb was replaced by her brother next day; it was true that despite bright starlight the corner where Miss Francine had parked would have been 'black as the pit' when she was about to leave, and might have been so on her arrival. She wouldn't have known, because light was flooding out from the hall as Mattie waited at the door.

'I should like to push this inquiry further,' Yeadings told Mott, 'but there's a report in from Holtspur of a missing child, and that has to override everything. A girl, seven years old, left for school this morning at eight-twenty and didn't arrive. She's never played truant, and her absence was only remarked on when the mother took in something for her lunch-box. There have been reports of a phoney social worker calling in the neighbourhood last week asking to see children on the 'at risk' list. There could be a connection.'

'Was this girl considered at risk?'

'No. Nothing known, and apparently a respectable family. Father's a building society clerk. There are two younger children, and since November Jane has been going to school with one other child and no adult. It's a quarter mile along the main road. Uniformed men are making the usual door-to-door inquiries, and I've offered your team for follow-up.'

'Right. I'll take Z with me to see the family. The other two can check on accounts of the phoney social worker.'

Mott ran the trio to earth in the canteen and explained the switch of cases. Rosemary looked apprehensive; Beaumont put his nose up like a setter scenting rabbit. Silver accepted it as the next chore to get on to.

The Hunters were an articulate couple, deeply anxious but controlled. The father had been summoned home from work and a neighbour had taken the two younger children out for the afternoon. The parents sat close on the settee, occasionally holding hands, trying to think of ways in which they might help the investigation.

A phone call to his place of work confirmed that Colin Hunter had been in his office since eight-thirty that morning. The journey would have taken him over twenty-five minutes at that time of day. That was one worry removed.

Both officers were shown the little girl's room, which was freshly decorated with a frieze of brightly coloured farm animals. There was a neat single bed with a sprigged duvet which matched the curtains, a child's desk in pale wood which had arrived last month from Santa Claus. A white-painted set of shelves held a surprising number of illustrated books, many of them well-thumbed.

'She's a great reader,' her mother said, 'and really keen on school, especially this term now she's got Miss Rampton as class teacher. I expect you've been given the list of – of what she was wearing?'

Rosemary read aloud from her notebook: 'Red woollen

cloth coat and hood, lined with grey fur fabric; hand-knitted red woollen gloves attached to the cuffs with a crocheted chain of the same wool; navy and white checked trousers; white sweater; red ankle-boots.' She smiled at the woman. 'That sounds quite distinctive. It would help if you could also lend us a recent colour photograph, Mrs Hunter.'

The little girl with whom Jane had been walking to school since November half-term was a Daphne Bowles, aged eight. That morning the child had been starting a heavy cold and her mother had kept her at home. For the first time Jane had continued on her own.

'If only she'd rung to tell me,' Mrs Hunter said in anguish, 'I could have left the little ones next-door and gone with Janey myself. What I can't understand is how any child can disappear on a main road in broad daylight. She'd never talk to strangers or accept a lift unless Daddy or I gave permission.'

DI Mott and Rosemary Zyczynski returned to their car. 'How did they strike you?' Angus asked.

'Genuine distress. I didn't get the feeling they were holding anything back.'

'A little too innocent for their own good, maybe?'

'Nothing so bad has ever hit them before. This sort of thing only happens to other people. Mrs Hunter . . .'

'Yes?'

'Feels guilty. She's wondering where she went wrong: meaning to encourage Jane's self-reliance, was she too ready to jettison her own responsibilities, exaggerating her ties to the younger ones?'

'Is that the full extent of her guilt? Why today, for the first time ever, did she call in at school at lunchtime? You don't think there had been a spat before the child left home, something upsetting enough to make Jane rebel and the mother feel a need to check on her later?'

Z shook her head. 'I think it was how Mrs Hunter said: they'd run out of fruit and Jane always liked an apple with her sandwiches. The fruit bowl on the sideboard was empty. I looked in her string shopping bag, dumped in the hall. She'd bought oranges, apples and bananas.'

'Right. Let's move on to Jane's little friend's house, see what the mother has to say.

Mrs Bowles answered the door in her curlers, fat plastic rollers of pale blue visible under a tired wisp of pinky-grey chiffon. There was a pungent smell of setting lotion.

'Oh, not more of you,' she said in disgust when Mott showed her his warrant card. 'There's been nothing but coppers all day. I'd've been better off going in to work. Well, you'd better come in. Rather now than later, I suppose. My bingo evening. Wouldn't want to miss that.'

'A few more questions about Jane Hunter,' Mott warned her. 'Could you tell us in your own words exactly what was said when she called here this morning?'

Mrs Bowles nodded Mott towards the settee and took an armchair beside the gas fire. A matching chair, occupied by a large china-faced doll and a bundle of comics, was turned to face the blank screen of a large television set.

Walking past the patio doors towards a corner seat, Z darted a quick glance at the garden. She saw a solid little girl in a navy duffel coat slouched on a motionless swing, unconcerned by the lazy flakes of snow settling on her from a sky as brooding as she seemed herself. Hardly suitable conditions for the heavy cold that had excused her from school attendance.

Mrs Bowles was ploughing through an account she must by now have committed to memory word for word. Mott interrupted her, and after answering his query she resumed a sentence or two back.

'So, on the doorstep, you explained about Daphne's cold, and she went on her way quite happily?' he recapped.

'Like I said.'

'So how long would you say she stood there, between arriving and departing?'

'No time at all.'

'Did she make any remark, say she was sorry about Daphne's cold? Ask to see her?'

'Lord no! You wouldn't get a word out of that child with a squeegee. I just said, "Daph's not well, duck. I'm keeping her in bed. You'd best get along on your own." So she did, see. Turned and went off, good as gold.'

'Are there any more children from the same school, about the same age, living near?'

'You mean, who might have joined her on the way? A couple of kids from the back road. You could ask them. Couldn't say what they're called, though.'

'Maybe Daphne would know if we asked her,' Rosemary put in quietly.

'Oh, I shouldn't bother her, nasty business like this.' Mrs Bowles began to look belligerent.

Rosemary caught the quick nod from Angus that meant she should take over the questioning. 'How did this arrangement start, Jane and Daphne walking together? Are you close friends with Mrs Hunter?'

'Never heard of her till she rang my bell. This was sometime early last term. Said she'd noticed Daph walked to school on her own, so would she like a lift in the car when it's raining really hard. I didn't see why not. Then on nice days they started all walking together, only Daph couldn't stand dawdling for the toddler, because of course both the little ones had to come along too. It was our Daph's idea they didn't need any grown-ups. She'd been managing all right up till then on her own, see. She fussed a bit, that Mrs Hunter, but once Daph's made up her mind she can be real awkward. Anyway, they been doing it on their own now – there and back – ever since the end of November. This is the first time the silly little kid got it in her head to do anything daft.'

'So do you think she's playing truant, Mrs Bowles?'

'Stands to reason, dunnit? Kids will be kids. Here, I'm just going to make some tea. Don't suppose you'd want a cup?'

'That would be very welcome,' Mott answered for them both.

'Let me help you,' Rosemary offered quickly.

While the two women moved off to the kitchen Mott went across to the patio door towards which the WDC had stabbed a finger. Under a lowering sky the garden looked more like a junk-yard, stacked with leaning timbers and panels of wattle fencing. Mott remembered Mrs Hunter mentioning that the man of the house worked at a joinery. The swing, at the end of the concreted yard, was a solid affair, like the subdued little figure idly scuffing at the earth with her foot. In a world of her own, she was unaware of being inspected.

Mott switched on the overhead lights and a square of warm yellow fell across the terrace. It must surely make the garden seem a gloomy place by contrast.

He watched the child let down the foot she had been sitting on, rub her numb leg and start to limp towards the house. He tapped on the window and, having caught her attention, mimed that he would let her in.

'Where's me mum?' she asked suspiciously as he slid the patio door closed behind her.

'Getting us some tea. Aren't you frozen?'

She stood on the carpet shedding her coat and lied valiantly. 'Nuh.'

'How's your cold?'

'What co——? Oh, you mean like Mum told Jane. It's a bit better. Not much.' She sniffed dramatically.

Mott winked. 'Useful.'

She gave a sly grin. 'Swallowed it all right. She said her mum always made her stick her head over a jug and sniff in some smelly stuff in steam. She wanted to go home and get me some. I said she better run off to school like all the other little goody-goodies. My dad had promised – he *promised* – to take me out in the van today and I wasn't going to stinking school whatever my mum said.' She stuck out her bottom lip and scowled ferociously.

This was a different version from Mrs Bowles's dismissal of a silent Jane on the doorstep. Mott smiled falsely. 'So where did your daddy take you?'

'He didn't, did he? That's what they was rowing about, him and me mum, and then he went slamming out and I told her I wasn't going to give up my day's holiday just because she wanted to spoil it. She might stop me going out with Dad, but she couldn't stop me staying at home. And then she screamed at me and said that would mean her staying off work, and she tried to send me upstairs.

And that's when the kid arrived wanting me to walk her to school.'

The kid. Possibly as little as a year younger. In age; but much more in experience, he guessed. 'So how about tomorrow? School again?'

'S'pose so. It's more fun than here, with *her* around.'

There was a bump on the door and Mott went across to let Rosemary in carrying a tray. Mrs Bowles from the kitchen roared, 'Did I hear that kid in there?' She came in fit for battle and bearing a boxed sponge cake iced and scattered with jelly fruits.

'Says she feels better. Might even try school tomorrow,' Mott got in quickly.

Mrs Bowles stared suspiciously at him and at the damp coat dropped on the hearth-rug.

'Wonderful how a breath of fresh air helps to clear the snuffles,' said Rosemary in a gullible-aunt voice.

Unconcerned whether they defended her or not, Daphne was circling the tray. 'There's no milk.'

'Yes there is, miss. Use your eyes.'

'Oh, you've put it in a *jug!*' jeered the little horror.

Rosemary drove round the corner and parked by the kerb. She left Mott reading her shorthand notes while she rang the nearest doorbell. At the first house the elderly woman who shuffled to open up was not only deaf but uninterested in her neighbours. The second house appeared to be empty. At the third house she learned that Ruby and Grant Johnson who lived opposite attended the primary school and were 'dear little kiddies'. Armed with this information, Rosemary rejoined Mott and they went together to knock at the Johnsons' door.

Ruby, aged six, and Grant, nine, had only just returned home. In their mother's presence the boy informed them that he never walked with Daphne Bowles because she was common. Presumably that would have automatically proscribed Jane Hunter too by association. They had seen Jane entering the Bowleses' corner house that morning but she hadn't caught them up on the way to school.

'Would you expect her to?' Mott asked. 'Were you dawdling?'

Not really, he was told; but there'd been an electric train set working in the toyshop window and they'd stayed to watch it and were nearly late. (Guilty glances in Mother's direction.)

'So Jane could have gone by while your backs were turned?'

The boy supposed so, then decided otherwise. 'Roo would've seen her. She doesn't understand trains. She was looking for someone else to go on with.'

'Looking all the time, Ruby love?' her mother asked.

The little girl took her thumb out of her mouth with a soft plop. 'M'm.'

'She means yes,' the woman said. 'She doesn't talk a lot but she never misses anything.' Which Mott could well believe; the small child was all eyes, like a newborn guppy.

'Concentrate on the houses between Bowleses' and the toyshop?' Rosemary asked as Mrs Johnson closed the door on them.

Fourteen doors and two turnings farther along the main road, the toyshop proved to be a newsagent's, but one counter inside was given over to fancy goods and stuffed animals. The train set in the window was marked down by twenty per cent from its pre-Christmas price and now bore a 'sold' notice.

Uniformed branch had already gone house-to-house in the area asking routine questions without raising a clue. But somewhere on that route the child had disappeared.

'Nothing else for it,' Mott said grimly, 'but to visit them all again.'

SEVEN

CROSS-CHECKING AND ANNOTATING STATEMENTS in the Webster file, Superintendent Yeadings too felt burdened with repetition. More a matter of *déjà fait* than *déjà vu*, he told himself, but the case had a hold on him. He had officially taken the others off it, but even the urgency of tracing a missing child could not totally distract him.

Mott was running the CID end of the search for Jane Hunter, and at this early stage the inquiry must follow established patterns. Only when some positive discovery was made would Yeadings be required to make decisions. Meanwhile he remained haunted; by the image of a wrecked car and the lovely face of a lame girl.

The circumstances of the car accident, if accident it was, had been as provocative as Francine herself, and as open to opposing interpretations. Her presence lingered in his office; the contrast of her lurching gait with the delicate handling of the long, gipsy skirt; the fineness of face structure and yet the bald outspokenness of her approach; an abrupt challenge delivered in a husky, vulnerable voice. A young woman to be reckoned with. Formidable. Enigmatic. Of the kind who would once have been widely feared as a witch.

He tried to trace the point from which his own uneasiness sprang. It had been there before he met her, aroused by that self-mocking, subjective account she wrote of the family confrontation.

Were they really as she had described them, or had her sense of the dramatic created caricatures out of quite normal people? In so doing, had she fixed in his mind an image of them which would colour his own impressions on

67

later meetings? If such were found necessary.

And in her presentation of herself, how much truth lay under the wry humour? Was she, as she'd claimed – or regretted – a genetic echo of the bizarre old man at whose behest the family had felt obliged to forgather?

One way to lay the ghost was perhaps to trace it back to source. He ordered a car and gave the driver directions to Lynalls, the country house above Wendover where Hadrian Bascombe supposedly lay recovering from a stroke. Supposedly, because he couldn't be sure that anything to do with Francine Webster's family was quite what it claimed to be.

The smooth-faced, respectably drab elderly woman who answered the door must be Francine's 'Old Mattie'. 'Mrs Cooper?' Yeadings asked.

She regarded him levelly, explaining – politely firm – that Mr Bascombe was not receiving visitors.

'This isn't a social call. Thames Valley Police. Detective-Superintendent Yeadings. I should like a word with Mr Chadwala, if he's available.'

She frowned but moved back, leaving him room to enter. A young girl in maid's uniform appeared and took his overcoat. 'If you'll wait in the library, sir, I'll see if Mr Chadwala is free to see you.'

The woman was gone over ten minutes, during which time Yeadings trod the thick Wilton carpet picking out titles from book spines. Some of the snuff-coloured leather-bound volumes were extremely old, but on the wall facing the long windows he met the bright dust jackets of non-fiction bestsellers of the past fifteen years.

Someone, perhaps the old dinosaur himself, had catholic tastes and kept abreast of serious publications on travel, biography, popular science, medicine and economics. It would seem to indicate that Hadrian Bascombe remained as keen-witted as Francine had implied. On the other hand – and Yeadings intended bringing scepticism to all his dealings with this family – it could be that the old man had failed to cancel a long-standing general order to his bookseller. But the books had been read. They opened easily, right back to the bindings.

Mrs Cooper had come in silently and stood directly behind him. 'If you would care to go up, sir? Mr Chadwala is in Mr Bascombe's suite.'

The Indian nurse was waiting in the gallery above the hall, and showed him into a fair-sized room which appeared to double as his private sitting-room and dispensary. 'I have told Mr Bascombe that you are here,' he said in his gentle manner, 'and he indicated that he would be pleased to see you.'

'Indicated?'

'Mr Bascombe is not speaking any more. Except with his eyes and his hand. He has suffered a stroke.'

'I see. That must be difficult for you.' And a hell of a job for me if I want to question him, Yeadings thought.

'I have the honour to be with him many years, sir. We do not always need to speak aloud.'

'Then perhaps, rather than risk tiring him, you would answer some questions for me yourself, after I have paid my respects?' (God, I shall be falling into the fellow's courteous ways myself any minute.)

Old Bascombe was in the adjoining salon, tucked into a winged chair and wedged in position with several cushions. His body was lopsided but his face less so, and with a start Yeadings briefly recognized a cruel caricature of Francine. Thus far, then, her observations were valid.

It was left to him to manage the dialogue on his own. He explained who he was, although certainly Mrs Cooper would have quoted his credentials. Old Bascombe grunted and permitted a trail of spittle to tremble on his lower lip and spill down his chin on to the brocaded dressing-gown. Yeadings steeled himself to continue blank-faced.

'Although we have as yet no positive indication of any interference with Miss Webster's car, we have thought it necessary to follow up certain suggestions made that the incident was not entirely – er, accidental.'

A sparky reaction in the old man's eyes could have been anger, eagerness or mockery. The locked features gave no clue to which it was he felt.

'Miss Webster herself regards any suspicions as

69

mistaken. Mrs Morton Webster on the other hand – perhaps because of the serious nature of the injuries to her son – considers every aspect should be carefully examined.'

Now there was an audible response. Yeadings was almost ready to believe it a repressed chuckle. Old Bascombe's eyes were brightly unwinking.

Right, press on, the policeman told himself. Get some specific indication, if it's only outrage.

'So we are interested in the meeting with your family which preceded the incident.'

Now one hand made a snatching movement on the man's lap and then hung still. Hadrian Bascombe's eyes held steady as if he waited for more.

'I understand from remarks made by various members of the family,' – (best not mention written statements yet) – 'that you called them together to discuss the provisions of your will. This may be entirely irrelevant, even if it were found that the car had been deliberately tampered with, but at this point I think we must take it into account. The *future* provisions, as I understand it, because you had not then made up your mind.'

The paralysed man blinked both eyes together.

'Mr Bascombe says that that is so,' Mr Chadwala interpreted.

'May I ask whether during the course of the evening you were able to come to any decision?'

The eyes blinked twice, then once again.

'No and yes?' Partly due to the temperature in the room, but mainly because of the foolish role he was being forced into, Yeadings felt a prickling of sweat under his collar. The inflamed side of his face was thumping again despite the generous dose of codeine he'd taken before setting out. The pain seemed to have spread and settled in his jaw. He remembered Dr Harris suggesting he let the dentist take a close look at his teeth. He wished he were on his way home to bed and a knockout brandy instead of sparring with this obstinate old porcupine.

He stifled a sigh and determined to be patient. Nobody asked to be paralysed. Bascombe was as much the victim of

70

events as the young man at Stoke Mandeville waiting to learn if he would ever stand or walk again. Strange, that. The oldest and the second youngest present that night both struck down within a matter of days. Different causes, but the same effect.

'Superintendent?' Mr Chadwala said gently, recalling him to the one-sided conversation.

'Does that mean you were in two minds?' he suggested.

Two blinks.

'No?' That message had been vehemently passed on. So consider what alternative there was: 'no' first, and then 'yes'.

'So perhaps you decided only after the family had left?'

Bascombe's face twitched. He blinked once and made scrabbling movements with his good hand as if writing.

'You wish to write something down? No? ... You *did* write something down? ... The will itself? ... With a single legatee? ... Properly witnessed? ... Yes, I see.'

Yeadings took a deep breath. 'Did you disclose to anyone – anyone at all, Mr Bascombe – what decision you were likely to make? No? Or give anyone a hint, even a deliberately mistaken one?'

The old man seemed to consider this. His eyes were like a malevolent monkey's.

You did, you old horror, Yeadings appreciated. You played them all along. They all have suspicions, and nobody's going to know for sure until you finally snuff it.

Now Bascombe had got hold of a corner of his nurse's white jacket. Mr Chadwala leaned towards his charge and made soothing noises. 'I think,' he said, straightening, 'that Mr Bascombe wishes me to give you an account of what happened that evening.'

'Is that so, Mr Bascombe?'

One blink for yes.

'Has he your permission to be utterly frank about everything that occurred?'

One blink.

'Enough for now,' the nurse cautioned. 'He will rest a while and we can talk in my room.' Smoothly he reached under the chair and pulled a lever to change its angle so that the old man lay almost horizontal. At the door he operated the dimmer light switch. At the touch of a button the heavy champagne velvet curtains silently closed out the darkening afternoon.

Dusk, Yeadings thought. And perhaps, somewhere out there, little Jane Hunter alone and terrified as night came on. He would record the nurse's account as briefly as possible and get back to find out what progress, if any, there had been in the search for her.

They returned to Mr Chadwala's sitting-room and Yeadings nodded towards the pocket tape-recorder he had placed on the low table by his chair. 'This could save us time.'

'And guarantee accuracy.' The nurse nodded. Voluntarily he began to identify himself, as if accustomed to interrogation. 'I am Atul Chadwala, naturalized British Citizen, State Registered Nurse trained at St Mary's Hospital, Paddington. I first met my present employer when working at the London Clinic. Mr Bascombe was there for a short period twelve years ago to have prostate surgery. He afterwards offered me a post at his home and I accepted. I have been here ever since and enjoy some degree of his confidence.'

'Splendid,' Yeadings approved. 'You've evidently done this sort of thing before.'

'I am accustomed to making résumés of newspaper articles and recording them for Mr Bascombe. In that way he can easily refer back to subjects of interest.'

'And books too, I imagine.'

'Mr Bascombe does not approve of books in abridged versions. He prefers me to read them aloud in full. I spend several hours each day at his lectern.'

'So you are much more than his nurse.'

'I – serve him in whatever way he requires.'

Yeadings paused to find the right words. 'And of course he values your opinion on matters which he is prevented by his health and age from participating in himself?'

Chadwala hesitated. 'I keep him informed, but I am not a spy, sir.'

'There is no need to call me sir. We are both

professionals, Mr Chadwala.' He settled more comfortably in his chair. 'My questions stem from necessity, not curiosity, so I hope you will feel able to answer freely. They concern mainly your employer's family and the evening of their recent meeting with him.'

'I have a clear recollection of the occasion.'

'Perhaps in your own words, then?'

'The invitations were given by Mr Bascombe himself by telephone and he made arrangements with Mrs Cooper to order a buffet supper for seven guests, Mrs Godden having declined on behalf of herself and her husband, although Miss Francine, her daughter, accepted. Mrs Cooper was to receive them and show them to the ballroom while I attended Mr Bascombe and made him comfortable at the head of the extended table set up there.'

'Rather a grandiose setting for a small gathering,' Yeadings murmured. 'Some might have found it overwhelming.'

Mr Chadwala looked down his nose. 'Mr Bascombe has a sense of occasion. He wished to observe closely his kinsmen and their responses.'

Put their backs up and make them feel small, was the Superintendent's private paraphrase. And in Francine's case something more, because that place, the Hall of Mirrors as she called it, held an unholy fascination for her. Asked for a statement, in shock still after the crash, she had been unable to get to the nitty-gritty of the family gathering without revealing her hang-up. She'd romanticized it, but the fact remained: the huge room of the glass walls had bad memories. Perhaps as a child seeing herself repeated into infinity there, she had fully realized for the first time the shocking distortion of her own small body.

Had old Hadrian, who seemed to miss nothing, known what effect the room would have on her? Was that, in her case, part of the testing he had set up for his putative heirs?

'I was not present during the meeting, so I cannot say what transpired,' said Mr Chadwala. 'Mr Bascombe rang for me when the family was invited to go downstairs for refreshments. I took him a tray and his medicines, and when he was ready to receive the guests individually I saw that they came up in the right order and did not speak to the others on leaving.'

'But Francine Webster spoke to her cousin, to invite him to return with her in her car.'

'I asked Miss Francine to call Mr Dominic discreetly herself. This was on Mr Bascombe's orders. If she mentioned more, that was entirely on her own account.'

'Do you suppose Mr Bascombe guessed that was what she would do?'

Mr Chadwala looked slightly shocked. 'I could not conjecture . . . It appeared to me that he needed my attention at the time, and that was why I could not go down myself for Mr Dominic.'

'But you did so for everyone else?'

'Mr Dominic summoned Mr Alastair. After him I went down to escort Mrs Halliday, then Mr and Mrs Morton Webster together, and finally Mr Joshua Webster. By the time that the last one had left, Mr Bascombe showed signs of strain and I helped him to bed.'

'Go on. There's something more, isn't there?'

Chadwala looked uncertain.

'You had Mr Bascombe's permission to speak frankly, and he can't tell me himself. Was there something significant he said to you that night? Or did?'

'When I had given him his milk drink he asked me to ring down for Mrs Cooper to come up. When she was there . . .'

'Yes, Mr Chadwala?'

'He signed a document which was already made out, and both Mrs Cooper and I were witnesses.'

'His will.'

'So I believe.'

'And what has become of it since?'

'It was enclosed in a sealed envelope and sent with a covering letter next day to a solicitor, with instructions for him to take care of it until Mr Bascombe's death.'

'I see. So did either you or Mrs Cooper read the terms of the will, or did Mr Bascombe give you any hint what they were?'

'I have no idea what provisions were made. About Mrs Cooper I cannot say, but it is doubtful she would have had the opportunity.'

'Fair enough. Well, I think that's about all I need to ask you. Oh, one other thing. Did you have any cause to go outside between the arrival of the first guest and the departure of the last?'

'Outside?' Again Mr Chadwala seemed hesitant. 'Only once, for ten minutes, to look at the stars.'

'The stars. Yes, I understand the sky was clear that evening. After midnight it clouded over and there was quite a heavy snowfall.'

'That is so, Superintendent. I am, in my way, a student of the heavens, and when Mr Bascombe was speaking with his first two guests he gave me permission to plot my chart. I went out on the tower . . .'

'Tower? Not down in the garden or courtyard?'

Mr Chadwala smiled patiently. 'I am a Parsee, Mr Yeadings. We are a race descended from the Zoroastrians of Ancient Persia who were persecuted and fled eastward. We have always followed our stars, even to the Christ Child's birth, it is said. And for us there are always towers, the high places of our religion. It is partly because of the tower here that Mr Bascombe thought to invite me to his service. I will show you, if it is of interest.'

Curiouser and curiouser, Yeadings told himself. Either my face infection's sent me bonkers or I really did fall down the rabbit hole.

But he had to admit he was indeed interested, even intrigued.

The Parsee nurse led him back into the gallery, along a narrow passage to the house's rear and up two flights of stairs to an unused attic floor. From there an aluminium ladder led up into a small hexagonal turret which commanded a view of the whole roof and part of the courtyard, as well as an unrestricted panorama of fields and sky. The glass panels on five of its six sides were removable, and the room was dominated by a large mobile telescope. It was impressive, and Yeadings said so.

'It is useless for the moment, I regret,' said Mr Chadwala.

'Too much cloud, yes. But do you use it to look at other things? Views, distant roads, people?'

'They would be distractions.'

Yeadings considered him, head tilted. 'At just what point did you come out here on the night which interests me, Mr Chadwala?'

'The time I do not know, but I could estimate it according to the rising of Orion's belt.'

'How about according to what was happening in the house?'

'That would be when the first guest was speaking privately with Mr Bascombe.'

'Miss Webster? Did you happen to notice the courtyard then? You can just see the corner where she left her car. Do you recall whether the bulkhead light was on or off?'

'I regret. I did not look. But I think . . . I think it must have been dark. Otherwise why should someone be shining a torch there? It was not a strong one, but it distracted me as I sought the azimuth.'

EIGHT

'BETWEEN EIGHT-THIRTY AND NINE A.M., a street outside a newsagent's,' Mott recapped. 'How do you fancy that for the scene of a snatch?'

'Lots of come and go,' Rosemary offered. 'Drivers parking briefly for a newspaper, then off at speed to work. Children on their way to school; older ones returning from a delivery round. Who's going to notice one small girl resisting being hustled into a car? She could have been protesting at not being given a lolly or a comic, or scolded for holding up someone who'd be late at the office. Unless she were recognized as not belonging to the adult with her, no one would think twice.'

'Exactly. So premeditation or impulse?'

'A bit of both? If it had to be Jane specifically, then this was a chance in a million – a grab on impulse. If any unguarded child would do, someone could have been seen hanging around before, on the off-chance.'

'Uniformed men will have covered that. If the little Johnson girl is as observant as her mother claims, Jane Hunter never got as far as the shop. Let's look at the lane that turns off just before it.'

He waited for a clear space and did a fast three-point turn, doubling back and easing into the narrow road five doors away from the newsagent. He bounced the nearside wheels on to the kerb and was scowled at by an old man leading a dog from a garden gate opposite. 'All right if I park here a minute?' Mott asked cheerfully.

The man came close. 'Wudden make much difference what I said, wuddit?'

77

'Get a lot of it, then?' Mott sounded sympathetic, untypically abashed.

'Alla time. You shud see it mornings. Folks on their way to work, goin' for fags and papers. No consideration for them as has to live here. Hey, you anythin' to do with the perlice? They bin askin' my missus all sortsa things.'

'CID, yes. Weren't you questioned yourself?'

'I wuz out. Walk the dog three times a day reg'lar. That's how they missed me.'

'So I'll ask you now. Did you notice anything unusual this morning between eight-thirty and nine?'

'Much the same as always. Usual character with an old van where you're parked. Came back with a newspaper under his arm and started kickin' the nearside tyres. Glared at me as I got back, just as if I'd bin droppin' tacks to give him a puncture.' The old man's indignation faded into wry regret. 'Mighta done it if only I'd thought.'

'We'd better contact him for a statement. Maybe he saw something. Did you notice the van's number?'

'Nuh. Blue one, it was. Seen if often. He must live somewheres around.'

'Did you see him drive off?' Rosemary put in.

'Didn't stay to watch. Ugly mood he was in. When I shut me door he was just gettin' in, only he stopped and went back. As if he'd seen someone he knew. He was wavin' his paper towards the main road, last thing I saw.'

Rosemary looked hard at Mott who nodded. 'Maybe,' she ventured, 'we should ask Mrs Bowles what colour her husband's van is. That's one person we know wasn't in too sweet a temper at that time, according to Daphne.'

Mott set his teeth. 'You're right. Look, Mr – er . . .'

'King. Ernest King. If you wanna follow up this feller, you go after him. And tell him he can park somewheres else in future. I'll be in when you come back. Or jes' a dog's lead away.'

Mott decided against a second visit to Mrs Bowles. She might ring ahead to warn her husband they were coming. Better to chance confronting him at his work. She'd mentioned Cabury Joiners as his employers. Mott radioed through to Control to send out a DC to Ernest King for a description of the van driver.

The joinery was down at Wycombe Marsh. There was just space to park between two pick-up trucks being loaded with timber frames. As Mott and Z got out, their ears were assailed by the high-pitched scream of a power saw. No one was in the office but the receiver was off the hook, and as they waited an officious little man with a bald head came galloping up to take the call, followed by the office secretary. Rosemary, finding Mott had drifted off, explained to her that they wished to talk with Bowles.

'He's out on a replacement window job,' said the girl. 'You could see Mr Ashdown if it's about having your measurements taken.'

Rosemary stifled a grin. 'It's rather more a personal matter,' she explained. 'A bit of family trouble.'

'Oh yes?' The girl looked hopeful, but when Rosemary displayed her warrant card and said, 'Thames Valley Police,' her curiosity dried up.

'He's out at Jordans. You know the Quaker village? I'll get you the address he's working at.'

'Did he take his van?' Rosemary thought to ask.

'No. He wanted to, but Mr Polly made him unload it and take the two-ton truck, because of the weight with double glazing. And a right fuss he made about it too. I thought there'd be a fight.' She wrote out the address, adding the name Healey as assistant fitter.

Mott had quietly come back in and was standing behind them. 'A blue van, already loaded, you say?'

'Blue, yes. Actually he hadn't taken on the window units and frames. He was still carrying stuff from yesterday and he thought the Jordans order could go in on top. No way. Mr Polly made him shift the chests back into the store and booked the van out to the varnisher.'

'Chests?'

'That's right. We do a bargain line in whitewood chests. People use them for storing blankets or as toy boxes. You interested?'

'That might be just what I'm looking for,' said Mott ambiguously.

They followed her to a store-room off the rear yard.

'Have a look around,' the girl invited. 'There's two sizes. You can have them primed ready for painting or one coat polyurethaned. 'Scuse me; I've got to get back to the office.'

'You don't really think . . .?' Rosemary appealed to the DI.

'Depends how much time he had. We'd better check.'

The chests were stacked three deep. The first Mott opened held nothing but a little powdered dust from planing and a pleasant scent of fresh pine. Together they lifted it down. The second had a darker mark on the chicken-flesh paleness of its interior. Rosemary put a damp finger on it and was relieved to find the colour didn't come off.

'Just a knot in the wood.'

'It's got something snagged on it, though. See?' Carefully Mott pulled at it, unwinding a thread of red wool.

'Red coat and red gloves.'

'Off to the car, Z, and put in a request for immediate backup. I want SOCO out here and this chest bagged for removal. And a patrol car to meet us this side of Jordans. I'll get the secretary here to order the varnisher back with the original van before he roots around in it and destroys any evidence.'

While they waited for the relief to arrive, Mott spread an ordnance survey map on the car roof. 'Here, the place he's working is a turning off the north side of the village green. Woodland and open fields on the far side. Doesn't look good at all.'

'Bowles had promised to take his daughter out for the day but his wife wouldn't have it,' Rosemary reminded him. 'If he happened on Jane Hunter and somehow persuaded her to go instead, it might still be fairly innocent.'

'Invitation to a picnic? At this time of year? Anyway, little Jane would have turned it down.'

'If she knew what he intended. But if he made out he was giving her a lift to school, because Daphne had let her down . . .'

'M'm. And she wouldn't see him as a stranger.'

'She could have overheard him rowing with his wife. She wouldn't risk upsetting him again. Yes, I see her getting in the van, just to keep the peace.'

'And then? At some point she'd realize he was going the wrong way. She'd make a fuss. Which he'd have to stifle. And then somehow red wool from her coat or gloves gets snagged on the inside of one of the chests in the van's rear.'

Mott was interrupted by a voice on the car radio. He identified himself.

'Message from DS Beaumont. A Daphne Bowles has recently been queried for the "At Risk" register. Social services are still waiting for a doctor's report. The query raised by her class teacher, a Miss Monica Foster.'

'That figures. I want Beaumont here immediately, to take over this end.'

'That's it, then,' said Z grimly. 'We know who these kids are most at risk from, don't we?'

Mott darted her a swift glance. He'd forgotten for the moment that Z had first-hand experience of child abuse; a ten-year-old orphan terrorized by the aunt's husband in whose house she'd been offered shelter. This would be a sickening case for her to tackle, but she'd be the right person on hand when they reached the child. If they got to her in time.

'He'll try persuasion first to keep Jane quiet about it, then threats,' the WDC said, staring woodenly ahead. 'But Jane seems to be open enough with her parents. They would notice her distress later. I wonder if he understands her background? If his own daughter has kept it from her mother, maybe he'd hope . . .'

A patrol car came sweeping into the joinery yard and two uniformed men tumbled out, keen to share the action. Mott gave a few terse instructions, then he and Z packed into their own car and accelerated out, heading for Jordans.

Superintendent Yeadings returned from rinsing his mouth with salt water and looked sourly at the barely tasted cup of tea which, gulped too hot, had exploded a pain bomb in his upper jaw. Cautiously he began to sip at it again when his black phone gave a buzz.

'Yeadings. Who? – ah, of course.'

Matthews, Aylesbury vehicle examiner, had gone down

to Aldermaston on another case and so been the first to hear the positive find on the Webster car. Definite evidence of interference; nothing in the usual area; quite a cunning little bit of sabotage. Small perforations under the metal part of the feed pipe from the master cylinder. The instrument used could be something like a nutcracker with a line of fine, sharp teeth. Possibly with a vice attachment, because the slim pipe was tough and considerable force would have been needed. Not like cutting the ribbon to open a bazaar.

He thanked the examiner and replaced the receiver. He'd felt in his bones that the failure of Francine Webster's car was no accident. Modern brake systems were as near foolproof as dammit. Even with deliberate interference of this kind, brake failure would be only partial. It had taken the driver's panic over the long pedal action, plus the wrenching on of the handbrake and an icy road surface, to cause the crash. So what had the saboteur intended – death, or just a bad fright?

That depended, didn't it, on how well clued up he (or she) was on the technical possibilities? It was commonly supposed, but wrongly, that you cut the fluid supply and both pairs of wheels were affected. Francine herself might know better. Morton Webster, with his haulage fleet, undoubtedly would. But any of the others could have thought that on that road the interference would guarantee a fatal spill.

Now, once the missing child case was tied up, he'd put Mott's team back on an attempted murder inquiry. The trouble was, if there had been an intended victim, which of the two young people was it – Francine or her cousin Dominic?

DS Beaumont came round the corner into the joinery yard with a squeal of tyres and slammed on the brakes, almost catapulting Silver out of his already unlatched door. They were close on the arrival of two uniformed officers, and Beaumont's first concern was to keep them and the joinery workmen at a distance until SOCO had been in. With a guard on the outer doors, he walked through the delivery store-room. As he reached the far end a half-glazed door opened and a small, elderly man came through with a ledger.

'Who're you then?' Beaumont demanded.

'I'm Mr Ford. You don't work here. Customers aren't allowed . . .'

'Police.' He flashed his warrant card. 'So what's your job?'

'Funeral requisites,' said the little man with dignity, and blinked. 'I am in charge of caskets, urns and boxes.'

'Does that include the chests over by the main doors?'

'They're a cheap domestic line my apprentice makes. The quality work is through here.' He turned and marched back the way he had come, Beaumont following.

In a fair-sized workshop there were two gleaming coffins standing ready for delivery. 'Know what this is?' asked Ford, laying a reverent hand on another, miniature casket.

It looked just right for burying a pet rat, the policeman thought, but he wasn't given time to utter the sacrilege.

'Myrtle wood,' Ford said in hushed tones. 'From Oregon. Special order for an American gentleman. For the ashes,' he added as Beaumont continued to look uninformed.

'I always thought coffins were mass-produced,' said the detective.

'They mostly are,' said Ford, snuffling a little. 'Chipboard with various veneers; but we craftsmen are still appreciated for the quality work. Thirty-five years I've been employed by the Cabury brothers. Once I had four cabinet-makers under me, but it's fallen away, sadly. I'm semi-retired now, with only one lad to assist.'

'Well, perhaps you'd assist *me*, as you aren't rushed.'

'However I can, of course.'

'Do you know an employee called Bowles?'

'There is a journeyman here by that name.' Marked disdain.

'Did you see him this morning? Have any conversation with him?'

'He was late, which caused considerable inconvenience.

It meant that the outgoing goods were stacked in the wrong order.'

'What time did he arrive?'

'It was after nine. He's due at eight-thirty, but most of the drivers are here ten minutes before that, for loading.'

'So you had words?'

'Not I. At the best of times he's not a man I care to deal with. This morning he was particularly offensive to Mr Polly who organizes Goods Outward. He was determined to keep the light van he'd taken out last night, but it was needed for another purpose, and I'm glad to say Mr Polly had the last word.'

'I understand there were things he had to unload from the van?'

'Yes. He returned two blanket chests which were sent out on approval. We make two sizes, you see, and . . .'

'Right. So did you actually see him carry them in?'

'I can't say that I did. I had no wish to cause embarrassment by witnessing an outbreak of violence.'

Chickened out, Beaumont translated. 'So, when he'd changed transport, Bowles had to load some heavier stuff. That right?'

'Yes. He called my assistant to help. It's company policy that the double-glazed units are always handled by two, because of insurance coverage.'

'Although he'd already replaced the chests on his own?'

'Certainly. Anyone could handle whitewood goods of that size. Er, has there been some sort of accident?'

Beaumont considered this. 'Not to my knowledge,' he admitted. 'I'm just interested in working practices.'

It didn't totally satisfy the little man, but just then the Scenes of Crime experts arrived. Beaumont waved DC Silver aside. 'I'm going after DI Mott. He may need a hand. Stay on here and get a statement from the man Polly and any eye-witnesses to the unloading.'

'How about the old gaffer back there?'

'The craftsman coffin-maker? Not much use. Too absorbed in his work.'

'Gruesome job.'

'Yeah.' Beaumont stopped half way into his car and

winced at his own coming pun. 'Probably gets good perks. Free bier, would you think? On the house?'

The address Mott sought at Jordans was a cottage at the hamlet's edge, in atmosphere midway between Disney and the brothers Grimm. Z felt that aged crones might at any time leap out cackling from the gingerbread buildings. Encroaching woodlands looked dankly menacing in the failing light.

Of the expected Cabury Joiners truck there was no sign, but they drew up behind a well-kept eight-year-old Ford Escort. 'That could be the assistant fitter's,' Mott guessed. 'Stay ready for take-off while I find out what's happened to Bowles.'

Healey was indeed within, enjoying a cooked meal in the kitchen, his arrival from the outer world a big event in the life of the pensioner who lived here alone. She wanted Mott to join them, incapable of grasping that any urgency was involved.

Healey was full of complaints against the man he had been sent to work with. 'Arrived late, said he'd got lost. Then I had to help dig his truck out of a boggy bit of lane before we could start. Next he takes two sodding hours off for lunch, and me with the big window to fit in on me own. Real swine he's been all day. Then he chucks his tools in, leaving me to make the plastering good. We'll be here all week at this rate. Mr Cabury'll go spare.'

'I don't think he was feeling very well,' offered the Quaker lady.

'When did he leave?' Mott demanded of Healey.

'Ten minutes back.'

'Going which way?'

'Same way he came. I wasn't going to tell him the shorter route.'

'Left or right out of here?'

'Left, and turn right after fifty yards into the wood.'

'Thanks. I'll talk to you tomorrow.' Mott ran back to the car. 'Straight on, and first right.'

The lane wound downhill, overhung by trees, the surface slimy with half-thawed ice from running springs.

No sound of birds came through the dank scents of rotting vegetation. Rosemary put on as much speed as the slippery track allowed. There were two S-bends and after another eighty yards or so a fork before both tracks began again to ascend.

'Left,' Mott snapped. Ahead the lights caught deep tracks in the black mulch by the verge where a large vehicle had run off the road and made heavy weather of reversing out. 'That's it. Stop ten yards past the mess. For God's sake don't spoil . . .'

But Rosemary had realized the tracks' significance and pulled well clear to avoid them.

Mott was out, treading cautiously, flashlight in hand. Z followed.

'Guv!' She caught at his arm, spoke barely above a whisper. 'Along the lane, on the bend. Could be the truck.'

He saw the dark mass she pointed to. So where was the man, ahead of them or behind?

Then they heard him retching, and a moment later the truck door slam.

'He's getting away!'

'No, listen! He's coming through the wood.'

Coming closer. They stood on the direct path between the approaching man and where the truck had first floundered. 'Down!' breathed Mott, and they both crouched for cover.

The man made no attempt at silence. He was lumbering through the undergrowth. They heard brambles tearing at his clothes. His breathing was heavy, almost sobbing. Mott was feeling around by his feet for some weapon, a stone, a club, anything, because even with the advantage of surprise there was too much to lose. A child sex victim already, and Rosemary Z alongside. Trained copper she might be, but a woman still.

The sounds stopped a short distance away. A moment of silence, then a small animal sound. The child? Still alive?

No. Something more eery, unhinged. It was the man keening.

The high pitch dropped to a subdued moaning. Mott rose to his feet and went quietly forward, Z close behind.

The trees thinned into a little hollow, and there they had their first sight of Bowles crouched in a bed of dead bracken, head in hands and sobbing, while the unused tyre lever lay on the ground beside him.

He was unaware of their presence, even when Mott stood over him and Rosemary slid the weapon away. 'Where is she, man? Where's little Jane?'

She wasn't far off, tucked behind a screen of bare elder branches. Wood shavings curled out from either side of the dirty handkerchief binding her mouth, and her wrists were still taped behind her. She lay stiff and cold, her eyes wide-staring.

But alive. Minutes more and Bowles could have steeled himself to use the tyre lever and silence her for ever.

Ever since they first entered the trees Rosemary had been holding a fruit knife open in her pocket. She slid it now through the gag and cut it away, emptied the girl's mouth with her fingers, talking quietly, comfortingly, as she worked. Next the wrists, but the child couldn't move them apart.

Z cuddled her close. 'Jane. Janey, believe me, it's all right now. It's over. We're going home to Mummy and Daddy.'

The child's first movement was a sudden recoil as Mott came close.

'He's a friend,' Rosemary assured her. 'We're police. You can trust us.' She turned swiftly, apprehensive. 'Bowles? Angus, he . . .'

'Cuffed. He'll be no trouble. When you're ready, take Jane back to the car and call in for support. I'll keep Bowles separate in the truck until the cavalry get here. No hurry. Let the little lady thaw out. Then Dobbin and the usual back at base. Call the parents in.'

Dr Miriam Dobbs (Dobbin because she was a great old war-horse) had no doubts. All the positive signs were there: tearing, semen stains, lumpy bruising. She gave a preliminary report and made her departure tight-mouthed.

She had been ready with a warm blanket when

87

Rosemary gently removed the shocked child's torn clothes and bagged them. 'I think one of my special sweeties in your cocoa,' Dobbin suggested. 'Then I'll have a little look to check you're all right before Mummy comes in. We don't want to keep her waiting, do we?'

'And the man?' she had asked flatly, scrubbing off afterwards. 'I suppose he's my next pleasure.' But a male colleague was already with him. This way no chance of a later defence of traces transfer through a third party.

Not until Jane was again in her parents' care could Z afford to ease up. Sent to Superintendent Yeadings on emerging shakily from the women's room, she found herself short of words.

'You did well. Get it typed up first, then straight home,' he ordered, familiar with the way of things.

'Yessir.' She stopped at the door and looked back, holding on tightly to the jamb. 'Do you know what really got me? Jane was scared she'd be scolded for staying off school.'

'Funny old world,' said Yeadings, 'or has someone already said that? By the way, tomorrow we're looking again at the Webster case. The girl's car definitely was monkeyed with.'

He cleared his desktop for going home, switched off the lamp. And realized his face pain had eased. Must be the antibiotics getting at the abcess. Another couple of days and maybe he could have that rotten back tooth out.

NINE

FRANCINE LOOKED AGAIN AT HER mother's ormolu clock. It agreed with her own wrist-watch: six-twenty. Surely by now Elinor should have been back to dress if she had a seven o'clock drinks engagement? The girl went across and checked the date on the invitation card tucked in a corner of the mirror. Yes, it was for tonight.

Outside it was quite dark now, and besides the shushing of soft snow against the window panes a rising wind was scraping across branches of some spiky shrub with an eerie screeching. The roads would be clogging with evening commuters from London. To stay on might risk a further encounter with her stepfather. Best to leave a note on Elinor's dressing-table.

She got away just in time, the lights of Frank's Mercedes coming at her as she turned out of the driveway. As he pulled to a sudden stop she waved a dismissive hand, noted that he was alone in the car, and drove on past. The drinks invitation had included him. It looked as though Elinor was standing him up again.

For whom? Francine remembered old Hadrian's smile, the malicious words: 'I know all about your mother – and her new lover.'

Isolated out at Lynalls, how could he learn so much when Francine herself had heard no recent scandal? The old man had probably been bluffing, counting on the leopard not changing its spots. She should have challenged him, demanded who the fortunate man was. But he would never have told her. He'd rather set her guessing, wanting her to start digging into Elinor's private affairs and so make trouble between them. Well, she knew better than to attempt that. But the question went on niggling at her.

She was unsurprised, just faintly curious about who the new man might be. It was little wonder that red-blooded Elinor looked elsewhere when Frank was such a wimp. She had surely married him because of her frustrated need to be maternal, Francine herself having opted out early and so deprived her of the function.

But mothering wasn't Elinor's strongest instinct. She needed a he-mate, a cave monster, someone who'd measure up to her own wild potential, fight and dominate her. It was fortunate that she encountered such a one only infrequently. On those occasions she was transformed with a surging dynamism. She became more beautiful, more animated, if possible more vital than before. There followed a period of ecstatic fulfilment, but too soon would come the uncontrolled furies, the shattering despair, the physical bruises, the emptied bottles; finally total silence, and after a long withdrawal an exhausted, quieter Elinor would be back in circulation being charitable, extending sympathy, running errands, putting herself out for anyone who would take advantage of her generous nature. Another protracted mothering phase while she rebuilt herself, until a new he-man claimant crossed her path.

It was her destructive fate to crave being mastered, but to find her only enduring rôle as a protector of men weaker than herself. And in each of her sexual disasters she poured herself out while the men, uncomprehending, leeched on to her as either a copulative stimulus or a substitute nipple.

How, Francine asked herself, can I go on loving her as I do and have any respect for males who misunderstand her so?

She had long felt that the only safe sexual path for herself was an uncommitted one, fondness and lust prudently segregated. Curiosity had led her to step experimentally on the biological merry-go-round, but she had never for long let both feet leave the ground.

Once as an adolescent unwillingly aware of the searing

stages of her mother's passion, she had asked herself *why?*, but she did so no more. Elinor was Elinor, made that way. It was organic.

And beneath the compulsions Elinor was subject to, some blame, she thought, must lie with herself, the sole offspring refusing to be sheltered. But by God, *his* had been the greatest guilt: her father, whoever he was. It all goes back to that. What kind of disappearing demon was he, to stir up such cycles of frenzy, setting in irreversible motion this mechanism of eventual self-destruction?

Traffic was still streaming out of London, all three oncoming lanes ablaze with headlights, her injuries sharply reminding her she'd been warned against driving too soon. She'd missed taking her pain-killers; lucky, that, because she was weary enough without. When she reached the flat she'd have a long, hot soak in the bath, with the water just waist-high to keep the rib-strapping dry.

She left the motorway at the West Slough exit, turned north, exchanging traffic for snaking lanes with high walls of greenery, then open fields and the final calm of her cul-de-sac. As she passed her flat she noticed lights in the windows, and tooted to bring Roddy down and save her scrabbling for the doorkey. She disposed of the hired car in the line of lock-up garages and walked the twenty yards back.

Roddy opened up looking tousled and in his dressing-gown. 'Did I disturb you? Sorry,' she said, and stomped past him. She went on up the stairs and he followed close, while someone from the lower flat closed the outer door on leaving.

'The place is a bit untidy,' he warned. 'I wasn't expecting you back for a few days.'

'I decided I'd do better back at work,' Francine said shortly.

'Good.' He rubbed at his spiky hair and gave his triangular, outdoor smile. 'I was hoping you'd come back because you missed me.'

'That'd be the day.' She went through to her bedroom and dropped her bag on the floor. But funnily enough, she supposed she had missed him, just a little. There had been a lot on her mind, so no room for cravings. But now, back among her familiar things and able to be private, to regain herself, she would admit it was comfortable to have him around. With the promise of his intelligent talk, and gentle love-making before sleep at the day's end.

She went to rejoin him in the lounge where he had turned on the television. 'How're things?' she invited.

Roddy stood, head on one side, zapping from programme to programme, and hummed non-committally. 'Plenty of work to be picked up, but low budget stuff. Everyone's feeling the pinch and the first to go is always advertizing. I've moved over to a pilot scheme Darby is scripting. Could be a good proposition.'

'Any star billing?'

'What do you think? Would-be starlets and producer's friends. I could get you in as an extra any time you want.'

'I've enough on my plate. Anyway, Josh wants to do a portrait of me. That should satisfy my amateur camera-lust.'

'You sound a bit scratchy. What's wrong?'

'Tired and sore.'

'Want me to help warm your bed?' He came across and put his arms tenderly round her.

'M'm, an early night might be what I need.'

'What *we* need. Tuck yourself in and I'll bring along some drinks.'

But he stayed to see the end of a documentary, and when he slid under the duvet Francine was already asleep, scented with bath gel, her chin tilted aggressively, the centre line of her mouth suggesting that whoever featured in her dreams could be in for a hard time.

She had been the subject of some uncharitable thoughts herself as Frank Godden swiftly showered, one ear alert for sounds of Elinor's return. In his bath-robe he looked into his wife's room, but the note under her hairbrush was only something from Francine. Wretched girl, why couldn't she have stayed on? Having her in the house was an interest for Elinor, something to keep her innocently occupied.

He sat down for a moment, conscious of the painful throbbing set up in his head at first sight of the folded paper on the dressing-table. Always at the back of his mind was the grinding fear that some day there would be a quite different note, addressed to him in Elinor's hand.

He returned to his own room, took two more tablets and lay a few minutes on the bed before dressing. When he was ready, and impatiently aware that they were already twenty minutes overdue for the party, the phone rang.

'Godden.'

The caller had engaged in some asides while he dialled and Frank caught the tail end: '. . . take them through, then. Yes, to the conservatory, you dolt.' In the background were voices and laughter.

'Godden,' he acknowledged again.

'Hello, there. Pat Knowles. Message from your good lady. She got somewhat hung up with her shopping in town, so she's come on direct. Last one to arrive's a cuckoo, or something.'

Frank replaced the receiver with a shaking hand. Bloody party parasite! And what did he mean by that dig at the end? Was that Knowles's sort of humour or had Elinor herself said it, gaily waving her glass, not bothering to make the call herself? In the vivacious little group gathered round her someone would have turned away, murmuring behind his hand the inevitable witticism, 'Cuckoo or cuckold, poor old Frank.'

Godden leaned over his hands as they steadied him against the table. He wouldn't turn up. He hadn't wanted to go in any case. Certainly Elinor wouldn't be concerned one way or the other.

He tried to convince himself he'd enjoy a quiet evening at home. But not on his own, with Elinor having her fling with God knows what lady-killer and either driving herself home after drinking too much or chauffeured by some shit who'd find a lay-by and start groping her on the back seat.

He re-read Francine's note while he poured himself a stiff scotch, then dialled the local taxi service. He was told there'd be a further twenty minutes delay. It was the last straw. He snarled a cancellation, swept up his overcoat and gloves from the hall and went out for his own car.

At Headington Edith Halliday sat on in front of the blank television screen, with her supper tray on her knees and the salad sandwich untasted. She lifted the letter from VSO headquarters off the chair-arm, and re-read it to make quite sure she hadn't misunderstood.

Further to her message regarding her son Piers, the writer insisted that it had been impossible to contact Mr Halliday. He had not taken up the vacancy offered with the North Africa Relief team and had written as recently as two weeks ago to withdraw his application. It was trusted that she would have more success in contacting him at his previous address.

She had already phoned through to the flat which he had shared with two other young men in Kilburn, and learned that he left there a fortnight back. About half his belongings were also gone.

Her son, disappeared, without leaving any forwarding address; it was so unlike him.

Her first impulse had been to notify the police, but second thoughts warned her that he might turn up at any moment, and whispers of unreliability could harm the chances of a young would-be solicitor. And then, just now, hadn't the police all sorts of ridiculous, unspecified suspicions about the family without drawing their attention to her branch of it? Not that there could possibly be any connection with the unfortunate business of Francine's car, even though they'd inquired how certain she was that Piers was away at the time.

The Palladian marble clock on the mantelpiece struck the hour and, setting aside the tray, from habit she went to switch on the television news, a new chill creeping over her at the fear that tonight might be different. This time it might not be happening to other people but to herself. Some horrible disaster read out by the familiar newscaster. Something had happened to Piers, something that would change her life in a moment.

But there was nothing; just the customary Middle Eastern disturbances, and on the local news a man, his head masked with a blanket, bundled out of a police car and into an official-looking building. One of those awful child-abusers who'd abducted a neighbour's little girl. Quite horrible, but no cause for personal concern.

What began to nag at her now was how knowledge of Piers' disappearance might affect his standing with old Hadrian. Provided she said nothing herself, was there any way it might become public property? Perhaps only if the police were to check on him again.

If Morton's wife Marcia were to guess that Piers had never arrived in Ethiopia, had finally decided against going, what would she make of it? Accuse him of causing the injuries to his two cousins to clear his own way to becoming Hadrian's heir? Such a vindictive and unreasonable woman! Marcia had gone too far already with her campaign against Francine.

And yet she had a point there because, however unlikely the possibility that the girl would deliberately harm Dominic, quarrelling with him as he drove she might well have upset him and so brought about the crash. Yes, one could see what had started Marcia off on that tack.

But the police were also inquiring into the movements of others in the family, surely with the implication that the car had been tampered with while Francine was upstairs with her great-uncle.

But they had all been together, helping themselves to the excellent buffet. Except for – except that Cousin Alastair had been absent for a few moments before his turn came, and while Mrs Cooper was pouring coffees. He'd have gone to the bathroom, almost certainly. Yet who was to know for sure? He could as easily have slipped back the front door lock and gone out into the courtyard unnoticed. There had been no other staff on duty that night to observe him.

No, not Alastair. He didn't admire Francine's brusque waywardness any more than she did herself, but he wasn't the sort to endanger anyone. Except by loose talk.

There, she was eliminating everyone from harming Francine on the score that it would be out of character. Which left motive (as well as opportunity) only for someone beyond the family. Any outsider could have meddled with the car while they were all occupied indoors.

But Piers hadn't been with the family. To a suspicious mind his absence could be misinterpreted. Supposedly in North Africa, it might be claimed he was actually somewhere quite close. A malicious woman like Marcia could say he'd set up a false trail.

Was there a chance that at the last moment he'd changed his mind and decided to attend the gathering, come as far as the door while they were all inside, and then—?

Then gone away. Anything else was unthinkable. Piers wasn't one for spiteful tricks. But then it wasn't like him to deceive her about his intentions of joining the relief team. Piers was a good boy. She'd brought him up to weigh his actions in advance and listen to his conscience. She had every confidence in him.

But the doubts went on circling on the clockwork wheels of her mind.

Beyond outlining a statement of arrest for Public Relations to hand to the local press, there was no need for Superintendent Yeadings to become more closely involved with the Bowles case. Next morning he was glad enough to leave it to those who'd already had dealings with the man. Feeling as he did about attacks on the defenceless, whether the elderly and frail or the trusting innocent, he considered it fitter to ride his desk on this one, merely ensuring that all necessary steps were being taken and no move made that could prejudice the hearing of the case once it reached Crown Court. Too often of late years had over-zealous members of other forces rejigged evidence, intending to make a leaky prosecution watertight. And so, on its coming to light, they had ruined the painstaking work of the sticklers for accuracy. It wasn't going to happen on this one. Thames Valley had a reputation for fairness to maintain. Mott, as arresting officer, would see to the committal proceedings with Z standing by.

Yeadings buzzed Beaumont to drive him, and opted for a visit to Henley. It would be interesting to see Francine

Webster on her home ground, or at least her mother's. Elinor Godden didn't sound the sort to let her daughter upstage her. Also he was keen to check for himself whether his own impression of the older woman would square up with the third-hand views of Hadrian Bascombe as passed on in Francine's statement.

A shallow horseshoe drive, well gravelled, showed deep ridges where a car had recently swept from the double garage at speed, showering pebbles into flower borders planted with winter pansies and primulas. The house was large, Victorian, and gave an impression of easy affluence. Nobody here, it appeared to say, lived in desperate need of a final handout from Hadrian Bascombe. But people's desires are in proportion to their life style, as he well knew. Houses can lie as easily as humans. Sometimes you had to dig around to find the underlying truth.

The doorbell was hardly audible outside. It brought a pleasant-faced middle-aged woman in a blue floral smock who said Mrs Godden was at home and she would inform her they were there. The two men stood in the hall until she returned, followed by a striking redhead in a willow-green silk kimono.

'Superintendent, I have been hoping to meet you. Do come into the breakfast room and join me for coffee. Sergeant, you too.' They followed in her wake and were waved towards chairs.

Elinor's was a mature, almost luminous beauty, barely marred by signs of recent fatigue which showed under her eyes. She moved with voluptuous confidence. Nothing so vulgar as a Monroe wiggle: her lower half statuesque, with a gentle, long-stemmed swaying at the waist. She used her arms in expressive, if exaggerated, arabesques, but the hands were large, almost ugly, he decided.

The room was comfortable, warm, and due to the peachy colourings of walls and hangings created an illusion of sunshine that belied the icy conditions outside. Elinor Godden made no apology for the débris of the past meal, which the housekeeper now began to remove. 'Or perhaps you're a tea man, Mr Yeadings?' Elinor invited.

'Coffee would be fine, thank you.' He scanned the used crockery while she poured. 'I had thought to see your daughter again.'

'Flown the nest,' said the woman with a brilliant smile. 'As is only proper, since she has her own. Have you children, Mr Yeadings?'

'They're still young as yet. I understand your daughter is a successful career-woman.'

'A scientist, no less.' Elinor Godden gave a mocking laugh. 'Yes, that's one facet to her.'

'And the others?' Yeadings smiled into her eyes as he took the cup she handed him.

'Find them for yourself, as we all have to. I'm sure I don't have to tell you, Superintendent, that women are quite complex cattle.'

'I've discovered she's a very independent young lady. I hope that won't prevent her taking the full time needed for recovery. She's had an unpleasant experience.'

'She revels in her toughness, yes. Even to calling herself "the old boot". Which in her case is, of course, rather too . . .'

Yeadings watched her search for the right word. '—apt but hurtful,' she decided.

Hurtful to Francine herself or to the mother considered responsible in some way for the deformity? he wondered. Just how far do these two challenging women go to wound themselves and each other? It could be an uncomfortable situation for any third party in between. Back to facts, however.

'You didn't attend the family gathering on the night of the accident?'

'You know I didn't. I don't believe in pandering to the old monster's whims.'

'You don't fancy yourself as heir to his supposed millions?'

'That's another statement masquerading as a question. Excuse me.' She selected a small cigar from a box on the table, then pushed it across to the two men. 'Do light up.'

Yeadings declined. Beaumont helped himself and sniffed at the cheroot. Impatiently Elinor Godden had already lit her own. 'Have you met my uncle, Superintendent? If so, can you imagine what it would be like with the two of us in confrontation? I can exchange insults with the best that come, but I draw the line when it really isn't to any point.'

'But Francine saw fit to attend.'

'Francine is her own woman.'

'As a claimant, do you think?'

'Ask her.' Elinor shrugged, then turned impulsively to him. The harsh daylight, falling across her cheek, revealed a tiny tracery of lines hidden till then. 'Money as money hasn't any great allure for her, but perhaps – and I have asked myself this before – she may have some use for it which she hasn't divulged.'

'A great deal of money?'

'M'm. She earns enough for her obvious needs, won't take a penny from us.'

'From you and your husband?'

'Nor from either of us singly.'

'Then, hopes of reward apart, did she attend in order to meet her other relations? Or Hadrian Bascombe himself?'

'There you have me. She certainly appears to have been entertained by the evening's outcome. Until the incident with the car, that is.'

'Yes. You realize that if she had been driving herself, the result could have been much more serious for her.'

'With Francine driving, the accident would probably not have happened.'

'So why did such an independent young woman opt for the passenger seat in her own car? Pandering to her cousin's sense of male superiority? I shouldn't have thought that likely.'

'No.'

'But she would have had a reason. And it was she who offered him the lift.'

'Elinor!' The caution was hurled at her from the doorway. Yeadings had been aware of the man's approach and now he turned to face him.

Godden was tall and thin, lean-cheeked, with a domed head and liquid brown eyes like a spaniel's, but he made a less than appealing figure in his dressing-gown with an overnight growth of stubble.

'Superintendent, my husband,' Elinor introduced casually. 'Frank, this is Mr Yeadings who is looking into the accident with Francine's car.'

'Superintendent?' queried Godden. 'Isn't that a rather rarefied level to be concerned with a road accident?'

'Not under the circumstances. We are CID, Mr Godden. Our vehicle examiners have reported deliberate interference with the car.'

'You mean – someone tried to injure Francine?'

'Injure or worse, yes sir. Miss Webster or any other occupant of the car.'

'Young Dominic. But who would – I mean, this is unbelievable, unless some mindless yobbo . . .'

Yeadings flashed a glance at Elinor. She was watching her husband with a sardonic smile. On catching the policeman's eyes she gestured with both hands, palms up. The ash which had accumulated on her cheroot fell to the tablecloth and she ran a casual index finger through it, smudging the mark in. 'Naturally we have discussed together all the possibilities.'

Her words were final, cutting through the man's act of shocked disbelief. Cutting his legs away from underneath, Yeadings observed wryly. How often was that her pleasure?

She rose, stretched exaggeratedly and said, 'Well, my dears, I really must go and dress. It's all right for Frank, taking a day off work, but I have things to do. It's been so nice meeting you, Superintendent, Sergeant.' She held out a hand to each, smiled with her strange, golden eyes, shook back the copper-toned hair and moved off, queenly and well-fleshed in the clinging wrapper.

Godden was looking sicker than before. He leaned over the table, supporting himself on his hands. Hungover, and being punished for it, Yeadings supposed. One paid a price for marriage to a challenging Amazon.

Yeadings and Beaumont moved towards the door. Limply Godden followed. 'If there is anything I can do, Superintendent . . .'

As if there could be, he seemed to imply.

'I don't suppose you'd have any idea,' Yeadings suggested on the doorstep, 'why Francine should invite her cousin to share her car like that?'

He shook his head. 'Seems quite out of character to me. Frankie wasn't really fond of him at all. Found him a bit of a drag. Maybe . . .'

'Yes?'

'It could be something to do with a photograph he had.' Godden spoke as if thinking aloud.

'What photograph would this be?'

'Oh, perhaps I shouldn't have . . . I don't really know anything myself. It was just something Frankie let out at the hospital, right after the accident. I went there with my wife, you know. She was babbling, only half-conscious, poor love. Frankie, that is. Thought she was still in the car with him. Now, what did she say? Something about a snap, then, "Dom, you swine, give it to me. You'll be sorry!" Nothing important, I'm sure, and for heaven's sake don't let her know that I said anything. My stock with her is already at rock bottom.'

TEN

'I – ER, TROTTED DOWN TO Henley to see the Goddens,' Yeadings told Mott when they met up over constabulary cottage pie. He made it a throwaway remark as he bent to pick up a fallen fork and wave it at the distant girl who had been serving their table.

'Oh yes?' Mott took the news po-faced, but his boss wasn't deceived. The lad was slightly shocked that he'd moved out of line, poached on his underlings' preserves.

'How did you find them?'

'In their dressing-gowns, at late breakfast. Somewhat hungover, but she less so. Formidable lady, as one was led to expect. The man – under the circumstances, I wasn't impressed, but he let fall something that you might well follow up. A possible reason for Francine offering her cousin a lift. It seems Dominic had a photograph, subject unknown, which the girl wanted off him. A "snap" he called it.'

Mott considered this. 'Nothing significant, surely, if she'd discussed it with the scorned stepfather.'

'She hadn't. Or not intentionally. Godden drove the mother over to see Francine in Casualty as soon as they had news of the accident. The girl was half-conscious, babbling a lot of nonsense, but he was sharp enough to pick up she was pretty desperate about this.'

'Or did he exaggerate, out of spite? The implication being that what Dominic had was a potentially embarrassing picture of the girl herself.'

'It could be like that, of course. But why should he manufacture trouble? He tried to cover up when it was too

102

late. I hadn't seen enough of the man to know if that was a genuine reaction.'

'By now he must realize we'd probably question her about it. Better get on to it before he warns her. I'll ring and fix a meeting.'

'She's moved back to her own flat in Stoke Poges. Probably returned to work too. So leave it till this evening. Have a word with Dominic in the meantime. The doctors can't hold us off him forever.' Yeadings belaboured a crusty roll with butter and changed the subject. 'How's the Bowles committal material shaping up?'

Mott and Z found Dominic Webster alone, wearing a padded headset attached to a tape-machine. No mere Walkman for him, Mott observed, his eyes taking in the expensive equipment. 'No visitors today?' he asked cheerfully.

The young man carefully removed the earpieces with one hand and grinned. The other wrist was still connected to a drip, but he had clearly recovered movement in both arms.

'Mother's bridge club afternoon. And yesterday was the hairdresser. Two days free of being coddled. I got her to bring me in some tapes, or she'd have arranged a baby-sitting roster. Get yourself a chair, Inspector. Oh sorry, is the young lady with you? I'd taken her for one of our more ravishing doctors.'

When they were both seated and Mott had asked the expected questions about his health and learned that the previous day's operation to relieve pressure on the nerve had exploded the boy's gloomy foreboding, they added their own congratulations.

'Look at the pile of mail already,' he said, pointing to the opposite wall. 'The phone wires must have been buzzing all night. I was even allowed a glass of Moët with the doctors.'

'A ticklish bit of surgery, I imagine,' Mott offered.

'So I believe. I'm going to have the best X-ray framed.'

Mott dived in. 'Which reminds me, do you have the photo with you, the one Francine wanted back?'

It caught Dominic open-mouthed. 'She told you?' He flushed, seemed unable to reply, then said hurriedly, 'No, it's at home somewhere.'

Momentarily all the bounce had gone out of him. The two detectives watched carefully while trying to appear casual.

'I should give it her as soon as you're on your feet again. Let her off the hook, don't you think?'

Almost imperceptible changes of expression flickered across the young man's face, discomfiture replaced by puzzlement, caution, a fleeting impression of calculation. Damn, Mott thought; I've messed it somehow. It wasn't the sort of snap we supposed.

He shifted on his chair. 'Photogenic girl, I imagine. Who took it? Was it you?'

'Well, hardly. I wasn't that precocious. Josh, I guess. He's the family photographer. I found it among some old books Dad had off Frank Godden.'

So Francine must have been just a child then. Try another tack. 'Your father collects old books?' Mott was groping about in the dark now.

'Not as a rule, but Frank was clearing junk to have a new bathroom put in. These were old histories of the area Dad was buying into. Domesday, squirarchy and land ownership, that sort of thing. Dad was having treatment for a patch of rosacea and it came up in the small talk.'

He's talking more freely now; hustling me away from dangerous ground, Mott thought.

'I see. So the snap was tucked in among these books. A picture of Francine.'

'With her mother.'

'And father?'

'God, no! That'd be worth a fortune!' The words were out before he could stop them.

Mott watched the flush creep up Dominic's neck and cheek as he turned his head away. The eyes, he decided, were like Webster Senior's, packed too tightly against the nose. An avaricious face, and hadn't the young man's outcry confirmed that trait? Photographs of Francine with a money value put on them.

But why should the girl be so keen to lay hands on a picture of herself, presumably as a child, with Elinor Godden? There must be dozens of similar ones in the family albums.

Dominic's flow of patter seemed to have dried up. Mott made one or two more efforts to get him going, with lacklustre results, concluded he was understandably tiring, and stood up to leave.

Dominic offered his hand limply to each of them. 'Any time you feel like calling in again, lighten my life,' he told Z.

'At this rate of progress, you won't be here that long,' she said sweetly. He took it as purely a reference to the speed of his recovery.

'Well?' Mott demanded of her as they reached the outdoors.

'You're smelling blackmail.'

'Aren't you? But if Dominic claims he'd have been precocious to take the photograph, then Francine was only three or four at most. So was the valuable subject matter her mother and not herself?'

'Or the place it showed as background – some clue to who her father might have been?'

'You could have a point there. But if it *was* Joshua Webster and not the father himself who took the snap – as Dominic assumes – then Joshua could even know the father's identity. Would Francine have realized that?'

'We don't even know if she'd had a glimpse of the snap or was merely going on Dominic's description .'

'She'd have seen it,' Mott insisted, 'or it wouldn't have got to her so badly that she babbled about it in delirium. He'd have shown it to her earlier, somewhere where he was safe from her snatching it off him. He considers it's of reasonable value, and an old snap like that, it's unlikely there's still a negative knocking about. If Dominic was actually holding something over her, whether blackmail or a high-priced identity clue, it could give credence to the idea of Francine's arranging the accident to get it. In which case the boy would have been carrying the picture on him, by pre-arrangement. Otherwise she might never get to lay hands on it.'

'So did she pull it off, or did her own injuries prevent her? In which case, had he still got it on him when he was carted off to hospital?'

Mott grunted. 'His clothes would have been listed on entry. Let's go back and take a look.'

But they found no mention of the contents of his pockets, and Dominic's mother had taken everything away days ago. By now the clothes would have been laundered or sent to the cleaners. His personal belongings were presumably back at home.

For a second time they left and made for their car. 'Angus, maybe we're making too much of this mystery father. Illegitimate children are given every chance nowadays to learn who their parents are. Why shouldn't Francine know already? And even if she hasn't discovered, with Elinor claiming not to know, would it bother her all that much?'

'We'll see what the Boss thinks. I got the feeling he has more than an ordinary interest in this girl.'

But they found that Yeadings had abandoned his office, leaving instructions for Rosemary Zyczynski to have another talk with the Hunter parents concerning little Jane's abduction. Which left Mott alone to wait for Francine Webster's return from work.

Angus dropped Z off in Holtspur, drove out to Stoke Poges and parked outside Francine's flat. He had been there a little over ten minutes when a stocky, red-haired young man issued from the front door and came stalking over with a belligerent gleam in the eye. 'Move on, feller,' he said, his chunky face levelling with the open passenger window, 'unless you've got a legitimate reason to hang about here.'

Angus lowered the window further and flipped his warrant card at him. 'That's who I am. Who would you be?'

The young man was frowning over the ID. '*State* police?' he queried.

'Thames Valley Force, like it says. That's all we have here. You're not local?'

'From Hastings, New Zealand. Rod Carradine. Sorry,

mate. That was my Neighbourhood Watch routine. What can I do for you?'

Mott explained he was waiting for Miss Webster's return. 'Does she leave her car at the kerb overnight?' he asked.

'Nup. See those lock-ups? Third along. She always puts the car away. That's why I don't think anyone got at it this end.'

'You know about the accident, then?'

'Should do. I'm the temp flatmate, stand-in for m'cousin Sarah, who's abroad.'

Mott thought he'd heard of him now, but not by name.

'Better come up and have a cuppa,' Rod Carradine invited.

'Thanks, I will.' Mott eased himself out and straightened. 'Actually I'd like to take a look at the garage first.'

'Nothing simpler. Use my key.' The young man burrowed in his jeans pocket and brought out a key-ring attached to a square of polished hide. 'That little feller with the square end. I'll get the kettle singing. Jes' stomp up when you're done looking. Door's on the latch.'

The garage was minimal. Mott reckoned there'd be care needed to get the little Panda parked alongside the Yamaha motorbike on its rests beside the left-hand wall. Probably Carradine's machine.

There were old stains of oil leaks on the concrete floor, although someone had provided a photographer's developing tray to catch any more recent drips, and the bottom of this was dry.

At the rear, three shelves crossed the whole width of the garage, and they were filled with a collection of partly used paint cans and cardboard cartons labelled with their contents. Most of these boxes had originally held computer stationery or hardware. A wooden one, labelled 'tools', he lifted down and carefully went through before returning it to the middle shelf. He would have liked to examine some of the envelope files crammed into cartons alongside but he didn't want Francine to return and catch him at it. There was nothing here, he decided, to indicate

107

that brake fluid had been extracted. But then he hadn't expected any easy answers offered him on a plate.

The New Zealander had the teapot ready and waiting under a blue knitted cosy with drawstrings and pompoms. 'That thing really gets to me,' he said, noting the detective's eyes on it. 'Essence of England. I asked Fran if she'd made it herself and I barely escaped with my life. Came from some church bazaar.'

'How is she settling down after the shake-up?' Mott asked, dropping into a basket chair.

'Says she's fine. A bit scratchy, mebbe. Takes time. Hasn't decided yet on the replacement for the Panda. I guess that bugs her more than most else.'

'Not a bad little flat,' Mott suggested, feeling his way. 'Been here long?'

'Me? Five weeks. The girls – eight months, I think.'

'Still a bit impersonal.'

'They're neither too flush with money. All the prettifying's been done in the bedrooms. I guess you're getting round to asking to look. Go ahead. It's all right by me.'

Mott hummed, stood and moved back into the little hallway. He opened the first door and saw luggage piled in one corner, a man's scuffed leather jacket lying across the bed. A few male accoutrements, superimposed on a lush décor of ivory satin ruffles and gilt-framed mirrors, spoke of the New Zealander's temporary occupancy.

The next room was Francine's, tidily feminine, the floral colour scheme peach and cream on dark blue, her toilet things grouped on a narrow shelf, the dressing-table dominated by a word processor.

He walked across to the three-quarters bed. No cuddly toys. A tailored pair of blue cotton pyjamas folded under the single pillow. His toe-cap knocked against something solid under the bed. He bent and investigated: perspex boxes of filed data discs and four cartons of books ranging from childhood's fairy tales through technical texts to modern fiction in paperback. No photograph album.

Here, in a space twelve feet by fourteen, was the bare summary of a solitary life. And here, he guessed, she was more herself than any outsider ever saw her. It seemed reasonable to him that maybe she'd felt a need for some image of a richer phase now lost, a photograph of her childhood self taken with her mother.

In the street outside a car hooted twice. 'That'll be the lady,' Rod Carradine said, coming to stand in the doorway. 'I'll jes' go down and unlock the door.'

He stayed below to wait for Francine and warn her there was a visitor. By the time they came up together Mott had the bedcover straightened and was back in his cane chair sipping cold tea. He stood up. 'Inspector Angus Mott, CID,' he told her, holding out a hand. 'Thames Valley Police.'

She unloaded a carrier bag of groceries on to the kitchen table and ignored his hand. He had the full force of her dark eyes searching his face for symptoms of animosity. Not afraid, not even defensive, as most people were at an unexpected incursion by police. Simply assessing the newcomer, evaluating the situation. He took it patiently. When she started to turn away he asked, 'OK?'

He got a small smile in return. 'I've written up the rest of my statement for Mr Yeadings. It just needs printing out. I'll set it up now. Back in a minute.'

Carradine squeezed another two cups of tea from the pot. 'How about Miss Webster?' Mott asked.

'She won't have this stewed stuff.'

Francine came back, easing past their chairs to the fridge and poured herself iced orange juice. They heard the chatter and whine of a computer printer from her bedroom.

'Look, I'll leave you to it,' said the New Zealander. 'Got a camera to fix.'

Which gave Mott the chance he needed to slide the topic of photography in as an incidental. She explained what Carradine's work was at Pinewood. He asked if there was any connection with her uncle Joshua Webster. None at all, it seemed. They'd not so much as heard of each other. Two different worlds, fine art stuff and video.

Which reminded him, he said casually, that her cousin Dominic had a snap for her. Not at the hospital, but back home. Would that have been one Joshua took?

Momentarily she froze, then caught up on herself. 'What picture would that be?'

'One of you with your mother,' he said lightly. 'I think he'd promised it to you.'

'Oh, maybe.' She sounded a little too casual. She sipped her fruit juice and replaced the tumbler on the table, slid on to the empty chair. 'How is Dom now? I haven't liked to bother the hospital with inquiries, and I don't welcome the sort of outburst I'd get if I phoned Marcia.'

Mott gave her the latest news: Dominic with what appeared full use of his arms and torso; expectations of almost total recovery, given time.

'God, that's a relief.' she said whole-heartedly. 'I don't blame myself for anything, but it was my car, even though I knew it was roadworthy.'

He could see her weariness. Too much had happened of late and she'd allowed herself no recovery time. There was no call to beat her into a corner. Change the subject. 'How about the car? You'll be getting a replacement, I suppose.'

'Something or other. Are you a car buff?'

'Afraid not. More of an A-to-B travel person,' he lied. 'Have you any preferences?'

'Prejudices, mainly political. That's the only kind of politics I've got. Seeing the way British manufacturing's dwindling at present, I'd avoid Jap or EC products.'

She sat, untidily relaxed, with her elbows on the table between them. A domestic scene. If it had been Paula sitting there exhausted and dispirited, he'd have reached over and fondly ruffled her hair. Francine, it seemed, hadn't anyone to do that, unless the self-styled temp flatmate had taken on the rôle.

'Maybe,' she decided, 'I'll go for a Vauxhall. People are saying nice things about them. Only it will have to be a price to suit my bank manager. He rather disapproved of our mortgage on the flat.'

'We live in hard times,' Mott agreed sombrely. 'Look, if I may be so personal, I'd say you need to knock off and get your head down. Today's taken it out of you.'

'It was good to be back, though. Working, I mean.' She rose, smoothing her dark green skirt. 'Printer's gone quiet.

I'll get that statement for your boss.' At the door she turned and asked abruptly, 'What's he like to work with?'

Mott crossed his fingers under the table. 'There are worse. A bit paternal.'

Francine gave a lopsided smile. 'He struck me that way too, both things. But a wise old bird all the same.'

She went out, leaving him to reflect that she and Yeadings had struck up a note of mutual admiration – but with a faintly grudging tone, which was only natural between investigator and suspect.

The present Francine, tired and seemingly defenceless, didn't square up with the image of her Z had given in her account of the deliberately outrageous interview of yesterday. But trust the Old Man to see through to the real girl underneath. Angus thought he'd been fortunate himself to catch her with her defences (and hackles) down. The Boss wouldn't be the only one saddened if Francine was proved to have set up the accident to injure her cousin.

ELEVEN

WDC ZYCZYNSKI HAD TO RING three times before anyone came to the door, but she persisted, having seen the furtive movement of an upstairs curtain. A dim light, filtering into the bedroom from the landing, had shown up the darker bulk of someone staring down.

It was the man, Colin Hunter, who eventually opened up, but the door was still on the chain. 'Yes?' he asked doggedly.

Rosemary identified herself and asked for a few moments of his time. He stood there, blocking her.

'It really isn't convenient. My wife's had so much to put up with; neighbours and reporters . . .'

'We want to get the whole thing cleared up as quickly as possible,' Z said crisply. 'I know it's a nuisance, but the sooner we have all the details the sooner it will all die down.'

'It never will,' he said with some passion. 'Can't you see, our lives have been ripped apart.' Nevertheless he took off the chain and stood back to allow her in.

'So how are things?' she asked quietly.

Hunter looked guiltily along the passage and lifted his shoulders. 'I thought I'd best stay at home today, but it seemed to upset her. My wife I mean. We had to take the phone off the hook. She's pulled down the blinds in the front room, as though there's been a death. Well, it feels like that. Yesterday we were just glad to have Janey back, safe and whole. Well, not whole really. That's the trouble. She'll never . . .'

'Is it that policewoman again?' came a voice from the kitchen. 'Tell her I can't stand any more.'

112

'Enid, it was her brought Janey back. We can't send her away.'

'Hallo, Mrs Hunter,' called Rosemary, unabashed. She walked on in darkness towards the crack of light where the woman was peering through. 'I know you've had a really awful day.' And then she was inside the kitchen and recognized at a glance the state of siege.

'I'll put on the kettle,' said Hunter and went to busy himself at the sink. His wife had gone back to her chair, a padded one brought in from the lounge which was now enemy territory, bordering as it did on the outside world. She sat crouched there with a car rug round her shoulders. You would have taken her for the child's grandmother.

'Janey tucked up for the night?' Z asked comfortably.

'Been asleep nearly all day,' Hunter offered over his shoulder. Water hit the bottom of the kettle with a harsh splashing and he seemed to be shouting over the top of it. 'Doctor gave her something to keep her quiet. Gave Enid some too but she won't take it. Awake and worrying nearly all the night. Now look at her.'

That last was the wrong thing to say. The woman gave a little animal moan and pulled the rug over her head. 'Go away,' she shouted through it. 'Leave me alone. Both of you. I told him to go to work. We don't want him around.'

Hunter turned an ashen face to the policewoman. He opened his mouth but seemed unable to speak.

None of the usual approaches seemed possible here, Z thought. Clearly the woman hadn't ventured outside the house yet, and wouldn't in this mood.

'Look,' she said quietly, 'this has been a terrible shock for everyone. You need all your strength to help each other. Doctors know what's best. They've seen all this before, many times. You must have rest. Will you let me make you a milky drink and then take whatever's been prescribed for you?'

Under the rug the woman was shaking her head. Hunter looked across to Z, helpless, the half-filled kettle still in his hands. 'You see?'

'Mrs Hunter.' Rosemary was kneeling beside her.

'Tomorrow morning, when Janey wakes up you're the first she'll turn to. She'll be needing you to make the world look as normal and kind as it ever was. It won't be easy, but you will try, won't you? We all want her nightmare to be over soon and forgotten.'

'I'll never forget,' came the muffled voice. 'Why did she have to go off with him?'

On the rising wail, Rosemary impulsively reached for her hands, but it was too soon. The woman pushed her away, dragged off the rug and stood, fiercely threatening. 'Get out of my home! D'you hear? Go away, or I'll do something horrible. I will! Go now, while you can!'

'You'd best . . .' said the desperate Hunter, but Rosemary had already stepped back, out of the doorway. She groped her way along the dark passage. Lights out, like wartime, she thought. The husband followed and she stood aside as he fumbled for the lock of the outer door.

'Where are the two little ones?' she asked.

'My sister has them. Enid didn't seem able . . . You'd have thought she'd never seen them before.'

'Who's your family doctor? I'll get him right away.'

'That'd finish her off.' Hunter almost wept. 'A man, see. If there was a woman in the practice . . . That's why I'm no use, just make her worse. Being a man. She thinks we're all filthy. Things she says . . . about sex!'

'I'll get a woman doctor,' Rosemary promised. 'She'll be here as soon as ever we can manage.'

Mott had taken the car, assuming she'd go home by bus at the end of the interview, so now she walked to the road's end and radioed to be picked up. Back at division there was nobody senior available for her to report to. She asked the duty clerk to look up Dobbin's number and took it on herself to call in the woman police surgeon.

Advised by phone of a cancelled appointment at his dentist's, Yeadings had seized on the opportunity to go in and get the obscene molar extracted. After steeling himself to face certain torture, it was deflating to learn that the job must wait for tomorrow.

'Give the antibiotics another day to settle things,' he was told. By then there seemed to remain neither time nor energy to make a return to his desk worthwhile. With a covert sense of truancy, he headed for home.

A shared pot of Earl Grey with Nan began to boost his faith that the infection was well on its way out. He felt brave enough to confront the frost damage wrought on his garden, and he was out there, peering into sackcloth screens protecting hydrangeas and hebes, when Nan came on to the terrace to announce a phone call for him.

'It's Angus,' she told him, nodding towards the receiver dangling by the kitchen wall.

'Right, lad, what have we?' Yeadings demanded.

'Nothing new, sir. Just an up-date, but I thought you might like to know that Francine Webster overdid not knowing what photograph we were interested in. So, being in the neighbourhood of Beaconsfield, I dropped in on her uncle and aunt. As it happened, they were both out, visiting Dominic. The housekeeper had seen to his clothes when they were returned and had emptied his pockets into a plastic bag, which I was shown. The photograph was there all right, an old three-and-a-half-inch colour print of the child with her mother. I'd say Francine was little more than eight months old, just able to pull herself upright, still in a nappy. On the back was written, "With my little darling, June twentieth", no year.'

'Presumably Elinor Webster's writing.'

'I'll get that checked.'

'What about the background?'

'No clue at all as to where the shot was taken. A few square yards of lawn, smudgy trees behind, no buildings. Both subjects in normal summer clothing. Anyway, while the housekeeper went to answer the phone, I used my Instamatic, so you can see a copy tomorrow.'

'Right. Anything else?'

'There's a note on your desk from Dr Dobbs. It seems Z ran into trouble with Mrs Hunter, the mother of—'

'I know who Mrs Hunter is. What happened? Why Dobbs?'

'Mrs H was hysterical, refused to see her own GP again

because he's a man. Z got short enough shrift herself, decided to go for the only female doctor she knew. Anyway, Dobbin went round and persuaded the woman to take sedation. She wanted you to know she'd squared it with the family's GP. She explained about the woman's state of mind, and he understood why he'd been passed over, almost apologized for his all-male practice. Even recommended a female shrink he knows.'

'Good old Dobbin. Without her tact it could have been awkward. So Z assessed the situation and acted on initiative. Make quite sure she knows she took a risk there, Angus.'

'Yes, Boss. You OK?'

'Hope to lose the Demon Tooth tomorrow. Dentist's against extraction, but for me it can't be too soon.'

Mott sympathized and put down the receiver thoughtfully. There was more than half a chance Yeadings wouldn't be at his desk at all next day. And that offered a chance for any quirky moves of his own to go unremarked. He fancied a quick tour of all the protagonists in the Webster crash case, to duplicate interviews already covered by others of the team. He had faith in the accuracy of their reports, but it never did any harm to check on impressions received at second hand.

Stepping into the hallway, Rosemary Zyczynski removed her key and closed the outer door behind her. Beyond its glass panels the kitchen was in darkness, but it opened on to welcome warmth and the tantalizing aroma of a recently baked ham which stood on its cooling tray, glazed and studded with cloves in a diamond pattern. She walked past with eyes righteously averted and went to pick over the fragments of its pastry crust discarded in the fat pan.

Too salty, more to her plump little landlady's taste than her own, Z assured herself. Boiling would surely have suited it better. But so succulent. Her mouth watered even as she resolutely filled the kettle and set out her coffee things. From her own half of the fridge she removed a foil-wrapped package of cheese and coleslaw sandwiches.

Tray in hand, she reached out at the door to switch off

116

the light, and at the onset of darkness she sensed a sudden disturbing shift of location. Right, she was tired, low blood sugar and all that, but why for an instant was she back in the kitchen of the Hunters' house?

She switched the light on again and looked around. The layout was the same: same relationship of entrance, window, sink, range, back door. But how different. Instead of the shining, neat precision imposed on the other house, this room was witness to Beattie's extravagent, slapdash cheerfulness, her warmly comfortable presence.

If Janey had been brought back here after her ordeal she would have been wrapped around with affection, reassured. There would have been no inference of guilt. She would have recognized that the familiar was safe reality and that the outrage belonged to nightmare. But in Janey's home there was no Beattie, and everything surrounding the child was new, even to the freshly decorated bedroom, the hygienic, tidily arranged toys. How could sterile respectability dispel confusion when you felt soiled, degraded?

Z steadied the tray that was shaking in her hands. Stupid, how after all these years memories could still disturb her so. Of course she saw herself in the abused child, but she had fulfilled her police rôle, had no further responsibility – officially. And personally? Appalled: how she could feel otherwise? And because much the same thing had happened to herself, wasn't there a moral duty to offer understanding, which only someone having suffered the shame could give? And she knew, felt it physically like slime creeping over her flesh, that it was far from all right now for little Janey Hunter, restored to her shattered, scandal-stricken parents.

She went up to her room, set down the tray and carefully hung her coat on its padded hanger, hooking it on the outside of her wardrobe door. She stood a moment fondling the pliant softness of the silver-grey sheepskin, and let it comfort her.

Maybe that was luxury's real function, as a distraction from the unbearable. Just the same, she remained scornful of the overindulged who inhabited a privileged world unknown to the striving Hunters.

She ate her supper, leafed through a few pages of a paperback novel which failed to grip her, turned out the light and shrugged off the day.

Next morning began with her recalling what Mike Yeadings had once said. 'We follow what clues we can find, identify the crime, then the criminal, make a good case and hand it all to the courts. Responsibility ends there. We are not, repeat *not*, welfare workers.'

In the abduction case she admitted they'd been lucky to get straight on the trail; not lucky enough to arrive before damage was done. But Janey Hunter was alive, the man caught; there was incontrovertible proof of what he had done. A good case could be made against Bowles.

But it wasn't over. The suffering had only just started, would be reinforced when the man faced public justice. How long before the healing process could get under way? A chill fear remained that for the Hunters there would be no full cure. Young children often censor what they can't understand, but for Janey's over-nice mother, so dependent on respectability, the whole structure of life was under attack, her marriage, her own sexuality, sanity itself. And Colin Hunter – how would he respond? Was his attachment enough for him to overcome her initial revulsion, or would he be pulled helplessly into despair, destroyed by his wife's suffering?

Z admitted it wasn't in her gift to help. Time, love, and wise counselling were the only viable remedies. She had to turn her back, assume that there were others at hand to cope, and pass on to routine matters.

So – a final bash at the Webster case.

She tried to suppress her aversion to the elitist family and their trivial concerns. Francine was a spoilt bitch using her physical disability as an excuse to override others. Not that they seemed, any of them, specially endowed with sensitivity: vultures, hovering over the not-yet-dead prey, or jackals jealously snapping at each other's heels. Did they matter enough to justify the work that must be put in on them, arising from their family greed?

Impatiently she flung off the duvet, stood shivering a moment at the parting of the curtains, seeing again dull skies with the yellow threat of more desultory snow. And was suddenly, inconsequentially unsure.

Greed? Could she say for certain that it was simple greed behind the damage to Francine's car? A lot pointed to it, and wasn't the girl's own account of the family meeting loaded with implications of it? But surely there were other complexities in their inter-relations that night?

There was a deviousness about these well-heeled, educated people, and mightn't confidence in their own superiority convince them they were above laws made for the common herd? There was something period about their way of living. Not just their servants and the left-over ballroom with its chandeliers, but their assured disdain, secure in their successful careers and invested capital. They belonged to body-in-the-library crime fiction, the Christie world of slightly unreal subtleties. It seemed likely they saw the police as inconvenient, slow-witted meddlers, only a minor threat since there was no super-sleuth Poirot to give a pointer to the truth.

Fanciful? she asked herself, as she flung her hair back, soaped and rinsed off under the shower. Exaggerated, perhaps; but she thought she had touched on some truth there. Complexity, rather than the obvious. Maybe the Boss had scented it too, and that was what made him hang on when others would have filed the whole business away as a probable accident. He had a sensitive nose for the devious.

Already her mood had changed. She felt eager to resume the challenge, shake out the mysteries. But at the same time she sensed a degree of shame, as though she reached again for an uncompleted crossword puzzle while the sound of quiet weeping came from a neighbouring room.

Mott phoned Z while she was eating cornflakes in her landlady's kitchen. She was to wait there and he would pick her up.

He elected to drive. Not the same car he'd used on the last case, Z noted, but a plum-coloured TR7 with a tuneful throb under the bonnet. She wondered wistfully if he'd give her a chance to try it. She took the passenger seat and received a sheaf of notes with a handwritten list attached to the upper sheet.

'The station first, then we're duplicating some visits I wasn't in on,' he told her briefly. 'Hopefully in the order given.'

She glanced through the names, noted those missing, and asked, 'How did you get on with Francine last night?'

He grunted, waiting for traffic lights to change. 'She was a little low key, considering what I'd been led to expect. No trantrums, no exhibitionism. In no way upset that I called, until the subject of the photograph came up. Then she went into elaborate casual mode.'

'Did she admit Dominic was holding a picture over her?'

'Vaguely recalled he was going to give her one. I mentioned it showed her with her mother. No reaction, so I think Dominic was telling the truth about that. Except for her attempted cover-up just before, I'd have thought they were involved in a quite normal exchange of family snaps.

'Both Francine and Dominic are trying too hard to play it down. The trouble is it's a perfectly ordinary picture of a toddler with her mother. I left a copy of it on the Boss's desk in case he goes in after facing the dentist, but you'll get a chance to see it later.'

'How did you get hold of it?'

'Called at Dominic's home. The housekeeper had removed the picture from the suit he was wearing at the time of the crash. I had my Instamatic with me and snapped it while she went to answer the phone. Luckily I found her alone at the house and she's an obliging woman.'

Z nodded, running a finger down the list. 'You'd seen Dominic's father out at the house earlier, and the mother when she came to see the Boss. Which leaves the Goddens—'

'Yes. The Boss stole a march on me there, so we'll try for them first, then Edith Halliday at Headington, and back to Francine's Uncle Josh at Turville Heath. Finally up to

London, to Tottenham Court Road, where Cousin Alastair runs a second-hand bookshop.'

'Leaving only old Hadrian Bascombe who, presumably, can't be pressed because of his stroke. Is there any news how he's getting on?'

'Nothing since the Boss called on him. I get the feeling that even if he could make himself understood it would be designed to muddy the waters.'

Rosemary stared ahead at the road. After a marked pause she asked, 'You know I visited the Hunters last evening?'

'So tell me.'

He listened while she gave an account of the situation she'd walked into. 'Didn't you consider that calling in Dr Dobbs could get her accused of poaching on others' preserves?'

'It was a petty risk compared with the need to get Mrs Hunter sedated.'

'As it happens old Dobbin had a word afterwards with the family doctor, who was willing to hold back. He even recommended a female shrink.'

'That's all right, then.'

Mott risked a quick glance in her direction. 'I have to deliver a caution just the same. Boss's orders. And watch it, Z. Don't get emotionally involved over the child, eh? There's adequate professional help on hand.'

'Right, Guv.'

She agreed with him, of course, but she didn't see that psychiatry was the only and ultimate answer. The best antidote to vicious evil was a persistent application of good. Which meant love. And love, for the respectable Hunters in shock, wasn't standing up well to the onslaught. If incapable themselves, where, in this world of whispering neighbours and salacious media, were any of them to find it?

TWELVE

'BETTER RING AHEAD AT THE station and find out if the first lot are in,' Mott advised.

A woman answered the phone, deep-voiced, melodic. 'Mrs Godden?' Z asked.

'It depends what you're after.' Humour, with a hint of invitation.

'A few minutes of your time, this morning, Mrs Godden.'

'Oh dear. Red Cross, Church Bazaar or Friends of the Earth?'

'Try Thames Valley Police,' Z offered, picking up the tone. 'Inspector Angus Mott of CID would like a word. We could be with you in half an hour.'

There was a slight pause, then brightly, 'Why not? But what's happened to the delightful teddy-bear who came before?'

'Superintendent Yeadings has a number of urgent cases on hand at present.' Rosemary kept the smile out of her voice with an effort. She was quite sure the woman was aware of relative ranks in the police.

'I shall look forward to meeting you and this – er, Angus someone.'

'Thank you, Mrs Godden. Will your husband be at home? We should like to have a word with him too if possible.'

'Frank? Yes and no. He's here, but in bed. He seems to be starting flu. I'm sure you'd prefer to see him some other time. Thursdays he normally has an NHS clinic in Wycombe, but he's had to cancel. Probably the rest of the week at his private practice too.'

Z thanked her, repeated the Inspector's name in full and heard Elinor Godden ring off.

'Well?' Angus demanded. 'What sort of reception did you get?'

She repeated their conversation to him and added, 'She sounds very confident, in command of whatever turns up, but I had the feeling—'

'Right, let's get full value on the feminine intuition thing.'

'—that it's partly cover-up. She started off with what appeared to be her routine whimsy. When I mentioned police she broke off, then decided to go on the way she'd begun. Under the bluff I think she may be as keen to meet us as we are to see her.'

'Reasonable, if she believes someone has been trying to injure her daughter. We'll have to leave the husband until we've seen the others. Assuming they're not all about their business in the daytime.'

They left the motorway at Booker, taking the scenic valley route. Overnight frost had crisped up the fallen snow. The deep, winding road was black tracked with grey, between stacked woodlands topped with sterile white. The slightest touch of colour – a roan pony ridden through the trees by a girl in an emerald anorak, a yellow Telecom van parked by a junction box – were alien, with an exaggerated contrast. There was little traffic in either direction until they reached the outskirts of Henley.

Elinor Godden was waiting for them, framed in a long window to one side of the substantial porch. She came to open the door herself, letting them into comfortable warmth with the faint fragrance of woodsmoke. Logs were burning in the open hearth of the drawingroom into which she ushered them.

She was a drawingroom character, Z decided; along with the thornless, long-stemmed pink roses in a crystal vase, the chinoiserie wallpaper and the silky cream rugs. Nothing home-grown, natural or ordinary. Definitely hothouse-inspired. But not artificial: the direct eyes stated that here was a real personality, as the voice on the phone had hinted.

Mott was aware of her physically from the first. Well-built, well-fleshed, high-breasted, smooth and highly touchable. Redhaired. Her face was a credit to one of the outstanding skin-care specialists. Behind the maquillage was elegant bone structure, firm lines, a beautifully modelled mouth, eyes that sought his own and challenged him. And then he sensed, as Z had suggested, that while being socially gracious the woman was covering up; impatient, possibly anxious.

They were barely seated when a thin, young girl in a beige uniform wheeled in a trolley with both coffee and tea. Elinor poured in silence, and the youngster, inexpertly handing out the china and napkins, darted curious glances under her lashes at the two visitors.

'Thank you, Kerry. That's very nice. We can manage on our own now.'

As the door closed on the girl, Elinor smiled. 'If she'd half a notion who you were she'd be off down the road like a gun-shy rabbit. I shall tell her after you've gone. It will be an education to her.'

'One of our sometime "clients"?' Mott asked, smiling back.

'And inner-city waif,' Elinor explained. 'One of our neighbours is a liberal magistrate, and we're expected to back his hand. Another is Master of the Beagles, so we have a pair of those to look after as well.' She raised her eyes drolly. 'One has to do the right thing, of course. Part of country living.'

'Your daughter doesn't care so much for the country?' Mott suggested, and they were away. Not that Elinor told them anything about Francine that they didn't already know, but it was interesting that she was so perceptive and unprejudiced. She understood the girl's pride in building herself a career, her liking for independence.

'You must be very proud of her success,' Z ventured.

'Proud? I don't know. I admire her enormously, perhaps envy her a little. If I had been of her generation I should have liked to live the way she does.'

'Not that you're anything but a liberated woman yourself,' Mott challenged. He made the suggestion with a

124

smile and a hint of admiration.

'I make damn certain of that,' said the lady.

'Don't you miss each other, though?' Rosemary asked almost wistfully.

'Because we don't live in each other's pockets? No, it doesn't do to continue yanking on the umbilical cord once the child is on its own two feet. All the time they're growing up, you have to keep taking one more step backwards, leaving them room to expand. It's even more essential with an only child. You find alternatives to busy yourself with. Luckily we're both able to take a detached view of family life.'

'Maybe she's less detached than you think,' said Mott. 'That's partly what's brought us here. Concerning a photograph. Do you have one missing from the family album?'

Elinor stared at him fixedly. 'I don't understand. What photograph is this?'

'Mrs Godden, when you rushed to your daughter's bedside, after the accident, do you remember her rambling on rather oddly about a photograph Dominic was to give her?'

'No, I don't. Who says she did?'

'It was your husband. He accompanied you there and—'

'It must have been when I went to speak to the doctor. Francine was still anaesthetized but restless. I left them together for a few minutes. When I came back she was quieter, in a proper sleep. We stayed on for about half an hour, then left. He never mentioned that she'd spoken.'

She left her chair and went to stand by the hearth, the blazing logs staining the paleness of her fine wool dress with fiery patterns. She seemed lost in thought. When she turned away and walked slowly back her face was flushed from the reflected heat. She stayed standing. 'Could he have been mistaken? Perhaps she was just mumbling. It isn't always easy to make out what's said when someone's only half awake.'

'No mistake. You see, we've found the photograph she was talking about. It was taken when she was very small, just beginning to stand. You are with her, sitting on a fallen tree trunk and she's beside you, holding on. You're wearing a fawn and white striped dress with . . . Mrs Godden, are you all right?'

'Oh my God,' she whispered, holding on to her chair back. Rosemary was swiftly beside her, guiding her to the seat.

'I . . . yes I have these odd little turns. It will be over in a moment. Just give me . . . time.'

Rosemary held a cup to her lips. Elinor sipped, smiled, shook her head against being offered more. 'There, I think it's passed. It's always just momentary. Wasn't it lucky I'd come away from the fire? Now, what were we talking about?'

'It doesn't matter, if you're feeling unwell,' Mott offered.

'No. I remember. It was some photograph Francine mentioned after the accident, wasn't it? And you say Dominic has it. A snap of Francine as a tot, taken with me. Yes, I'm almost sure I remember it. Probably one of those Josh took. Let me fetch my baby album and we'll see if I still have my copy.'

She crossed to a lacquered cabinet and opened it with a key. Inside there were shelves filled with books. 'Here it is. I haven't looked at this for ages. Let's see.'

She placed the album on a small side table and the other two came across. The photographs were mounted neatly in adhesive corners. Among those of Francine at an early age there was no space left empty. Nor was there a copy of the picture Dominic held.

'That would be the dress you were wearing,' Z remarked, pointing to a picture in which Elinor and another girl were walking side by side along a road backed by a hillside with cypress trees.

'Holiday snap in Italy,' said the older Elinor. 'God, I was never as young as that.'

'How old would you be then?' asked Mott.

'Eighteen, nineteen. My dresses had to last more than one season in those days. Well, it looks as though the photograph you mentioned isn't here. If it was one Josh took, Dominic might have had it off him.'

'Apparently not. He found it tucked in the pages of a book your husband lent, or gave, to Dominic's father.'

Elinor looked startled. 'What kind of book?'

'On land tenure, or something of the sort.'

'He did clear out a lot of useless books a few months ago,' Elinor remembered. 'Well, that solves the mystery, then. It must have been a lose snap I never stuck in the album, and Frank used it as a bookmark. All the same, I'd like it back. It can't have any value for Dominic.'

Mott watched her. 'I think Francine wanted it herself.'

Elinor opened her mouth to speak, closed it, then started again. 'Did she – did Francine – see it?'

'Possibly. But he may just have described it for her.'

The woman considered this. 'How unexpectedly sentimental of her to want it,' she said. But the thought brought her no pleasure. Her vital face seemed drained of life.

Mott drove away in silence. Z, looking sideways, noted the puckered mouth. She badly wanted to know what he'd made of the woman, but knew better than to ask while he was working things out. At last he said abruptly, 'We could be wasting time over this photo.' It sounded provocative to Z, and she rose to the bait.

'Not on your nelly. Too many people reacting strangely. You said yourself—'

'Francine, yes. Her mother—?'

'That was the first she'd heard of any photograph. I believe that. She didn't like the sound of her husband overhearing Francine's ramblings, but she wasn't rocked back until you started describing the actual picture, herself and the toddler together, and what she was wearing. And what she meant us to take for a "nasty turn" wasn't entirely physical. Her hand on the cup was quite controlled. I saw her eyes. She wasn't faint, but thinking furiously.'

'Playing for time. So you thought so too. And yet there's nothing about the picture itself that suggests anything special.'

'She may think it does, because she remembers the circumstances.'

'But Dominic seems to have known it would have quite an effect, and he was too young to have known what the circumstances were.'

'Unless he connects it with something he's heard from his parents' generation.'

'We could press him for it. I'd rather get it elsewhere, though.'

'Do you want to go straight to Uncle Josh? It sounds as though he may know the answer. Both Dominic and Mrs Godden thought he would have taken the photograph.'

Mott peered up at the sky, which had darkened ominously. 'No, we'll get the Headington end done and see him on the way back. I don't want to get caught too far out in heavy snow.'

Edith Halliday had put in her two hours at the hospital shop and been busy enough – Surgical Appliances clinic and diabetics morning – to keep her mind off personal problems. But once she was free of the tea and sandwich service which she shared with a fellow voluntary worker, the worries came flooding back. And the question of whether she should or shouldn't confide in Cousin Alastair who, living in Maida Vale, might be supposed to know what young men in the capital got up to when they went missing.

The house as she entered it seemed only briefly warm after the outside chill. Too soon she was regretting the overheated luxury of the Outpatients' Department. There was still half the day to get through before the comfort of a hot water bottle and bed. She had performed all the physical jobs which kept the blood circulating. If she sat down to her accounts, and to think what to do, she would really have to turn up the heating a couple of degrees.

She stood undecided between the faded velour drapes of the sitting-room windows and watched a sports car pull up at the kerb opposite. Hopefully she leaned forward as driver and passenger emerged, heads down against heavy flakes of snow that had started falling a few minutes before.

Neither of them was Piers. She recognized the

silver-grey suède coat of the woman detective, but the tall young man with her was somebody new.

With a sickening dread she went to open up the front door, certain now that any news when it came must be the worst.

'Mrs Halliday?' said the man.

She found she couldn't speak. Her eyes took in the halo of white already stuck to his crisp blond hair.

'Have . . .' she managed to get out. 'Have you news of him?'

She discovered they had hustled her indoors and into a chair. The man was rubbing her hands in his own. The girl had gone off towards the kitchen.

'My son,' she pleaded. 'Please, you have to tell me. What has happened to Piers?'

While she sipped hot soup which Z had warmed from a can, they covered their own ignorance long enough to grasp the gist of what she was so desperate about. Piers Halliday had never arrived in Ethiopia. She was convinced something terrible had happened to him.

Eventually she remembered the letter from VSO and had Rosemary fetch it from the bureau drawer. 'May I?' Mott asked and scanned it rapidly.

'It says your son cancelled the appointment,' he said. 'So it's likely he's still in this country.'

'I've been in touch with the two he shared a flat with in London. They say he moved out, with most of his things.'

Mott and Zycynski exchanged glances. 'It does sound as if he made his own plans,' Z said persuasively. 'There may be some very good reason why he hasn't yet got in touch to advise you.'

Edith Halliday began to regain some colour. The supply of medicinal whisky which Rosemary had unearthed and poured into the tomato soup was having its effect. Sitting dumpy and truculent on the edge of her armchair, the woman began to look for others to blame. 'You didn't even know he was missing,' she accused. 'What good are the police if they can't help in a case like this?'

'We can only move when a person's reported missing,' Mott countered. 'Look at the date on this letter. You could have told us days ago. The information was relevant to the inquiry we're following. Is there anyone you can think of who might have an idea where he's gone?'

'Only these two friends he lived with.'

'I suppose they might tell us something they've been warned not to mention to you. Anyone else?'

'Well, perhaps Alastair. He lives in Maida Vale, not so far from the boys' flat. If anything was wrong Piers just might have gone to see him. Not that they're friends really. Just related.'

'Anyone of his own generation? How about his cousins – Francine or Dominic?'

'I'm sure he wouldn't have anything to do with them.' The note of censure was marked. 'Piers is such a steady boy. He's always so careful . . . not to give offence.'

This was the description Mott and Z turned in their minds as, having persuaded Mrs Halliday to ring Cousin Alastair, they left her, still distressed, awaiting his arrival. He had fussed a little over the need to leave his bookshop in his assistant's care, but responded to Mott's suggestion he should come, obviously pleased to be involved in this new family scandal. Edith Halliday had had no wish to call on any of her neighbours for company in her desolation.

'Careful not to give offence,' Z quoted, once in the car again. 'That could mean that Piers is probably skilled in keeping his less savoury doings dark. And he'd probably have got away with it this time, except that because of the family meeting and the accident, his mother tried to get in touch. VSO must be accustomed to people dropping out, and would normally carry on regardless, but Mrs H cabled him and he wasn't there to receive it.'

'We did put through our own inquiry about Piers,' Mott reminded her grimly, 'and haven't had an answer. If it has arrived and been bogged down in the machinery, heads will roll.'

'So are we to consider him as a possible saboteur of Francine's car?'

'Until we find an alternative reason for his dis-appearance. But if he had done it, wouldn't he simply delay departure for Africa, rather than cancel the trip altogether? Then, by the time news reached him, he'd be settled in and nobody the wiser.'

Z grunted agreement. 'Did you get anything out of Alastair on the phone?'

'All I needed. He'd no idea what I was talking about when I mentioned the photograph, although he said he'd had old books handed in by both Godden and Dominic's father. Valueless junk, he said they were. As for Piers, he denied all knowledge of his doings. Odd bloke; he sounded quite excited at hearing the boy had disappeared.'

They drove on through increasing gloom, cocooned in warmth and lulled by the rhythmic swishing of wipers clearing the windscreen. A few miles from Turville Heath, Mott climbed out and removed a weight of snow from the juddering blades. The sky looked as if it could go on dropping the stuff right round to next Christmas.

Rosemary was thankful that the phone call to Alastair Bartholomew had saved them continuing to London. Perhaps forty minutes questioning Joshua Webster, and then they'd be heading back to base, a hot meal, and the accumulated paperwork.

They overran the driveway to the house, turned in the yard of a farm where they called in for directions, and drove half a mile back. Then Rosemary saw the long line of hothouses on a southern slope and remembered hearing that Josh exhibited and photographed exotic blooms. The modern chalet house lay beyond, but as they passed the glass buildings Rosemary called out sharply, 'Angus, look!'

The car slithered to a skidding halt, one wheel overhanging the ditch at the side of the road. Before Mott could protest, Z was out and away, running towards a door hanging open on its hinges.

Inside, the whole place was frosted, glass panes opaque, dead green slime writhing on the carefully turned earth. Puce and brown tatters of vegetation, still caught in plastic rings against wooden trellises, were the shrivelled remains of vivid blooms. The place was as cold as the world outside.

Z ran on across duckboards, through a second door. In a sort of grotto pool, iced over to within an inch around it, lay a sprawled figure in a Shetland sweater. Face down, utterly still, frozen like all his cherished blooms, this had been Joshua Webster.

Not drowned, but burned, his ankle still wrapped round by the trailing cable of an arc light that lay across his crushed head. Beyond his farther outstretched hand a camera was equally trapped in ice, its tripod legs splayed crazily above it.

Mott had caught Z up. She was steadied by his hand on her arm. 'It's him,' she said with certainty. 'An accident with the electric power. He must have tripped and dragged the light in with him.'

'Accident-prone, the Websters,' Mott said tightly. 'In this case, a little more. Death-prone.'

THIRTEEN

THE POLICE SURGEON WAS A new one to Z, young-faced but paunchy and already going bald. She found his chirpy self-importance jarring and would have been happier with Dr Littlejohn. However, in view of rapid temperature changes, unavoidable once emergency lighting was fixed up, time was of the essence and the pathologist, already notified, would take another hour to get there. At least Dr Salem was in there working on the body, even as screens were being erected in case the unusual activity, bright lights and blue flashers of police cars brought morbid sightseers from the not so distant cottages.

With familiarity, violent death should be getting easier to stomach, Rosemary told herself. And in general it was. Perhaps her present queasiness was because of the bizarre setting. With glass walls all around throwing back the lighted interior, she felt herself encased in a brilliant fish tank, the outer world invisible and alien. The Scenes of Crime officers, moving efficiently about their tasks, finned past swiftly, unconcerned. She drew aside and found somewhere to sit. Like an anemone anchored to a rock of the death pool, she made herself small, extending only the tentacles of her mind to pick up whatever plankton might drift within her limited reach. Mott had ordered her to stay, while he went to radio for the team and make a preliminary examination of the house, ensuring minimum interference. So far he had found no cause to call her in.

She forced herself back from the fanciful to reality. Dr Salem was making his observations aloud. She took out her notebook and jotted down the air temperature found on entry; night temperature outside; rectal temperature of the body; temperature of the pool water; thermostat settings on the blown electric heating system.

'This'll be a nice mathematical teaser for someone,' the doctor said brightly, beaming around. 'Thank God for pocket calculators.'

'Can't you even hazard a guess how long ago it happened?' Rosemary pleaded.

'Not my business.' He was suddenly cautious, anxious not to let enthusiasm lead him beyond his function. He came across to her, snapping shut the catches on his case. 'Tell you one thing, though. My guess is it'll be measured in days, not hours. First limit – the last time anyone saw him alive. Last limit – a few hours before you found him. Like bread stored in your freezer, a week's as good as three months. If it hasn't been too long, though, the excellent Dr Littlejohn will find our mannie's not quite so solid under the crust.'

He walked off before Rosemary could betray her distaste. At the outer door he turned back. 'Oh, by the way – he's dead, of course. That's all you really need from me.'

A uniform flat cap came round the edge of the door. 'WDC – er . . .'

'Zyczynski.'

'Yes, well, your guv'nor wants you inside now.'

She went out into a sharp night of broken cloud, a few bright stars and four sets of blue lights flashing. Cars and men had been kept at a distance from the hothouses and chalet: more signs that Mott wasn't yet accepting the death as accidental.

And she had this feeling herself, not just because the outer door was left open. In such extreme weather Josh Webster would have taken great care not to disturb the sub-tropical conditions essential for his tender blooms. If the latch hadn't caught, wasn't it more likely that some stranger, leaving in haste, had been less bothered?

The handle was smudged now with grey powder. My own fingerprints, Rosemary thought. But no, she had rushed straight through, hadn't handled anything. Not that there'd be any useful clue there. In weather like this no one was foolhardly enough to be abroad without gloves.

But something else was niggling at her: the body itself.

There would be countless reconstructions of the act of tripping, the angle of fall, the strength needed to rip the lighting off the wall, the weight of the lamp and the injury it could cause dropping from a given height on the back of a skull, the thickness of the cranial bone. As Dr Salem had said of the temperatures question, a nice little teaser for someone.

It could so easily have been the way it looked – was made to look? Josh Webster coming in to set up a photograph of his prize blooms. Forget the open outer door for the moment. He fixes the camera and tripod, stands on the edge of the pool and leans over to adjust the angle of the lamp affixed to the wall. But the cable is round his ankle and it trips him. Desperately he reaches out. His full weight suddenly on the lamp pulls it out of the bracket. He falls with it into the water, a crack and a flash and it's all over. A huge discharge, so the entire electric system blacks out.

Only, wouldn't the lamp have gone in *under* him? Instead, his arms were flung wide as if to maintain balance. And the lamp followed after, lacerating the blackened back of his head.

She took her query to Angus Mott who was standing in the centre of the kitchen, hands plunged in pockets, eyes taking in everything.

He nodded. 'I wondered myself. It's something we'll have to try out. There could have been a moment when he clung on, then felt the bracket giving way and fell clear, the cable round his ankle pulling it after him.'

He regarded her, head tilted challengingly. 'But there's something else, more significant. Did you look at both ends of the cable? No? Well, SOCO will be reporting on it fully. The cable wasn't that much too long, but the plug hadn't been wrenched out of the socket, and there was no stress shown on the wires or casing. The scenario as I see it is this: Webster went into the water first. While he floundered, the lamp was wrenched off and thrown in on top and the cable looped round his ankle. The head injury may have been incidental or it may have been caused first by the proverbial blunt instrument. Almost certainly the intention was to electrocute him.'

135

The Scenes of Crime Officer appeared in the kitchen doorway. 'We'll be doing in here next.'

'Right, Bob. Z and I will wait in the car. You'll find something of interest in the sink.'

Following the direction of his glance, Rosemary saw a partly-filled glass coffee flask with two used cups and saucers. The SOCO went across and grunted encouragingly. 'Cups were never rinsed. Good-oh.'

Z followed Mott out to the car where he switched on the engine and let the interior warm up. Radio 210 came on the air with a programme of bouzouki music. 'If it is murder,' Rosemary said as he turned the music low, 'how does it fit in with the accident to Francine's car? Or doesn't it?'

'Interesting possibilities, aren't there? Whatever we assume about that, there's one other connection we shouldn't overlook. First our attention's drawn to the mysterious photograph, and now we have a dead photographer. We came here to ask Josh Webster where, when and how the picture of Elinor Webster and her baby daughter came to be taken. Among the possible motives which doubtless we'll be turning up soon, there is the way-out chance that he was killed to stop him telling anyone what we wanted to know.'

Mike Yeadings had been at home when the call came through. His mouth was still distorted from the tooth's extraction. He spoke through swollen lips numbed by the local anaesthetic, but mostly he was listening. 'Nine-thirty, tomorrow,' he finalized and laid down the phone.

'Something bad?' Nan asked, putting her mending aside. 'That was Angus, wasn't it?'

'He's got a body. He and Z were the ones to find it.'

'Locally?'

'Over at Turville Heath. Someone – unexpected. Now why should anybody kill the one person in a family whom everyone seems to get along with?'

Nan waited, knowing that in his own time he would tell her more. 'Will you risk a hot drink yet?'

'If you make some tea, I'll wait a while and drink it cool. The hole's still bleeding a bit.'

She brought a tray and set it up between them. 'Milk or lemon? Help yourself.' Mike reached for the jug and poured. As ever, he ignored the little table alongside and put the cup and saucer down by his feet. For a while he sat hunched, his clasped hands hanging down between his knees. Then he started to tell her about the Bascombe–Webster family.

It should have cleared his mind enough to let him get a good night's rest, but there was still pain in his upper jaw. While he lumbered off to look in on the children Nan warmed more milk and laced it with brandy. Then she took it to him with the sleeping tablets he'd declined until then.

'You've this new case to tackle tomorrow,' she said crisply. 'Knock yourself out and you'll wake up feeling fine.'

He grinned feebly. 'They say "Once a copper, always a copper". But nurses are worse.'

'Just as you like. But do it.'

He gave in. There was no need to count sheep. But he seemed to hover in limbo, neither asleep nor properly awake. While his body coasted restfully, a small, clicking part of his mind remained computing, putting up photographic stills, like mug shots for identification. And then he came totally, abruptly, alert because one had flashed up out of sequence, a face from many, many years back: a personal snap that had irrupted into his current case-load.

Moura.

He reached for the light stud, then realized his fingers too had regressed, moving towards another lamp, another bedside, twenty years back. He located the pull-string and the present room was restored, with Nan's patterned cream wallpaper and peachy looped curtains.

Moura had dispersed with the blackness. Or rather, in the image which his mind retained, the outline of her face was changing, the eyes darkening, the hair paling to cornsilk, the features reassembling yet still retaining the essence of his first, dead love. But now it was also the girl Francine Webster, challenging and angry.

There were no accidents, the Freudians said. If so, this interchange implied a connection already registered in his mind. The two girls, separated in time, were so different. Yet had something in common, if only their ability to move him. Moura, whom he had been duty bound to destroy: Francine, who seemed to expect him to fail her. Both rash, both demanding. And he a common factor in their lives.

His last sight of Moura had been on Hampstead Heath, where they met to make love. Two days later for a quite different appointment – at the Yard – she never appeared. Could not.

Other officers had written the case off, OD at twenty-three. At hospital he had faced the Casualty Sister's judgmental eyes. 'We did all we could,' she said, 'but it was too late.' And there had been stress on that first syllable. He had not gone to the mortuary.

Moura, and he'd failed her; Francine, who expected little else of him. Admitting so much wearied him. He closed his eyes. Nan, looking in on him, adjusted the duvet to cover his exposed shoulder, leant over and turned off the light.

It was already midnight before they finished at Turville Heath, because Mott and Z had stayed on to wait for the pathologist. Dr Littlejohn was insistent on viewing the body *in situ* whenever possible, and he'd had further business to delay his arrival.

Rosemary could have left with the SOCO's team but she wanted to see the next stage through. Leaving the Coroner's Officer with the body, they had moved into the sitting-room where she and Mott began a search through Josh Webster's papers.

Beyond his professional interests of photography and the cultivation of exotic flora, Josh had seemed to have simple tastes. On his shelves were the expected reference books and magazines, but no fiction; works on racing form; portfolios of his professional colour prints showing a sensitive eye for lighting, line and texture. In a burr yew desk receipted bills were neatly pigeon-holed and his bank statement showed a healthy current account. There were two passbooks for the Woolwich Building Society, gross and net, and a list of shares held in his name with a city broker. In the same drawer as his passport and four earlier cancelled ones they found his birth certificate and a sealed foolscap envelope marked 'The Last Will and Testament of Joshua Martin Webster'. Nothing appeared to have been disturbed, and there was nothing among his papers or possessions to indicate whether he had ever been married.

'So it's his brother and sister we have to notify,' Mott said sombrely. 'You'd better break it to Mrs Godden first thing tomorrow morning. I'll see Morton Webster myself and get him to identify the body.'

There was a sharp tap on the window. Mott flicked back the curtain and the constable on outside duty pressed his face close against the glass, mouthing. Mott passed back the message: 'Littlejohn's car has just turned into the drive.

'You may have to stand in for me at the post-mortem later, Z, while I report to the Boss. But for now it's back to the ice-cold hothouse.'

They reached for their heavy coats and turned out again into the dark.

Dr Littlejohn, in the manner of genuinely busy people, insisted on swift attention to the corpse. As expected, Z was assigned to stand in with the Coroner's Officer at the post-mortem next morning fixed to take place as soon as she would have returned from informing Mrs Godden, and DI Mott had brought in the brother to identify Josh's body.

Identification in this case was a formality, but one that distressed Morton Webster more severely than Mott had expected. Perhaps, he thought, the man's financial successes and the status they brought him had insulated him from the very idea of death. This had been, after all, the first of his generation to go, bringing him into the direct line of fire, reminding him that he was not immune from the ultimate certainty.

Coming on top of the shock of his son's serious injuries, this second blow had reduced the man to a jellyfish, leaving him even more inadequate in the critical and calculating eyes of his wife.

Marcia's immediate reaction to news of her brother-in-law's death had been to arm her husband with a double brandy, ring to cancel a theatre engagement with two friends in town for that evening, and prepare to accompany him and the detective at least as far as the precinct of the mortuary. Beyond that point she was prepared to find her presence unnecessary.

When Morton emerged, shaken from viewing the body, Marcia advanced and demanded sharply if it had indeed been Joshua. She might have intended to be bracing, but Mott saw her attitude then as something more like morbid excitement.

Morton was unable to say who his brother's lawyers were, nor the executors for his will. In business matters, he explained, there had been no common family connections.

'As his nearest relative,' Marcia put in quickly, 'you will naturally be expected to make all the arrangements.'

'But we don't know what he would have wanted. I mean, we've never discussed things like burial or cremation,' the man protested.

Mott produced the sealed envelope from Josh's desk and handed it to him. 'Perhaps this will say,' he offered.

Marcia reached for it, opening her handbag to put it away.

Mott turned to her husband. 'If you would read it when we get back to the car, we could find out the executors' addresses and help you get in touch without delay.'

'Yes. Yes, of course.'

From the driving seat Mott twisted back to watch as Morton started mumbling his way through the introductory words.

'Here,' said the woman impatiently, stabbing a finger at a lower paragraph. ' "I appoint as my sole . . ." But that's ridiculous! The girl wouldn't know where to begin.'

'Yes. Yes, it just mentions my niece, Francine Webster, and the address given is her mother's at Henley,' Morton babbled.

'I don't suppose he expected to go so soon. If he'd enjoyed his normal expectation of another twenty or thirty years, it would have been eminently sensible to choose someone much younger,' Mott placated.

'Would she have known about this arrangement?' Marcia wondered aloud. 'It's a very short will. See what else it says, Morton.'

'Marcia, I don't think we should. Josh meant it to go to Francine . . .'

'Let me have it to deliver, then,' and Mott tweaked it away quickly. 'I'll be getting in touch with Miss Webster after I've taken you both home.'

'There's no need for you to do that,' Webster assured him nervously. 'Take us home, I mean.' Perhaps at last he was sensitive to being seen in the back of a police car, even an unmarked one.

'I'm very grateful for the lift here. I wasn't feeling up to driving just then, but we can call a cab to get back.'

'Certainly,' said his wife, tight-lipped, reaching for the door handle. 'I think that would be much more suitable.' The icy look she directed at Mott was rapier-sharp. If he hadn't represented authority, he guessed she would have snatched the paper back.

As they walked away Mott waited a moment before starting the engine. 'That almost makes me hope,' he muttered, staring after them, 'that when I die I'll have nothing to leave anyone.'

He gave the retreating couple a final sour glance. 'And I'll bet my best boots that that little spat's only the beginning.'

He radioed back to base and was told that Superintendent Yeadings was waiting to see him. WDC Zyczynski was already on her way to attend the post-mortem due to take place in three quarters of an hour.

FOURTEEN

HER PRESENCE ON SEVERAL PREVIOUS occasions had not yet toughened Z's mind to the gruesome proceedings, but she had discovered a technique that served towards bracing her stomach muscles against physical protest. While the pathologist delved, explored, measured and weighed, dictating into a microphone clipped to the front of his plastic apron, she practised deep breathing, diaphragm-lifting, alternate buttock-flexing and relaxing: all designed to keep her occupied and slightly distracted from the grisly task in hand while her eyes continued to take in relevant matter.

Of all her rebellious senses, it was hearing that caused her greatest distress and could later provoke the worst dreams. All sounds in the overbright room were intensified by rebounding from white-tiled walls. The clang of instruments dropped in steel dishes, the slop of soft tissue in transfer to them, the perpetual gurgling of gutter and drain as networks of glutinous blood were reluctantly flushed from the surfaces undergoing examination – magnified acoustically – took a direct passage from ear to stricken sense-centres under her waistband. Despite any mental digression she could devise, her body responded with a fear all its own. Her flesh quivered for that unfeelingly under the knife. But she did not – as she saw it – disgrace herself.

Facts helped, and she computed them silently as Littlejohn droned on and grunted over his survey. He would phone in the bare outlines soon after the examination was through, and his written report would be

142

available within twenty-four hours. Nevertheless facts were a lifeline to the watchers, the straw that kept them afloat: bruising of the rear of the skull sufficient to cause unconsciousness; absence of water in the lungs, so the man hadn't drowned; cardiac arrest and widespread burning from electrocution. The last meal, taken some eight to ten hours before death, would be analysed later, but certainly contained something like cottage pie, white cabbage, carrots and fruit yoghurt.

And this, Z totalled the information, had once been a living, breathing man, the uncle for whom the unpredictable Francine Webster had admitted some affection.

By early afternoon, in addition to Dr Littlejohn's telephoned outline of his findings, there was considerable information gathered relating to the death at Turville Heath. The local police had reported Mrs Todd's arrival at the chalet to begin cleaning at nine-thirty. This she was accustomed to carry out twice weekly, on Tuesdays and Fridays.

In her capacious bag were a home-baked fruit cake for her employer and some items of shopping which tallied with a list in his handwriting which he had given her three days before. These and her state of profound shock on hearing of Webster's death seemed to prove that she'd had no previous knowledge of it. Her account of last seeing him alive was attached to the report.

On the previous Tuesday afternoon, when Mrs Todd had completed the cleaning and picked up the envelope containing her wages and fifteen pounds to cover the shopping, Mr Webster had seemed well and cheerful. Miss Francine had been visiting, so she'd made a late lunch for the girl, washed up the dishes afterwards and left. Mr Webster had offered to make the coffee as she had to catch the eight minutes past five bus at the corner of the lane. When she went for it, Mr Webster and Miss Francine were about to go out and look at the flowers in the hothouses. It hadn't been snowing at the time, but it started again soon after. She couldn't think how the accident had happened. Mr Webster was normally so careful with electricity and that. He'd certainly never mentioned to her having any dizzy spells.

A note was attached quoting statements from witnesses who confirmed Mrs Todd's presence on the bus she claimed to have caught.

'So for the moment the buck passes to Francine Webster as last person known to have seen the deceased alive, although, according to Littlejohn's statement on stomach contents, the dead man seems to have survived lunch by several hours,' Yeadings commented. 'We'll need to know what time she claims to have left him.'

Mott agreed. 'Do you want her brought in?'

He certainly didn't. Last night's image was too recent, confusing a long-dead love with the suspect in question. One needn't be a shrink to recognize what prompted his subconscious to bracket them together. Both had affected him in the same way, presented an almost identical appeal. Even in a middle-aged grizzly who'd seen a host of pretty faces go through the courts, Francine had managed to reawaken the most poignant moments of his early days as a copper and resuscitate his guilt – at having denied his own love, to serve what he saw as right and lawful. Because of him Moura had died, had taken her own life, fearful of inevitable sentencing and shaken by his betrayal.

A sick fear warned him that if he made a wrong move here the act could be repeated. He wouldn't be responsible for another young girl's OD.

'No, I'll leave her to you. I take it she's been notified of the death?'

'Elinor Webster was going to ring her at work after Z left. To insist she came out to Henley. Then she would break it to her when they were alone together.'

'Was that precaution necessary, I wonder?'

'Mrs Webster seemed scared of the effect the news would have on the girl.'

'Only that? No intention of hatching a mutual cover-up? I want you to follow up and question them both, with Z along. See how the girl reacts to being her uncle's executrix. And, Angus, tread carefully, eh? Still nothing to hint it could be more than an accidental death. We don't

144

want to – panic anyone.'

Could Francine have killed her uncle, that evening three days ago in the hothouses? he asked himself when the others had left. She had seemed genuinely fond of Josh. But she was impetuous, foolhardy. Could she, in a moment of exasperation with something he'd said or done, have given him a push as he balanced on the pool's edge? Then, seeing the appalling results, had chucked in the lamp and camera? If so, would her vaunted frankness finally stand up to admitting what she'd done?

The alternative scene, still accepting Francine as the killer, was a premeditated act. In the earlier incident – the car crash which could have resulted in Dominic's death – there had certainly been forethought plus a certain amount of technical knowledge. And hadn't the uncle's death shown familiarity with the electrical arrangements? Both were areas Francine would have been quite at home in.

The thought that the girl was only one of several suspects gave him some relief. It was likely that the alimentary contents would fix the man's death for a time when Francine could prove she was elsewhere. And Angus could be relied upon to get a full account of her movements after leaving her uncle at Turville Heath. Her *claimed* movements. There still had to be checking and independent corroboration.

So, supposing for present convenience that the car crash and murder were related incidents, which of the suspects on option did he fancy, assuming that this was indeed a family affair?

There was no denying that the missing Piers had a lot to account for.

There was also Mr Chadwala's sighting of torchlight moving about in the courtyard while the family was taking refreshments downstairs. Nobody had yet been fitted to that incident. It might have been the housekeeper's handyman husband investigating the loss of the bulkhead light. On the other hand, hadn't Cousin Alastair gone absent from the company while Francine was with her great-uncle? There was no witness to his claim that he had spent all the missing time in the library.

145

Then again, it mustn't be overlooked that Mr Chadwala could have invented the torch detail, to cover for himself in case he'd been glimpsed prowling outside the house when supposedly charting the stars up in his observatory. And beyond all these intriguingly possible suspects, as ever there had to be added the as-yet-unencountered X.

But the murder of Joshua Webster, unlike the car sabotage, could probably be fixed quite precisely in time. Which meant that alibis could prove the main means of eliminating the impossible.

At Henley the sun was trying to break through for the first time in three days. The driveway had been partially cleared, ramps of tea-brown slush lining its curves. Icicles at the edge of the porch overhang were slowly dripping. Mott nodded for Z to ring and they waited while footfalls approached over the hall parquet and the inner glass door was unlocked.

'Mrs Godden is in the morning-room with her daughter,' said the quiet woman who let them in. So they were expected. Mott let Z go in before him.

Elinor and Francine sat at either end of a chintz-covered settee, daughter tense, mother lying back like an invalid. Neither troubled to rise, but Elinor motioned towards easy chairs that were arranged to complete a cosy circle. 'Back again,' she said wearily to the WDC. 'Fran, dear, have you met WDC Zyczynski?'

Francine nodded. 'She was with the Superintendent, taking notes.' She faced Z, almost belligerently. 'You found him.'

It sounded like an accusation, but Rosemary felt a sudden rush of understanding. Fierceness was all the girl could manage as yet. 'Yes,' she admitted. 'I'm so sorry.'

'Was he – awful?'

Rosemary drew breath. 'He was simply dead. It was instantaneous.'

There was a short silence. Mott opened his leather coat and took out the envelope. 'Miss Webster, it seems your uncle made you his sole executor. I'm afraid that, in ignorance, we handed the will to Mr Morton Webster first,

146

so it's been opened already, but not read through.'

'Executrix,' Francine corrected expressionlessly. 'That's not quite as bad as executioner, is it?' She turned the envelope wonderingly in her hands.

'Fran, my dear . . .'

'It's all right, Mother. I'll behave properly in a moment. I'm just a bit out of practice.'

Her eyes were tightly shut, shining at the edges with unshed tears. 'It was nice of him to appoint me. He was – a wonderful person.'

'We're trying to fix the time of death,' Mott said. 'It would be helpful if you would tell us when you left his house on Tuesday. From what Mrs Todd said, you must have been one of the last people to see him alive. Was he expecting visitors at all?'

'I've no idea what time it was. That day was all upside down. It was the afternoon after I'd been to see Mr Yeadings. I was a bit upset. I drove around for a while, then I thought I'd go and talk to Josh.'

She fixed her eyes on the carpet, close to the hem of her long tweed skirt, and seemed to make an effort of recall.

'Yes, that would be Tuesday,' she told them, 'and I went back to work next day. The first time since my accident with the car.'

'What happened when you arrived at your uncle's?' Mott prompted.

'He was on his own. No, actually Mrs Todd was still there finishing off, but he'd sort of dug himself in for the day, because of the weather. I'd missed out on lunch, so Mrs Todd made me an omelette, with salad. We sat and talked, then later he made me a cup of coffee.'

'Just a cup for you? Nothing himself?'

'It was proper coffee in a flask, not instant, because he knows just how I like it.' Her voice almost broke. 'He must have had some just before, because he didn't pour any for himself then.'

'You talked. What about?'

Now the young woman was silent for a while. Then she seemed to rouse herself. 'Obviously, we discussed what had happened to Dominic. The crash. Josh had phoned

147

me at Mother's as soon as he heard, but we hadn't really gone into it before. And he asked me what old Hadrian had said that night. I asked him the same. He told me about some money, a thousand pounds, my great-uncle had given him to put on a horse, and how he'd made money on it. Only, when he rang up to tell Great-uncle, Mr Chadwala said he'd had a stroke and couldn't be disturbed. God, isn't it awful? Everybody at once – Dom and old Hadrian, and now Josh. It's like there was a curse on the family.'

'And then you left?'

'No, we went out to look at the flowers first. Orchids mainly, in the far section. He'd been setting up his camera to take some shots.'

'Lights as well?'

'Yes, he was waiting for the right moment when the petals were perfect, he said.'

'And then?'

'He potted up a rooted cutting for me on the way out, sealed it in plastic and put it in the car. Then we said goodbye and I left.'

'Was Mrs Todd still there then?'

'No. She'd left just before we went out to the hothouses. She said she had a bus to catch at the corner.'

'Was she still waiting for it when you drove past?'

'No, or I'd have given her a lift.'

So nobody had seen her leave, Z noted, and heard her own pent breath released.

Francine looked up miserably. 'I remember now what his last words to me were. "Well, safe journey home, Fran dear." '

She lowered her head, her voice scarcely audible. 'And I never wished him anything back.'

'I'm glad that's over,' Z confessed, once again in the car, Mott driving.

'M'm. Interesting, the difference in reaction between those two.'

Z considered it. 'The mother's that much older and more used to hiding her feelings.'

'Yes. I'm sure she took it hard when you first broke it to her earlier, but back there you'd have thought she was less involved with her brother than the girl was. She seemed almost withdrawn, leaving her daughter to do all the grieving.'

'She's had a little longer to accept it. But I wonder if Mrs Godden could have resented being upstaged in the will; because Francine, not herself, was chosen as executrix? The girl and her uncle must have been very fond of each other.'

'People like that don't give a lot away. And they accepted it exactly as we told it. Neither Elinor nor Francine suspected it was anything but an accident. If you can believe appearances.'

'It's bound to strike them later, when they find the police interest continues.'

'And neither of them made any move to open the envelope,' Mott marvelled. 'It would have been perfectly natural to, if only to check what I'd said.'

'Perhaps they'd already guessed as much, though Francine looked quite blank when you said she was executrix. I couldn't read anything off that.'

'Nor I.' Mott stared ahead and swerved clear of a cyclist wobbling out towards the crown of the road. 'What I'm most intrigued by,' he said, 'is whether they knew what was in the main part of the document.'

Z had expected him to enlighten her after she'd caught him reading the unsealed will before they set out for Henley, but he'd kept its contents to himself. 'The bequests,' she prompted him now.

Mott gave her a quizzical look, then decided to share his secret. ' "... all my goods and estate whatsoever and wheresoever," ' he quoted, ' "to my beloved natural daughter Francine Webster." '

FIFTEEN

'GET YOURSELF SOMETHING TO EAT,' Mott told Z when they arrived back. 'There's no knowing when you'll get another chance. I'm going to have a word with the Boss.'

She would have liked to sit in on the discussion, particularly as, after his one astounding revelation about the Josh–Francine relationship, the DI had been unwilling to part with any opinions or further observations for the whole of the journey. But there was something pressing she had to do, and the prime need wasn't food, so she allowed herself to be packed off without protest.

She put through a call from the CID office on an outside line to the Hunters. All day the fear had been dogging her that Janey's mother would wake up to the same frantic anger as yesterday. The woman's need to allot blame – rebuffing her husband for being male, the child because she had gone off with a stranger – had seemed dangerous. Unless the sedatives prescribed for her were taken sensibly over a period, there could be further disaster.

She heard the double ring go on unanswered and her anxiety increased.

She next dialled Dobbin's number. A receptionist at the group practice answered. Dr Dobbs, Z was told, had finished afternoon surgery and gone on her rounds. It took an exaggerated piece of officialese and some bluff to persuade the women to offer up two phone numbers of patients whom Dobbin might at present be visiting. The second attempt caught the doctor as she as about to leave.

'WDC Zyczynski? Ah, yes. Well, it's really a confidential matter. I don't want the family bothered by outsiders at present. Superintendent Yeadings assured me you had enough information for the moment from their end.'

'I don't want to question them,' Z told her. 'I was worried, after the scene Mrs Hunter kicked up yesterday. I wanted to be sure little Janey was all right. All of them really.'

The doctor considered this. 'Yes, well, they've gone away for a few days, to avoid publicity. I persuaded Mrs Hunter it would be the best thing for them all. I shall be keeping in touch, indirectly.'

'And she was calmer? I mean—'

'She is in good hands, Miss Zyczynski, I can assure you.' Her voice dropped a tone. Perhaps she thought she had been too severe, considering Z's helpful involvement. 'And I do appreciate the interest you took. It was quite right to inform me as you did.'

But there it ends, Rosemary thought, replacing the receiver. Thanks, but no thanks. Now go and get on with your policing.

She still didn't feel like food.

Mott, accustomed to Mike Yeadings' facial expressions as no one else in the job was, kept watchful of the eyebrows while he unfolded the story of his activities so far that day. They shot high towards the central arrowhead of his dark hair, hovered and plunged into a solid angry line. His mouth puckered tightly. An explosion was imminent.

Yeadings fired himself from his chair and planted himself at the window, opened slats of the vertical blinds, peering out with pretended interest in the doings of whoever was shifting cars in the yard below. Uneasily, Mott, who had earlier been quite intrigued at the new turn of events, now had the distinct feeling he wasn't the Boss's favourite man.

'And you left it at that?'

'Two women, clearly upset—'

'Discretion be damned. You had Z along. Think, man! They were about to open and read through the will. Suddenly the girl will discover she has found and lost a father in one blow. And she's revealed as the product of incest besides. All that on top of grieving for a supposed uncle she was uniquely fond of. Not to mention that previous business with the bloody photograph.'

Mott gaped, then quickly recovered himself. 'What business with the photograph? It was a perfectly normal picture of—'

'Normal? Of course it was. That's what was wrong. Francine Webster *isn't* normal – not physically, anyway. In that photograph with her mother she's standing as straight as any toddler ever did. Haven't you looked at the way she is now, damn it?'

'She's a bit lame, yes. Doesn't move well, but—'

'Her right leg's two inches shorter than the other. There was an operation to extend it with a bone graft some years back but it didn't work out. All she got for her pains was ugly scarring, and the other leg went on growing faster.'

'How could you tell all that, with the long skirts she wears?'

'Because she showed me when she came here. Lifted her skirt in a sort of damn-your-eyes defiance. A great one for calling a spade a spade, our Francine. Z could have told you that, but she was sitting behind the girl and didn't see what I saw.

'But today Francine's suddenly got a chunk more reality to face than can be good for anyone. How do you think she feels now about a mother who produced her from an affair with her own brother? – who has always told her she was born deformed, to cover up God knows what accident doubtless of her own causing?'

'Wait a minute. If you're right, then when her cousin Dominic saw the photograph, he too realized this about her injury?'

'And was intent on making trouble between her and her mother, ensuring that Francine learned the truth about that deception at least.'

'So Francine already knew the significance of the photograph from his description, or at least guessed. That's why she was so keen to get her hands on it. And certainly her mother had been disturbed when Z and I brought the subject up. She knew which picture it was that Dominic held, because we described the clothes she was wearing in it, and that would have told her the date. She knew that Josh had taken it *before* whatever happened to injure Francine's leg.'

Mott felt the blood drain from his face. 'And now Josh is dead, murdered, probably on the very day the girl visited him! She'd always accepted the fact that she was a bastard, tossed it defiantly around, but she must have had secret feelings about the missing father. Pretty intense love-hatred, I should think. Suppose that on Tuesday she pressed him and he told her. And now, today's public statement of what he was, with her mother alongside to realize she knows – God, yes. I should never have left them together to read the will!'

'Was there nobody else in the house?'

'A woman let us in. Housekeeper or something.'

'Ring and say you left something behind. Sound out what's happened.'

Mott snatched up the phone, slammed it down because he hadn't the number to hand. 'Here.' Yeadings scrabbled among papers on his desk and came up with the list.

Mott heard the phone ring some eight or nine times before the connection was made. A man's voice repeated the number.

'Could I speak to Mrs Godden, please? Inspector Mott, Thames Valley CID.'

'She's just left. I'm here alone and you got me out of bed. I've got flu.' The man's voice was disagreeable, the complaint tetchy. But to Mott it was reassuring. If anything horrendous had occurred in the house Godden would have sounded a damn sight more distressed. As it was, he was merely mad at disturbance from enjoying bad health.

'And your stepdaughter, Mr Godden?'

'Gone with my wife. They took Francine's car, so I suppose they'll both be coming back.'

'Have you any idea where they would be heading?'

'God knows. The women don't consult me about their comings and goings.'

'Would the housekeeper perhaps know?'

'Shouldn't think so. Anyway she's not here either. Gone

for her free weekend. Now if that's all, can I get back to bed?'

Mott rang off, shrugged. 'The birds have flown, destination a blank,' he told Yeadings. 'But they're together in Francine's car. She can hardly do her mother any harm while she's at the wheel.'

'Unless she's prepared to have a second crash,' the Superintendent reminded him. 'We'll go over the SOCO's notes while you're here, unless you feel we should put out a Follow and Report call on the girl's car.'

Mott seemed undecided. 'We could give her half an hour's grace. She might even make for here. We'll see. So, what did Bob turn up at the murder site, sir?'

'I'll get Z in, then we'll go through it.'

They waited, Yeadings leaning back to flick down the switch on his coffee-maker. He eased back from the desk and pulled three mugs from the bottom drawer. His own had a picture of Snoopy taking a siesta. The other two were *Crimewatch* ones from the BBC.

'Sir?' Rosemary greeted him, following up a rap on the door.

'I don't need to ask if you two helped yourselves to coffee in Webster's kitchen last night?' Yeadings pursued. 'No? Then there was a point in getting checks on the two cups in the sink. One had faint lipstick traces. Not that the analysis on that will come through for a while.'

'Francine admits to being there on Tuesday, but is vague about when she left,' Mott offered. 'The cleaner washed up her lunch things, but it seems her uncle made the coffee after that. She said he didn't have any himself. So if the one with lipstick was her cup, still unwashed on Thursday night, where does the other one come from?'

'The fingerprints on it were all the same as the corpse's. SOCO says the quantity left in the flask was equal to two cupfuls. Maybe she'll have noticed how much he made while she was there. Perhaps enough to allow each of them to have two cups; then he delayed drinking his until after she'd left. Or it could be that he made fresh coffee on a later occasion, to share with another female visitor. Either of which set of circumstances would appear to clear

Francine from involvement in his death at that time. Though it could be Francine herself who came back later and she's keeping that fact to herself.'

There was a buzz from the intercom. Yeadings switched it to open speech. The duty man up at Josh Webster's had radioed through that two ladies of the family had arrived and wished to see where Mr Webster had died. He had explained to them that the police seals weren't to be broken, and the older one had said that that was officious interference. No, they hadn't left. They were sitting in their car waiting for him to report back. A Mrs Godden and a Miss Webster.

'By now they must be aware we're not treating it as an accidental death,' Mott remarked. 'Do you want me to go over, or shall the constables send them away?'

Yeadings grunted. 'Z, I think this is one for you. Go over and let them in, keep the uniformed man with you and don't miss a move of either of them. I want to know what they ask about, what they want to see, their exact reactions to everything. Find out as much as you can about the coffee. I'm sorry it'll do you out of joining us with a cup now, but don't leave them too long waiting. I'll send a message that someone's on the way.'

The line of white plastic tape still stretched across the drive, a uniformed constable, stamping to keep his feet from freezing, on duty alongside. Francine's car had pulled up just short of it, some twenty yards before the hothouses. Elinor was stomping up and down in fur-lined boots and a wide-skirted black mink coat. Her daughter, looking white and ill, sat crouched over the steering wheel. Rosemary got out, locked the car door and strolled over. 'Me again, I'm afraid,' she introduced herself. 'All the senior people are out on jobs.'

'Does all this mean what I think it does?' Francine demanded abruptly. Her face was white and showed strain. 'A guard and seals on the doors and everything?'

'We aren't entirely satisfied that it was an accident,' the WDC said, as gently as she could put it.

'Of course it bloody wasn't!' The girl thrust her feet out

155

on to the icy path and almost slipped as she twisted to slam the car door shut. 'I'm sorry. It's not your fault, but are you going to let us in now?'

'We'll let the constable see to the seals. Ah, there he is. What exactly do you want to do here?'

Francine stood with head bowed, silent.

'She has to see the place, of course. How else can she ever come to terms with what's happened?' Elinor Godden had come striding over, her red hair tumbled by the wind, her voice cutting. We've been waiting nearly an hour for someone to let us in. What right have you people to keep us out?'

'Every right, when there's an investigation under way, Mrs Godden. Mr Yeadings was willing to make an exception in your cases.'

'Mother,' the girl said wearily, 'they think Josh was murdered, as I do. It has to be that, if it wasn't an accident. Because he'd never take his own life.'

She turned to the policewoman. 'Look, I'm trying to be sensible about this. I know you're the professionals, but I can't just do nothing when there might be some little thing I'd notice, something un-Joshlike that would prove someone else had been here with him.'

'That's what we were hoping for,' Z told her. 'You were here as recently as two days before we found him. Come in and have a good look around now. See if there's anything significantly different.'

They entered in a group, Z behind Francine, then Elinor, the uniformed man locking the door carefully behind them.

'Oh, the poor plants! Nothing alive at all!' Horrified, Francine gazed all round her. 'Of course, the whole heating system must have blown.'

'It did. And the outer door was left open.'

'Josh wasn't careless. He'd never have done that. He was one of the most painstaking people I've ever known. That's why it's impossible he could have killed himself that way, even accidentally. One thing he always insisted on was that the current should be shut off before anything was shifted. He taught me to be just as particular when I started using electrical equipment. With him it was ingrained habit.'

They moved through to the orchid section. The skeletal débris of once rich vegetation writhed grotesquely against the trellised frames, slimed by frost. The pool, with its little cascade, had been emptied and a chalk outline indicated the earlier position of the body against the blackened rocks. Francine looked quickly away and then back again with an unrelenting stare.

Z darted an anxious glance at the young woman, but she was holding on to herself tightly, determined to continue with what she had come here to do.

Francine lifted her chin. 'You came in, like we've just done, and you found him. What then?'

Z explained. 'Actually I rushed in, the moment I saw the outer door open. I saw the glass walls were all frosted over, ran on in here, saw him iced in, face down. I knew then there was nothing I could do.'

'Nothing. I know. That's the most awful part of it. Nothing anyone can ever do to get his life back.'

'Just our utmost,' said Elinor grimly, 'to help find the monster that did it.' At last her anger had found its real object, but then it broke suddenly into open grief. She stood there, holding herself, pathetic in her fashionable furs, and tears streaking her cheeks with mascara. 'Josh, oh Josh! You were the most wonderful brother. Josh, *Jo-o-osh!*'

Francine moved to her and took her in her arms. 'Elinor, don't. Please, don't. Not now. I can't bear it, and we have to be practical, to help.

'Look, Miss Zyczynski, I can see nothing here that suggests anything to me. Could we go into the house now? My mother's half frozen stiff.'

They found the heating still on. Francine fetched tumblers and poured them all whisky from Josh's tantalus. Z noticed the familiar way she found her way about. Even if her father had never made a legal claim on her while he lived, it seemed he had contrived to make his house her second home.

Restlessly the girl started prowling about the ground-floor rooms. She came hobbling back so fast from the kitchen that she had to reach for the jamb for support as she swung through the doorway. 'His anorak's in the back porch! He wouldn't have gone out without that! What was he wearing when you found him?'

Z frowned. 'Beige Bedford cord trousers and a lambswool sweater with a Norwegian pattern. Brown Oxfords on his feet.'

'That's exactly how he was dressed on Tuesday. An off-white sweater patterned with dark blue frost shapes and maroon stars?'

'It sounds like the same one.'

'Well, when he left the house here to go with me to see the flowers, he took it off and put his anorak on, even for the short time we'd be out there. And as soon as we were in the hothouses he hung up the anorak. He always worked on his photography in his shirt-sleeves. I had to drop my coat off too. The steamy heat was too much.'

'But when I found him he was really dressed for indoors here?'

They looked at each other, neither willing to put into words the scene they envisaged: Josh Webster attacked in his own home, possibly in this very room, presumably by someone he knew well and had invited in; struck on the back of the head by some heavy instrument and carried unconscious to the hothouses where the mock accident was staged.

But it hadn't happened that way, Z realised. The scientific experts had found blood splashes on stones surrounding the pool; and nothing of the sort here. Since Josh Webster had been found wearing his sweater, either he'd suddenly changed his habits or he'd gone out to the hothouses in such a hurry that he hadn't taken time to change. And he hadn't yet stripped off to start on his photography.

'Look,' Z offered. 'I'll ask my boss if you can be shown the scene-of-crime photographs. Could you bear to look at them? It's just possible you might notice something that means nothing to the rest of us.'

'Anything,' the girl said tightly. 'I'd do anything to find out who did that to my father.'

She said it with such passion and conviction that for a brief moment Z didn't pick up the fact that Francine was admitting the relationship.

Then it struck home. So Francine had almost certainly read through the contents of his will. But was that just today; or had Josh Webster claimed her as his daughter earlier – say, on Tuesday, when she was last here?

SIXTEEN

Z WATCHED FRANCINE'S LITTLE HIRED car disappear down the driveway until a bend hid it between high banks and winter hedgerows. In the open fields much of the snow had melted, but quite solid stretches at their edges lay bleakly waiting for the next fall to join them. Out here, away from town streets, the afternoon light seemed to last longer. Unobtrusively until then, the days were actually lengthening.

Z waved a hand to the constable left on duty, made a seven-point turn in the narrow lane and regained the main road. On the way back she rehearsed how she would put to Yeadings the idea of Francine Webster being shown the murder photographs.

When she did so he looked long at her. Or through her, perhaps. He would be seeing not one of his team but the daughter of the murdered man. 'Leave it with me,' he said at length, as though the decision troubled him.

Well, that was one less burden on her own shoulders, Z told herself. He would probably turn the idea over until it went limp on him, and then let it slide away. And perhaps, on further consideration, the girl too would prefer to be spared the pain of it.

He had questioned Z about the two women, the atmosphere between them; and she had admitted that after Elinor's early outburst at what she considered police interference and delay, the older woman had been distinctly subdued. Francine had been left to cope with the situation for herself, her mother in the background. No, not cowed, Z replied when he picked up the point. More as though she had taken as much as she could for the present

160

and was cutting off. There had been no obvious animosity between the two, but no closeness either. Both were suffering their loss separately.

Where would Francine be heading for after she left the house at Turville Heath? he asked. Z didn't know.

'But she'd have to take her mother home. She might be at Henley still.'

'Right,' he said. 'Maybe I'll give them a ring.' And then he sent her off to bring the paperwork up to date.

For a while he sat hunched at his desk, examining his own motives. He knew he was in danger of doing what he insisted his team should avoid: getting personally drawn in. On the other hand, who else could do what he already half intended? Who could be trusted to know how far the girl might be driven in her grief and despair?

Because of Moura, he recognized, this case was different for him. Subconsciously recalling her, he had bracketed the two girls in a similar danger. Did that mean that he believed Francine guilty of the ultimate crime of taking a life, merely because Moura had been guilty of the lesser one of fraud?

There could be no true parallel. Over a period of two years Moura had with light-hearted deception indulged her love of high living with no consideration for moral values or others' loss. Francine, if she had killed, would surely have done so from passion, as a sudden physical outburst of anger. To discover she had been deceived over her lifetime by those for whom she felt most affection would have been shameful to her. If, after frenzied killing, she later protected herself by covering up, that was because she had intelligence as well as passion.

No, in their actions the two girls were utterly different. All they had in common was his own response to them, his guilt at past and possibly future involvement in the destruction of a young life.

Could he take the risk that, if guilty, Francine, now facing the consequences, suffering the loss, and knowing the outcome if she was found out, would as impetuously do away with herself?

He wished he could talk to Nan about it. For years after

161

Moura died, his sense of culpability had been an invisible barrier between him and other women. Until Nan. In her he had discovered a similar purpose in life, and eventually such intimacy that he had found no difficulty in sharing with her his earlier good and bad times. And so found release. The wound had scarred over, finally the scab had come off.

But now, if he started talking again of his long-dead first love and a present parallel, what was she to think? That in his middle years he was hankering after Francine Webster, almost young enough to have been his daughter?

So wasn't it partly true?

Absolute bloody rot! Except that he would sleep of nights, without bad dreams.

He let out his breath explosively and reached for the phone, rang the number at Henley.

Elinor had returned. She answered cautiously, as though expecting worse news, reluctant to give the information he wanted; but gentle persistence overruled her scruples. Francine had dropped her off. She'd begged her to stay on, but there were things her daughter had to see to over at the Playhouse, or so she'd said. The converted stables at Stoke Poges, yes.

Yeadings looked through the photographs of the hothouse interior with Josh Webster's sprawled body in the iced-over pool. He chose the least offensive, more distant shots, and put them in a manila envelope. Then he went out to the Rover, automatically noted his mileage, and set out to find the young woman who so disturbed him.

He found the Playhouse almost deserted. A whistling joiner knocking together the frame for a backcloth on the empty stage said Miss Webster had been sitting in the stalls, from there had given him a bollocking for a badly fitting door on the drawingroom set and then gone off towards the dressing-rooms.

Yeadings had twice seen plays put on here, during the rep season given by visiting professional companies. For the rest of the year local amateur productions were just well enough supported by voluntary jobbing and regular subscription to keep the place alive. Backstage was new territory to him, but he passed out through the wings, down some stairs and along a passage hung with old play posters and with four doors opening on the opposite side. The first two of these were labelled *Guys* and *Dolls*. The others had paper stars stuck on, one pink, the other blue.

The third door stood ajar and light slanted out across the passage. Yeadings approached quietly and stood looking in before he raised his hand to knock.

In profile to him, Francine Webster was sitting in the star's chair before the mirror surrounded by bare light bulbs. She was leaning forward, staring intently at her own sharply lit face, a stick of greasepaint in one hand. At his knock she seemed to come slowly awake. Only her head turned to acknowledge him. 'Superintendent.'

'May I come in?' As she stayed silent he advanced, looked round for a chair, pulled it close behind her right shoulder and sat regarding her in the mirror.

Her eyes met his defiantly. 'What shall I make myself up as? A clown? An ingénue? A – villain?'

'Why not yourself? You know now who you are. That bothered you before.'

'Who I *was*. I don't feel sure of anything now. I've lost everyone. Orphaned.' With the last word she had fallen back on irony. She suppressed the vulnerability he'd intruded on and became mocking again.

'I've been fed the wrong clues, Mr Yeadings. You must sometimes have had that happen to you. All my lifetime, though. So I have to start afresh, be born again. Find someone else to be.'

'And you've a need to fantasize, because acting is a part of your reality. Acting, reacting, distracting attention from the vulnerable parts of yourself.'

'—because I am a cripple,' she said loudly. 'So I need to smile at my pretty face – and I know it is pretty, Mr Yeadings – just to give the lie to my twisted body.'

She hunched her shoulders. 'So I'm brusque and outrageous, shocking people for fear that they might pity me instead.'

'No one who knows you could ever pity you, Francine.

Who pities the sea urchin whose spines break off to damage your fingers?' He changed position on the inadequate little chair. 'You've heard of inverted snobbery,' he assumed urbanely.

Francine sniffed and looked sideways at him, waiting for the épée thrust. 'There's a lot of it about,' she granted drolly.

'I've noticed,' he went on in a bumbling, fatherly way, 'that there's inverted invalidism too.'

She considered this, unsmiling, and he went on to risk a definition.

'The need to do everything better than someone who's one hundred per cent able. If you'd been born dumb, Francine, you'd have had to become a singer.'

She laughed aloud, harshly. 'Instead of which – and I've never confessed this to anyone – I had a fierce longing to do ballet. Ridiculous, isn't it? It's uncanny how accurately you've hit the nail.

'When I was quite tiny, before I properly understood how I was, I'd seen *Swan Lake* on TV and been enchanted. Soon after, on a family visit, I wandered into the ballroom at Lynalls. To me then it was the royal palace come to life.'

She shook her head, eyes tightly closed as if it might make her invisible. 'I . . . I started to dance.'

He could appreciate the compliment she paid him. Francine was quick to challenge, slow to confide. And there was more to come, something he'd already half suspected on re-reading her early account of the fateful family meeting.

'Then I saw myself, over and over to infinity, grotesquely reflected in the walls of mirrors. And for the first time I knew how hideous I was. That's when Great-uncle Hadrian came in and caught me. Ever since, when I've seen his wicked old eyes watching me, I've known what he's remembering – me discovering myself. From then on he saw through every defensive move I made, every pretence, every little trick of distraction I learned to practise. And he knew *why*.'

She opened her eyes, stood up and faced him. 'Oh hell, Mr Yeadings, haven't you any crimes to solve? Can't you leave me alone?'

But, despite the brimming eyes, she was smiling.

He grunted, perhaps overdoing the rôle of grizzly. 'I certainly have. That's why I came. WDC Zyczynski wanted you to have a look at some photographs. But only if you still feel you'd like to.'

Her face turned grave. 'Have you brought them?'

He laid the envelope among the clutter of make-up beside her. She opened it slowly and set out the glossy eight-by-tens. Colour increased the horror of them. She looked at them quickly, then away, came back to study each in turn.

'Yes, that's the way he was dressed on Tuesday, indoors.'

'But you say he changed the sweater for an anorak when he went out with you to see the flowers?'

'And removed it in the hothouses, yes. But today it was still hanging in the house.'

'Anything else you notice that's unusual?'

She went through the pictures again then stiffened, holding in her hand a shot of the hothouse interior. 'Yes, of course! Something felt wrong when I went in there with the policewoman. It was the floor, see? These cables, they're uncovered. Where are the duckboards?'

'There are two standing against the low wall there. Is that what you mean?'

Francine took a deep breath. 'Tuesday afternoon, he had it all set up for the photographs. The cables to the lighting were passed through under duckboards. He was always so careful. Are you sure your men didn't lift them up after they found – the body?'

'Nothing was moved. If the cables had been as you say, your unc– – your father – couldn't have been tripped up as it appeared.'

She looked momentarily unsure of herself. 'Perhaps he'd already taken the photographs he wanted and was clearing up? But then the current would have been turned off. Nothing makes sense.'

'There was exposed film in the camera. It hasn't come back yet from being developed, so we don't know how far he'd got.'

165

'When I left on Tuesday he said he'd wait an hour and the orchids would be at their best.'

'Then he must have finished with them. The pathologist found he died eight to ten hours after eating his lunch, which we assumed to have been about one o'clock.'

She stared hard at him in the mirror. 'But Josh never ate at midday, unless he was out with someone. He used to get up about seven, miss breakfast and have brunch at ten on the dot, winter and summer alike, then not eat again until supper about nine. And that means that if he died Tuesday he could have been killed as early as six that evening – probably about the time I left him.'

'That changes things.'

'It puts me in the forefront as a suspect. I should have kept quiet about his eating habits, shouldn't I?'

'No, it could be helpful. Francine, I find you every bit as exasperating as you could wish for. Come on, let's lock up here and go out for a ploughman's lunch.'

In the event, they went to her flat where she grilled turkey fillets from the freezer. As they sat down to eat in the kitchen she challenged him. 'You could have sent Miss Zyczysnki with the photographs. What makes me so serious a suspect that you had to come yourself?'

He could have turned the question, but for some reason he refused to. 'I wanted to see you again. I worry about you.'

'Why should you?'

She thought for a moment he hadn't heard her. Yeadings was looking away, his eyes focused distantly. 'Perhaps,' he said slowly, 'because you remind me of someone. My first love.'

She had to lean towards him to catch the last words. 'Ah, youth,' she mocked gently. 'When one still has ideals and believes everything will turn out well.'

'It seems you know all about it.'

'Oh yes. I had a first love myself.' Her mouth twisted. 'A consuming passion. Unfortunately he had a consuming passion too.'

Yeadings waited. As ever, his silence had the effect of making the other add more than first intended.

166

'Music. Stefan won a violin scholarship to the Academy. Then he took up the cello. He kept discovering more and more instruments to absorb him.' She shrugged. 'Another girl as rival I could have coped with better. But I wasn't one to be tied to his bowstrings.'

'You wanted to be his inspiration.'

'I expected him to be absorbed in me, as I was with him.'

'That's more than most people get. But it doesn't mean that that sort of devotion is impossible. For you . . .'

'How did we get to talking about me? What of this first love of yours? How was she like me?'

'Impulsive, demanding more than I had to give. I failed her.'

'Did you need to be her obsession?'

'Perhaps, then.'

'And now?'

'I'm older. I found something different. Loyalty and tenderness, principles that are just a little higher than my own and keep me in line.'

'The wife-type.'

'We have a good marriage.'

She felt resentful, and angry with herself because she couldn't see the reason for it. Perhaps because she had started to identify with his first love and felt sloughed off. 'What happened to her?' she demanded.

Yeadings knew who it was she meant. 'She died.' He was silent for a long moment, then added, 'She took her own life.'

Francine's eyes were boring into him hotly. 'Because of you – something you did?'

'Something I wouldn't do. I was a policeman even then. She was closely involved in a case I was on.'

The girl frowned. He expected some sour remark to follow, about a man of principle and feeble love, but she was defensive again. 'I'm not really like her. And I wouldn't kill myself for anyone, or anything.'

He nodded. 'You're too positive.'

She was frowning down at her hands tightly clenched in her lap. Her voice came out so low that he barely caught it. 'I wasn't always.'

He stared at the smooth crown of her upswept cornsilk hair, only half accepting what she seemed to be saying. '*You Francine?*'

She sighed, looked up, shrugged mockingly. 'Try everything once: isn't that what kids say in every generation?' She shuddered. 'Nobody knows, not even Elinor. A girlfriend found me in time, drove me to hospital, signed me in under a false name. As soon as I was cleaned out and could get on my feet I walked out, worked myself out of it on my own.'

Brave, he thought, and horribly alone. None of her family knew, but – 'Now you've told me,' he said.

'You won't give me away. I trust you on that. Anyway, you need to know.' She shivered again. 'You see, if anything were to happen to me, someone has to understand that it wasn't by my own hand.'

That settled it, Yeadings told himself. Any lingering suspicion he had of the girl as the killer was dismissed. Instead, there returned to him the dark premonition that more was to come, reinforced now by Francine's own awareness of being dogged by an unknown enemy.

SEVENTEEN

'THAT'LL BE ROD,' SAID FRANCINE suddenly, recognizing a double hoot in the street below. Yeadings became aware of a motor-cycle ticking over quietly.

The girl lifted a ring of keys off a cup-hook on the dresser, opened the sash window and flung them out. 'He's mislaid his set,' she explained. 'We've only the one between us now, and his brand-new Yamaha's too valuable to leave at the kerbside overnight.'

'Your flatmate?' Yeadings queried. He recalled the New Zealander who had offered Mott the freedom of Francine's garage.

'Temporarily, while his cousin's abroad.' She darted him a challenging look. 'And do I sleep with him? Yes, I do, when it suits us. We usually have tea about now. Would *that* suit *you*?'

Yeadings remained imperturbable. 'Kind of you to include me. You know, it's a sound idea to change your locks after any keys go missing.'

Francine grimaced. 'Barring the stable door after the horse has bolted? I mean, the damage to my car has been done. It's not likely to happen that way again, is it?'

He thought she was right there. If another attack came, it would be from a different angle, as it was in her father's death.

She seemed to be following the drift of his thoughts because, suddenly sombre, she demanded, 'Have you any idea yet what really happened to Josh?'

'*You* knew him,' Yeadings challenged. 'What explanation do you find for the unusual circumstances?'

'The wrong clothes and the missing duckboards? I think

he must have heard, or glimpsed from the house, someone inside his hothouses interfering with his things, and he dashed out to stop it. But whoever it was saw him coming and lay in wait.' She threw out her hands helplessly and shook her head, refusing to picture it further.

'It could have happened that way. Did he ever mention having trouble with the locals?'

'No. He wasn't one to make enemies. And I can't think why anyone should want to damage his property. Unless – well, the orchids are valuable. Marketable.'

She was avoiding his eyes. Something there she's covering up, he thought. 'You don't really believe that.'

'Anything else is so far-fetched: birds' nests from China.'

'Perhaps there was something significant he mentioned when you were with him?'

Francine's hands stopped moving among the tea things. She hesitated.

'You want to find out who killed him, don't you?'

'Of course I do. But I just can't believe . . .'

'Try it on me.'

Still she hesitated, then, 'It was the name of the horse old Hadrian told him to back,' she blurted out.

'And that was?'

'Tontine. I knew it was some sort of legal term, and Josh explained it for me: a bequest to a group of named people, but frozen until there's only a single survivor. Then that one takes it all.'

'Dear God,' said Yeadings. 'And you think someone who assumed that was your great-uncle's intention is now creating accidents to be sure he inherits? A mass murderer in the family? It would need someone to be out of his mind.'

'His or hers,' she said weakly. 'Don't tell me you've overlooked how I might have meant to kill Dominic.'

He was saved from answering by the appearance of a young man in the doorway. He had let himself in quietly and come upstairs in his socks. Now he stood there scowling, picking up the atmosphere and attributing it to the stranger.

'So who the hell're you?' he demanded.

Francine performed the introductions. 'There was another police feller here the other day,' Carradine said suspiciously. 'Are you any further towards finding who tampered with the car?'

'Oh God, you don't know, do you?' Francine said aghast. 'Look, a lot's happened since I saw you last, Roddy. I'm not sure I can go through it all again.'

The man turned on Yeadings. 'Have you been threatening her?'

'There's been a killing,' the policeman said simply. 'A member of Miss Webster's family. She's naturally upset.'

'You've heard me speak of Josh?' the girl asked.

'Sure thing. You were fond of him. He's dead? I'm real sorry, Fran.'

'Well, it turns out he was my father, which makes it worse.'

'Hell, I'll say so. But I thought . . .'

'He was Elinor's brother? Yes, he was. But it seems now that she wasn't my mother. Just took me over when my real mother died. Josh didn't know until afterwards. My parents weren't married, you see, and Elinor was adamant about having me. It was all a terrible muddle. I'll tell you all about it later. What matters is I've lost him. I haven't anybody now.'

Yeadings drew a deep breath. *Orphaned*, she'd said earlier, sitting before the Playhouse mirror. And he'd thought she exaggerated her misery and the need to find herself again. Poor little soul, she was orphaned indeed.

'I'll push off now,' he said gently, nodding the man to follow him to the door. Francine gave a derisory wave of one hand, ironic to the last.

Carradine opened the outer door on to a blast of chill air. 'Look after her,' said Yeadings.

'Too true I will! And you see they lay off the pressure now.'

The Superintendent looked at the scowling face. A toughie, this one. Maybe that was what Francine Webster needed just now; but almost as an afterthought and barely expecting a satisfactory answer, he asked, 'So where were you on Tuesday afternoon and evening?'

The man stepped back as if struck. Under his permanent tan he seemed to lose colour as Yeadings watched. 'I – what the hell right have you to ask me that?'

After the fear, anger; then something too fleeting for Yeadings to interpret. 'You think I—? I never even met the man.'

But he wouldn't need to, if somehow he'd discovered Francine was Josh's heir and he had it in mind to marry her. That, to a fortune-hunting rogue, could be motive enough: remove the barrier, make sure of the spoils. Suddenly Yeadings felt he was on to a new and important factor.

'You can answer now or come with me to police head-quarters,' he said coolly.

The colour came rushing back into Carradine's face. His hands balled on the door edge. 'On Tuesday I was doing what I've been doing all week: filming and post-production work at Pinewood. If you want to check you can come over and see for yourself.'

He gave it just the right amount of contemptuous indignation to be almost convincing, but it didn't cancel out the consternation he'd first felt at the question.

'We'll do that,' Yeadings told him. 'If not me, one of my team. I'll wish you good evening, Mr Carradine.'

At home Frank Godden sat with his head between his hands. The pain was barely stunned, not deadened, by all the analgesic he'd taken. It had the effect of distancing him from his own body, from unacceptable reality. His hands, when he moved them, seemed to belong to someone else. He stared at the long fingers, well tended as a doctor's should be, with filbert nails and pale half-moons. Hands that had brought him a measure of success in his chosen career. Hands that had once placed the wedding ring on Elinor's finger, so long ago, as it seemed. And as far as they meant anything to her now, he might as well have useless stumps at the ends of his arms.

Since Elinor's return in Francine's car she had stayed in her own room. Weeping, he was sure. The pity he felt for her was useless because he knew he'd not be welcomed to give her comfort. She'd made an outsider of him.

172

There had been a phone call over an hour back, and cautiously he'd lifted the receiver in the hall at the precise moment he heard the click of her extension. It had been one of the detectives inquiring where Francine was, and Elinor had told him: the Playhouse. As Stage Manager, the girl had things to sort out there. Francine callously getting on with practical matters while her mother wept for her dead brother!

But the police would be following the girl up. She wouldn't get away with it in the end.

He had hoped that when she came to stay after the accident with Dominic, everything would come all right. They would be a family again, united, and Elinor would turn back to him, need him. But, as ever, the girl had a disturbing way of making everything go wrong, deliberately provoking him so that Elinor thought it was he and not her daughter who was at fault.

It was just as well that she had gone back to her own place, leaving Elinor free of her malignant influence. Though Elinor would miss her. Now, with Josh gone too, she must feel totally alone.

And still there was no place for him in her grieving. She hadn't even troubled to stop at his door and ask how he was. Not that she need fear he was infectious. The flu symptoms seemed to have gone, except for the headache. Tomorrow he would go in to work. He couldn't bear to spend another whole day shut up here, useless, while she obstinately suffered alone.

Perhaps by the time he returned in the evening she would have recovered a little, dressed herself up for dinner. Or he might even persuade her to meet him in town for a show and supper afterwards. It would be an attempt to get things back the way they'd once been, when he was her lover as well as her husband. Now that she was alone he must start courting her over again.

At Turville Heath the Incident Room caravan had been set up on the B-road below the lane to Josh Webster's. Mike Yeadings drove there from Francine and checked on the information coming in.

173

The local houses had all been given initial visits and several callers had presented themselves voluntarily. The gist of it was that nobody claimed to have seen or spoken with Josh Webster since midday on Tuesday when he sent away a couple of Jehovah's Witnesses. When interviewed, they expressed self-righteous sorrow at the rebuff but could shed no light.

No newspapers, milk or bread were delivered to the chalet, Josh having been accustomed to call at the nearby farm if he ran out of supplies from his three-weekly supermarket raid. He picked up his own copy of *The Independent* each morning when he jogged his mile and a half to the newsagent-Post Office, but it was not a standing order as he frequently went away for days at a time without giving notice. At the shop it had been assumed he was on another of his professional trips. Neither the proprietor nor his teenage daughter remembered seeing him come in after Tuesday morning.

'That squares with the papers found among his rubbish,' the sergeant on duty told Yeadings. 'Last one was Monday's. And Tuesday's was still folded, with the crossword unattempted, on a chair in the sitting-room.'

Which certainly seemed to confirm that the last meal eaten had been Tuesday's brunch, the components of which Mrs Todd had identified as similar to Littlejohn's findings.

'What arrangements did he normally make to have his hothouses looked after when he was away?' Yeadings asked.

The local police had got there before him. He was shown a statement by a Richard Ford, aged seventeen, schoolboy and would-be botanist. He held keys to both the chalet and the plant rooms. Whenever Mr Webster intended being absent for more than a day he would ring and arrange for Richard to pop in and check all was in order. Not that there had ever been anything to put right, because the atmosphere was maintained on balanced thermostats and hydrostats. If there had been a power cut the emergency generator would have switched in within seconds. All the boy had ever done was dead-head the plants where required, and once, when Mr Webster meant to be away for ten days, he'd helped himself to some blooms to take home and draw.

'So what was the last occasion he was called in?' Yeadings asked.

'Three months back, when Mr Webster went to a horticultural photographers' convention in Cannes for five days,' said the sergeant.

So Francine was still the last known person to see Josh alive. Yeadings would have given a lot to be certain that she'd taken leave of him as her uncle, and still had to learn of the closer relationship.

Mott and Z were out working on the family's alibis for the three days preceding the discovery of the body. He rang in to have them meet with him in an hour's time at his office.

Rosemary was already in the building, typing up her paperwork. Mott came in not long after Yeadings himself, complaining that his shoes were killing him. He thought he must have chilblains. Yeadings suggested he wasn't drinking enough milk. 'Stuff they give to babies, don't they?' the DI muttered back.

There followed a small ceremony involving the coffee machine and an amber-filled bottle from Yeadings' bottom drawer. 'Right,' he said, when tempers had been cooled and bodies warmed, 'you'll be glad to know it's confirmed that the time of the crime falls within the narrower frame we favoured: from six p.m. to eight p.m. on the Tuesday, unless the dead man had precisely the same meal that night at nine, when we'd also have to consider five a.m. to seven a.m. on Wednesday. However, since he was still in his day clothes and hadn't opened Tuesday's newspaper, that's a pretty feeble alternative. So, Angus, what have you got?'

'Francine Webster's a possible. Her neighbour in the flat below heard her come in "after seven o'clock that evening, but certainly before *The Bill* came on TV at eight". The New Zealander was already in, according to her, and came down to open the outer door as the woman's husband left to go to the pub. I haven't caught up with Carradine yet for confirmation, but I got an earlier sighting, for what it's worth, from the girl's stepfather. He saw her coming out of the Henley driveway as he returned about six forty-five p.m. He's sure of the time because he was conscious of cutting it fine for an evening engagement with his wife.'

'You said, "for what it's worth". Why that?'

'Poor visibility, fine snow. I don't doubt it was her car, but we'd never prove she was the driver. However, it's within the time that interests us. And it doesn't necessarily clear her. She'd have had time to get there after the killing. No one was in the house to vouch for what time she arrived.'

'Godden himself?'

'Claims he had a full list of private patients at his London consulting rooms. I'll check that with the receptionist. Elinor Godden says she was at the massage therapy centre at Beaconsfield, but the girl I saw there today thought she must have cancelled. Her name was scored through instead of being ticked. It's possible that the new girl on the desk then could have checked her in wrongly. They'll look through their receipts and let me know tomorrow. Mrs Godden always pays by cheque.'

'Right. How about the Morton Websters?'

'Interesting. He said at first he'd been in his office, so I spoke to the secretary. She'd had to apologize for his absence from a lunch appointment and said he didn't come in again until Wednesday morning. When challenged, Webster said he'd mistaken the day. He remembered now he'd spent that afternoon at the gravel-digging plant. Then he changed his mind once more and said he'd meant to go there but in the end just drove around thinking.'

'So who was the broken lunch appointment with?'

Mott riffled back through his notebook. 'A machinery supplier called Madison.'

'M'm. Did you ask who was lunching whom?'

'Webster would be picking up the tab. His secretary made the booking.'

'I should have thought he'd be the guest, as a prospective customer. I wonder.'

Mott and Z looked at him with expectation.

'Just a passing thought, but we all know that the recession is putting back the road-building programme. And it's a domino effect. If Webster's heavily into new equipment and can't unload his stone, he might be cancelling new orders for plant or even trying to sell back. With bank interest soaring over the last few years, all businesses have had to trim down after heavy expansion. Find out if he's stood men off and is leaving plant idle. We've taken him for a wealthy man because he's clearly been a big spender. But he might be in hot water over borrowings, and that's enough to make anyone wander round the countryside instead of meeting people he could owe money to.'

'I'll take another look at him,' Mott promised. 'If he's in Queer Street it could give him the money motive we looked for in Francine's car crash. That's all I've got, sir.'

'Z?'

'I checked on Marcia Webster, Edith Halliday and Cousin Alastair. He's in the clear. He was at his bookshop all Tuesday and lunched with two customers from just after one until three fifteen p.m. at the Buttery in Duke Street. Edith Halliday spent the morning serving drinks and sandwiches to outpatients at Headington Hospital. She came off duty at twelve and says she went straight home. No witnesses. She used her car that day, so she just could have gone over to see her cousin Josh at Turville Heath.'

'And still nobody knows the whereabouts of young Piers, I suppose?'

'So she says. Marcia Webster claims to have been with Dominic at Stoke Mandeville Hospital that afternoon and evening, but I've yet to check.'

'Tuesday?' Mott queried. 'Hang on.' He turned back a few pages and grunted. 'I thought so. It was Wednesday afternoon we both saw Dominic. He was all bright-eyed and cocky about his mother not turning up. He mentioned she hadn't been in the day before, either.'

Rosemary hummed. 'I missed out on that. Sorry. I'll have a word with the Sister in charge there, though I suppose it's possible for a visitor to get in without the staff noticing.'

'I doubt it. The nurses are very quick to pop out and check on everyone. I guess they're afraid of addicts wandering in for drugs.'

'Mrs Webster did seem quite convincing. A bit out of patience with me. Hadn't we made any progress yet about the car crash, and so on.'

'Attack as the best method of defence,' Yeadings suggested. 'So we have both Websters and Elinor Godden to do a little more on, and keep an open mind about Edith Halliday. I'd hoped we might have eliminated more of them by now.

'Actually, there's another name we should add to the list: young Carradine, same address as Francine. Bear in mind he had access to her car, could more easily have sabotaged it than any of the others, though I've no suggestion as to motive. But he's an aggressive type, reacted oddly when I asked where he was on Tuesday afternoon. His transport's a motor-cycle. He could well have followed Francine out to Turville Heath, stayed on to quarrel and fight with Josh, and reached home before her if she called in at Henley first. And shorting photographic lighting is something that might easily occur to him as cover-up.'

'Where did he claim he was?' Z demanded.

'Working on some film at Pinewood. As I say, there's no obvious motive and we don't know he ever met the dead man, but he's a poor liar. I'd stake half my pension rights that he was nowhere near Pinewood, and up to no good wherever he was. You can follow up on him tomorrow, Z. See who actually saw him at work on Tuesday afternoon.'

He leaned back and treated them both to a waggle of the famous black eyebrows. 'And now, just to make your day perfect, I'll tell you a fairy story. About a magic horse that turned paper to gold. Its name was Tontine.'

And he proceeded to amaze them.

EIGHTEEN

'SO MUCH FOR THE ODD state of mind of old Hadrian Bascombe and the game of chance,' said Yeadings finally. 'There's a new factor now I want you both to consider in relation to each of the suspects: Josh Webster as Francine's father.

'We've already wondered if he revealed the truth to her on Tuesday and if that provoked a display of temper which ended with Josh in the pool. Let's suppose instead that Josh had mentioned to Elinor Godden his intention to come clean, and Elinor, quite naturally, was strongly opposed.'

'It would give her a motive to silence him,' said Z. 'I've been turning that in my mind. Of course, we're all aware nowadays that incest's not as rare as was supposed, but if the news got out it wouldn't do Elinor any good. Particularly with her daughter.'

'How can you fit her in with the timing, Josh's indoor clothing and the scene in the hothouse?' Mott cautioned. 'Josh was over six feet tall and well built. Elinor Godden couldn't have dragged him there from the house.'

'Suppose she arrives soon after Francine leaves, then it could be her lipstick on the second coffee cup in the sink. Josh would lead up to the subject gradually. She could have gone berserk on hearing Francine already knew the truth. Unable to wreak her anger on her brother, she runs into the hothouses intent on damaging his beloved orchids. He follows, they struggle. You can choose your own ending.'

'He's protecting the plants, turns his back. She dots him one with—'

'With the light fixture he's previously removed, after the photography session. She thinks he's dead, panics. Covers up with the electrocution business.'

'M'm,' Yeadings said, eyeing the enthusiasts doubtfully. 'You've got to make up your minds whether she does him in in a fit of passion, or if she calmly works out and sets up a spoof scenario. To be capable of both in a matter of minutes would require something like a split personality. She's a pretty remarkable woman, but not that much.'

'Someone else arrives and does the cover-up job?'

'Who would be prepared to do so much for her?'

'Francine, coming back for some reason. Or her husband. She treats him like a bit of junk furniture but he seems quite besotted,' Mott offered.

Yeadings grunted. 'I think we're entering the realms of fantasy there. Let's leave Elinor on record as a possible for the killing, and go back to the effect on others of the story of Josh's fathering Francine. How would if affect Elinor's husband?' he pursued.

Mott grunted. 'He's had plenty of his wife's scandals to put up with. This would merely be one more, and something that happened well before he knew her. I doubt if he's even got to know of it yet. Neither Elinor nor Francine is likely to tell him.'

'And what of old Hadrian Bascombe? Does he know already, or has he guessed? If it came fresh to him now, what difference would it make to his disposing of his fortune?

'No suggestions? I'll admit I'm in the dark myself. It's time, perhaps, I paid the old codger a second visit.'

'The others will probably enjoy the shaming of Elinor in private, and be thoroughly embarrassed if it becomes public property,' Mott hazarded. 'But beyond the possible reflected scandal they're not really affected.'

Z leaned forward. 'One thing I find strange is the way Francine has accepted it. She and her mother together, almost as if . . .'

'In collusion? Or at least in agreement over something?' Yeadings prompted. 'Yes. Today they were acting together, with Elinor in the supporting rôle. Then

Francine dropped her mother off and returned to her own place. No further support either way.'

'You mean the girl dropped her mother in the sent-to-Coventry sense?'

'I'd think so, but for one fact. Francine is handing out a quite new version of the parenthood story: that Josh was indeed her father, but Elinor only the adoptive mother. Now, instead of a missing father to find . . .'

Mott and Z stared at him. Both spoke simultaneously. 'Clever! It does away with the incest scandal,' Z broke out.

'But surely,' said Mott, 'mothers are easier to prove than fathers.'

'How?' Yeadings answered him, 'when Josh may have been the only one to know the truth. Francine, as a baby, could have had no idea. That leaves Elinor Godden, and she can say anything she likes. And don't remind me there's DNA identification. We have to have the woman's sample to work from. I don't see either Elinor or Francine eager to undergo tests right now, do you?'

Roddy Carradine eased himself free of the sleeping girl's arms and slid his feet floorwards. When he had groped for his clothes he stood a moment with the door ajar, looking down at the lovely face. It moved him in a way he had never known before.

The emotions arising from their complex relations were hideously mixed in his mind. Not until he'd come on her under threat from the big detective had he realized he actually loved her. Now the need to protect overrode all other considerations. He would do anything, anything, to ensure she wasn't hurt further; even knock her out with sleeping pills while he dreamed up more duplicity. It shamed him, and God knew he'd enough of that already.

He bent and kissed Francine's brow, her exposed shoulder, the tip of one pinky-brown nipple. Then he softly drew the duvet over her and went to dress in the kitchen.

He hesitated over taking the ring of keys from the dresser. But tomorrow was Saturday and she'd said she meant to go to London by train. If he wasn't back in time to return the keys, she could take a bus to Gerrards Cross station. He reached for the keys and quietly let himself out of the flat into the chill, starlit night.

Frank Godden heard his wife's door close softly and a moment later the creak of the third stair down. In the dark he listened apprehensively, but there came no dreaded sound of bolts withdrawn on the outer door, no footsteps on shingle, no car starting up.

He found himself out on the landing, with a rush of vertigo faced the long staircase, knew he'd overdone the analgesics. If he went crashing to the hall floor, would she come running or pretend not to hear?

Unsteadily he began the descent. Much later, it seemed, he was leaning against the kitchen door, fearful of the bright light beyond and the encounter that must follow. His weight made it move and the woman gave a startled cry.

'Frank?'

He went forward into the room, dazzled and defensive. 'I heard you come down. Are you all right?'

It was like talking to a stranger. They *were* strangers. He remembered then that he had meant to start again from the beginning, courting her, Elinor Webster, the beautiful widow with the poor little crippled daughter. He tried to remember how he had been before, in the days when she'd found him desirable.

'Of course I'm all right,' she was saying. 'Just couldn't sleep. Here, sit down. You look—'

'I'm fine now. The flu's cleared up. Just a four-day event.' He heard the nonchalance in his own voice and it almost convinced him. Over on the counter the kettle switched itself off. She'd put the teapot ready.

'What a splendid idea. Shall I make it for you?' His voice was eager, but he stayed fixed to his chair. 'No? Enough for us both then, eh?'

From the distance which now muffled everything external he heard the soft scuff of her slippers on the ceramic tiles, the comfortable chink of china, a tinkle of spoons, smelled the sharp tang of freshly cut lemon.

When they were sipping hot tea, side by side, elbows on the table, he found energy to go on. 'I thought in the morning I'd go up to Harley Street, sort things out a bit.'

'Tomorrow's Saturday. Today, actually.' She sounded weary. He actually faced her then, and saw how drained she looked.

'Miss Drake will be in. We'll book new appointments for the ones I missed this week. Afterwards – how about coming up for a show? I'll ring around for tickets, find something amusing to take us out of ourselves. Then maybe supper somewhere smart afterwards.'

It all came tumbling out, eager, young. She was looking at him as if surprised. But said nothing.

'Elinor, if there's anything else you'd rather do—'

'There's nothing. Nothing, ever.' She sounded despondent, past desperation.

'So you'll come?'

Her dark-rimmed eyes met his ironically. 'Why not? What else is there?'

Somehow he found himself in his room again. Only the taste of tea rough against the inside of his teeth was proof that it had happened at all. He needed to sleep, but he mustn't take any more of the stuff or he'd never wake in time.

And then, when he lay down and his head met the cool pillow, he found he *could* sleep, needed no inducement, was already sliding away.

Towards dawn there was a sudden change in the weather. The front promised by the forecasters had come in more quickly than expected. Already in the south-west there was rain. The Thames Valley awoke to heavy cloud and an absence of frost.

Edith Halliday felt the difference in her hands and wrists, which had begun aching with arthritis. She made tea downstairs and carried it back to bed as usual. Not for her the decadent luxury of an automatic Teasmaid. She lay back, physically at rest, but her mind alert for the expected three clicks of the outer storm door below. First the milkman, leaving her customary pint of semi-skimmed ιn the lobby; ten minutes later the newspaper girl in her clomping boots; lastly the postman. The trio having been completed, she donned her nylon housecoat and slippers to go down and encounter the main excitement of the day.

With the milk cage in one hand and the newspaper under her arm, she bent to gather in the post. There were three letters, but she deliberately kept her gaze off them until she was seated by the kitchen range. One, in a white envelope, she left till last, her heart beating fast while she slit open and discarded an appeal from The Samaritans and a prize-promising invitation to a ninety-minute sales drive on a timeshare.

Finally she looked at the handwritten address.

It wasn't from Piers. It wasn't for her at all. The postman had misread thirty-two for fifty-two. She would have to go along the street later and deliver it herself.

Hope had gone sour. She felt again the black depression she had been fighting against ever since the letter from VSO. Where *was* the boy? Why didn't he get in touch? Surely something quite appalling must have happened, to account for his silence?

Today stretched ahead with no distractions. She would make herself go and change her library books, although she'd only opened one of them and couldn't settle to it. Anything was better than waiting here, between the closing-in walls, for something that never happened.

She washed and dressed, made toast and put out most of it for the birds. She listened to the BBC news, looked aimlessly through the headlines of the paper, then read them more carefully, apprehensively, in case there was mention of some accident.

At nine-twenty she had her hat and raincoat on, ready for the street, when the phone rang. And she knew from the way it sounded that this time was different. It had to be Piers.

Alastair's voice came through, with other noises behind it; a scratchy shuffling of paper, the distant ping of his shop doorbell. 'Edith, it's Alastair.'

Well, of course it was. But then he was saying he'd had a letter. Yes, from Piers. In the post this morning. He'd just opened it.

'For heaven's sake, Alastair, *what does he say?*'

'Look, Edith, it's better I come and see you. I can't talk over the phone.'

'But is he all right? Where is he? Why hasn't he been in touch with me?'

'Well, er, there's quite a bit to explain. But he's all right. Nothing really to worry about. Yes, I'm sure he's absolutely fine.'

'Then why doesn't he come home? Did he say when—?'

'Yes, actually he wants to see you, asked me to arrange it.'

'*Arrange* it? To see his own mother? Alastair, there *is* something wrong, isn't there?'

She heard him groan. 'No, there isn't. I told you I can't say anything properly over the phone. I just rang to set your mind at rest. Look Edith, as soon as I've shut up shop this evening I'll come over, stay the night. How's that? I'll ring you from Paddington, so you can meet me at your end with the car. How's that?'

'Well, yes. But—'

'Sorry, I *must* go now. Shop's full of people.' And he rang off.

She put down the receiver and went blindly into the sitting-room, sank on to the settee, still in her outdoor clothes. She had so wanted news. Good news. Now this seemed worse than nothing. Piers had told Alastair something awful which he had to break to her in person. He was to arrange a meeting. Where? Why couldn't Piers simply come home?

Because for some reason he was prevented. Was in hospital? – no, Alastair had said the boy was all right. So where? Dear God, he wasn't with *the police*? What on earth had he done?

Frank Godden felt little better in the morning. He decided to leave his car at the station and go up to town by train. Miraculously Elinor hadn't changed her mind about joining him in the evening, and she would use her car. They could drive home together in that.

As ever on a Saturday, the streets between Paddington

and his consulting rooms were less crowded. It would be vastly different a few streets farther south because the January Sales were on, when women dragged their whole families around at weekends to look at doubtful bargains from the previous season's fashions.

Thank God Elinor had no need to do that. Apart from the ample allowance he gave her, she had been left well-off when her first husband died. Money wasn't important to her, because she'd never been short of it. Unlike the rest of her rapacious family.

He walked in on a startled Miss Drake sitting at her desk eating a cream slice. It wasn't a thing you could do daintily without a plate, and in her surprise she bit so hard that raspberry jam spurted across her face. She sat there gaping idiotically, the scarlet stain making her look as if her cheek had been slashed open.

Sudden nausea overcame him, and the looming headache burst out again from the repressive drugs. He watched the embarrassed woman wipe the sticky mess away. Surely he had phoned yesterday to let her know he was coming in? He couldn't remember clearly. It was his own professional suite, wasn't it? Suppose one of his best clients had arrived without an appointment and taken her for a facial surgery that had gone wrong. Stupid, stupid!

'I've put your patients on hold for Monday and Tuesday,' she said in a rush. 'What would you like me to do for last week's cancellations?'

'Phone them and fit them in,' he said shortly. 'I'll be in my office. I don't want to be disturbed. Oh, and try around for two good tickets to some show for this evening.'

She watched him go through to the inner rooms, heard keys clatter against the glass-fronted drugs cupboard. Silence for a few minutes, then slow steps and the faint squeak of castors on parquet as he lowered himself on to the chaise-longue. She looked at the clock. In an hour she would peep in at him. If he was awake she'd make coffee.

Francine Webster always relied on the twice-yearly Sales to set herself up in half-price or third-off bargains. If styles she picked up had a look of last year it didn't bother her. Of necessity, she told herself, her clothes were somewhat freaky, and it was the way you wore them rather than the garments themselves that mattered.

By a little after two p.m. she had window-gazed in Burlington Arcade, found an ankle-length cream raincoat at Fenwicks, on the way up Bond Street had tried on and turned down several pairs of fleece-lined slippers, staring out the salesgirl who had seemed almost about to mention that madam's requirements were not in the normal run of stock. Eventually she reached the hurly-burly of Oxford Street where progress was a form of contra-flow slalom. Hobbling gratefully into John Lewis, she made for *The Place to Eat* before starting on Fabrics. There she sat over prawn salad and a coffee for a full hour until she felt able to stagger farther. After that, Dickins and Jones. Finally, she promised herself, the euphoria of Liberty's. She would aim for a skirt and trouser-suit length of something really good this year.

When, burdened with carrier bags, she finally left the overheated shop for the drizzle of Regent Street, the lights were brilliant, shining on massed umbrellas as the crowds milled and seethed as boisterous as ever, the jammed traffic chequered with black taxis and red buses.

On the puddled pavement she found it hard to ease her way against the general flow, ducking under brolly spikes, avoiding elbows and linked-up lovers. She turned back to the Circus Underground entrance in Oxford Street, gathered her long skirts in one hand and tried to keep her balance in the human stream cascading down the stairs towards the ticket barriers.

Roddy Carradine had put in some hard work overnight, and when he was satisfied with the results he biked back to the flat, left the Yamaha on its stand by the kerb and let himself in. Francine had gone, leaving her washed-up breakfast crocks in the plastic drainer. He remembered then her intended raid on the London Sales. Just as well, because he was knackered. This was a time for a whole bed to himself.

He awoke about one p.m., showered, dressed and biked

back to Pinewood. It was pretty quiet and he made sure the gate security man saw him come in. He had put in almost two hours on post-production when the expected call came: Donovan from the gate lodge, to say a woman detective-constable from Thames Valley would like a few words.

'Sure,' said Roddy. 'Point her in this direction and I'll be looking out for her.' He checked again that everything was in place, then went out in the rain to greet his visitor with a broad grin.

Miss Drake hadn't had any luck with the theatres, but in the early afternoon she had sounded out her employer on the offer of two central stalls at the Festival Hall. She'd had the initiative to check on the programme and it wasn't too stiff. Frank Godden rang home and nervously inquired how that would suit Elinor.

'Depends,' she said. 'I couldn't take anything soulful just now. No Wagner, no Bruch Violin Concerto.'

'It's a Viennese Night,' he assured her. 'Mozart, the Strausses, the sort of thing.'

Still she hesitated, then suddenly, 'What the hell, I'll be there. Festival Hall. What time?'

Forty-five minutes before they were due to meet, Frank Godden left his consulting rooms. There was no taxi free. The few that went speeding past with their For Hire lights out threw up water on pedestrians unwise enough to walk near the road. He decided to make for Oxford Street and the denser traffic, but he had overlooked the shoppers thronging everywhere, most of them now bound for home. There were even little queues of them waving brollies or holding up imperative hands outside the main stores. And still the cabs splashed past unheeding.

He thought he would never get to her on time. It would be unthinkable, when he'd spent all the wakeful part of his day imagining and planning this, had even sent out for a special corsage. (Not an orchid, because that would mean Josh, but three tiny tight rosebuds, pink against the soft green of maidenhair fern.) He held the little perspex box containing them in both hands as he walked through the

188

rain, like a priest protecting the chalice.

It was drizzling at Henley. By Maidenhead it had become a torrent and Elinor was in two minds about going on. But she had always had an aversion to turning back on anything. Her fault had been in accepting, when he made the absurd invitation during the night. Just for an instant, when he'd sounded so urgent, she'd glimpsed the man he once was. That she'd once thought he was, because now, for so long, she knew he was hollow. She could forgive a man much, but not dullness. And the exterior promising so much, with his fine body and dark, almost Draculan beauty. But, as a man, empty, so she'd had to look for her excitement and danger elsewhere.

Once on the motorway, she responded pleasurably to the demanding conditions, three double lines of white lights rushing at her as London emptied, three double sets of red lights weaving ahead, all speeds well over the limit, and the road surface dodgy.

A wry little smile tugged her lips at the thought that the world might end for her not with a whimper but a mighty crash of metal and a shower of glass. But she instantly admitted she wasn't the sort to give up easily, nor to think of endings when there were always new beginnings just a little way ahead. Even now, cramped in her mental tunnel, she knew she would eventually be happy again.

Meanwhile one freewheeled, waited, put up with a Viennese Evening in the company of one's deadly dull husband.

She made it in good time, parked in a reasonably near position, went for a Martini and was again at the door waiting when Frank's cab disgorged him, barely on time. And he was clutching, in the name of all that was adolescent, a boxed bit of vegetation with a pin that would certainly draw the threads on her olive green watered silk.

At roughly the moment they entered the auditorium, across the river at Oxford Circus Underground an elderly woman fell in the push of bodies as the crowd was herded back from a down escalator. There were cries for first-aid, and the woman was found a space to lie at ease while an ambulanceman checked she was no more than bruised and breathless. Then he went down after his colleagues. Two minutes later the way was cleared for firemen to go through.

Word went round the booking hall that a blaze had broken out below, but before panic could spread an official made a broadcast announcement. London Transport regretted that because of an unfortunate accident the northbound Bakerloo Line would be temporarily closed. Travellers were advised to choose alternative routes.

'We all know what that means,' said a thin young man with an orange Mohican haircut. 'Some poor sod's jumped under a train.'

NINETEEN

ANGUS MOTT HAD COME IN to type up his notes of yesterday. Monday would have offered him the chance to share a typist, but there was always a backlog to clear before anyone got round to his requirements. At least Sunday guaranteed a free machine, and he was several stages better than a two-finger pecker.

Edith Halliday's call was put through to him. She sounded weary, confused and not far from hysteria. She had sat up all night, it seemed, waiting for Cousin Alastair to ring. She'd been meant to meet him off his London train. He was coming to give her news of Piers.

But it got later and later, and she'd finally fallen asleep, woke in her chair at about half past two in the morning. She was sure that the phone bell would have roused her. Something terrible must have overtaken Alastair, because she'd tried ringing his flat for over two hours and there was no answer.

'Is there anyone who normally helps him in the shop?' Mott asked.

'His partner, a young man called Timothy, but I don't know his surname or his address.'

'I see. Perhaps we can help. I'll get in touch with the local police. They may know something.'

'Dammit,' he said under his breath. He was almost at the end of his typescript and had intended going out to see Elinor Godden about her unsatisfactory alibi. Now it meant staying on until the Met got back to him about Alastair Bartholomew. From what Edith Halliday had said, he could be in touch with her missing son.

He finished off and left a copy for Yeadings in the

191

operations file. The top sheet was Z's interview with Roddy Carradine at Pinewood. He seemed to have given her the grand tour of the place. Or the runaround? he asked himself. Z was an attractive female and the New Zealander wasn't blind.

Mott lifted out the report and took it off to read more thoroughly over a coffee and Danish.

Carradine had been sweet reason, explaining the set-up, how mainly he worked alone or with one technician assisting, but on Tuesday he'd been all over the place. If she came back on Monday she was sure to find someone who remembered seeing him around. He'd even been on the set for the filming, did a Hitchcock and sneaked in on one scene as an extra. Would she like to see it if he hooked it out?

Since in itself the piece of film could save her returning on a weekday to check on staff not then present, she'd said she would. He'd run it for her, a short reel of pilot episodes for an insurance ad. True enough, Carradine had walked out of a shop doorway, stopped to light a cigarette and sauntered off, just as the foreground filled with the souped-up banger of the ad's handsome hero. She had checked the date on the film itself as well as on the can. It was Tuesday right enough.

But Mott recalled that the Boss had thought the lad was smart-assing. It could be that he reacted better to women. On the other hand, perhaps he'd just found Z easier to deceive.

Mott turned, to find the subject of his surmise standing behind him holding her own mug of tea. 'Hullo, you a Sunday volunteer too?' he greeted.

'On the same task as you,' she said shortly. 'I see you've found my report.'

'Yes. I've just filed a copy of mine. Help yourself.'

Instead of reaching for it, she stood there frowning. 'It didn't smell right, though.'

'What didn't?'

'Roddy Carradine's story. All so pat. And he was too pleased with himself by far.'

'It could be his antipodean manner. The Boss felt something too. Decided he was a bad liar.'

'Only he wasn't in this case, because the film proves he was there. It's digitally dated and timed at the start.'

'But the lad's into cutting and splicing, isn't he?'

'I thought about that. But they're frame sequences where he's there alongside the main story. They couldn't have been inserted.'

Mott considered this. 'Hang on! *Battleship Potemkin!* You must have seen that video where the tourists got mixed up in the original Russian film. They were climbing up the steps all among the bloodshed. One of them tried to stop the runaway pram. Not inserted, Z; superimposed! Very clever stuff. I can't quite remember how it was done; something about filming fresh shots against a blue background, then refilming the two layers together. God! If Carradine's gone to all that trouble to give himself a Tuesday alibi, he must have been up to something shady.'

'If he's been playing about with film wouldn't he need to get the new version printed? Which would involve someone else and a lapse of time.'

'But he could actually have been working on video. Are you sure he didn't mention video, Z?'

'Maybe he did. Does it make much difference?'

'I believe it does. One of our civilian video experts may be able to wise us up on it.'

'What do I do? See Carradine again?'

'Certainly, but after we've told the Boss. Ask how he'd like it tackled.'

'I think he was trying to see old Hadrian Bascombe this morning. I'll have to leave it until tomorrow.'

'Are you going off now?'

'Unless there's anything—'

'Z, what a foolish question! There's always something. Could you hang in here for a message from the Met, while I cope with the Elinor Godden end? Earlier Edith Halliday rang in in a tizzy because Cousin Alastair didn't make it out to her last night, and she's been trying all morning to raise him by phone. Apparently he's had some kind of message from Piers. So I asked for the Met to send someone to his address to see what's what.'

'Right, then. Off you go to Elinor, and be sure you wear

your asbestos suit. I'll hold the fort. I've a good paperback in my locker for times like this.'

Mott was in two minds about ringing the house first, but decided the bird might take flight if forewarned. Elinor Godden appeared to have scant respect for the police, as for any sort of authority. He didn't think they would be church-goers, more likely lazing around before a late Sunday lunch.

In that he was wrong. The house at Henley appeared to be shut up. While he was checking at the rear, a taxi decanted the housekeeper at the front. She was trying to get her key in the lock as he reappeared. 'Oh dear,' she said, 'isn't this awful. I hope you aren't bringing any more bad news.'

Her habitual calm had deserted her. Mott took the key from her trembling hands, unlocked the house door and followed her in.

'No,' he said cautiously. 'How do things stand at present?'

She had been at her sister's, it being her free weekend, but this morning there'd been a call from Mrs Godden. No details, just that she'd stayed in town overnight at the hospital with her husband. He was a little better this morning, it seemed. Out of danger. But she'd decided to come back straightaway because Mrs Godden was going to dash back for some clothes, and it wouldn't be nice for her in an empty house would it?

Mott agreed it wouldn't. He was glad there was an improvement this morning. Did she know just how it had happened?

'Well, during the meal, it seems. Mrs Godden said he'd been very quiet in the concert interval, half asleep. Then he went off to the – the gents, like, and when he came back he seemed better, full of ideas about where they should go on to. Mrs Godden was driving and she took him to some place in Soho. Foreign, I shouldn't wonder. It's come to a pretty pass when you daren't go out for supper in London without being poisoned, though!'

Yeadings had taken the precaution of ringing Lynalls

ahead of his visit, so he was shown up immediately to the first floor; but this time directly into Hadrian Bascombe's presence.

The old man was slumped behind a handsome mahogany desk and was dressed in a lounge suit and a tasselled pillbox of dark, gold-embroidered velvet, which Yeadings reckoned to be an Edwardian smoking cap.

His left hand twitched as it moved to pick up a ball-point pen. 'WHY?' it scrawled awkwardly across a jotter.

'You'd like to know why I've come this time? It's because I'd like to know some of the things you know, Mr Bascombe. You see, when I came before, Mr Chadwala made a remark that set me thinking. He didn't mean to. It was a simple denial, because he didn't want me to have the wrong idea about him. He said he served you in many ways, but he was not a spy. So I got to wondering who your spy was, since you certainly pride yourself on keeping up with the private and personal affairs of your family.'

The hand wrote again. 'SO WHO?'

'You let your money do the walking, Mr Bascombe. You employ professionals. A private detective agency.'

The old man cackled. 'TOUCHÉ.'

'So perhaps your man – or men – were wise to some of the things that puzzle me: like where the Morton Websters were at the time Joshua was killed. Elinor Godden too.'

As the policeman watched, the old man underwent a change, unbent and took a deeper breath. His lolling head straightened and he held out both hands, the fingers outstretched, palms down. 'Enough of this charade, Superintendent. We need to talk,' he grated.

'I'm delighted to find you so recovered,' Yeadings greeted him.

'I'm none the better for police incompetence,' said Bascombe sourly. 'After my great-niece's escape from death and my great-nephew's disablement, I should have expected more care exercised towards the rest of my family.'

Not only was the old man capable of fluent speech but also of rancour, Yeadings noted. He flicked a glance towards the Parsee nurse standing to one side and was rewarded by a lowered gaze and a slow blush.

'Uh,' said Bascombe, intercepting the unspoken query, 'the stroke wasn't as severe as it might have been, but it served to keep people off me.'

Yeadings nodded. He remembered Mr Chadwala had said, 'Mr Bascombe is not speaking at present.' A stickler for truth, he hadn't said the man *couldn't* talk.

'Didn't your charade amount to tempting fate?' the policeman asked blandly.

'Perhaps. Next time may be final.' Dry as a stick; reptilian, as Francine had said.

Yeadings returned to pick up the gibe. 'The police cannot provide personal bodyguards. There was no reason to expect an attack on Joshua Webster, Mr Bascombe.'

The man sighed. 'No. Who would wish to hurt Josh?'

'Who would wish harm to any of your family?'

There was a considerable silence while the man glared at his wrinkled hands on the desktop. 'You could start by asking why, rather than who.'

'Why, then?'

'Isn't money cause enough?'

'Greed is an acceptable motive in general. When people have riches dangled and withdrawn, and they're desperate besides, teasing may well push them over the edge of reason.'

'So you must look for someone like that.'

'Your nephew Morton? The recession could have caught him in over-expansion.'

'Morton's a short-sighted speculator; he doesn't see that the crest of any wave has to break. Though he may be pathetic, he isn't vicious.'

'Someone stronger-minded, then? We have asked for alibis for Tuesday afternoon. Francine Webster was at the right place at about the right time, but all the rest claim to have been elsewhere. Some of those claims don't stand up to examination. Elinor Godden was not at the masseur's; Morton Webster was not at his office; his wife Marcia was not at Dominic's bedside.'

'Indeed not.'

'I beg your pardon?'

The old man's eyes gleamed with malice. 'Marcia was indeed not with her son. But neither was she occupied in killing her brother-in-law. She was, instead, with the private investigator who is checking on Morton's finances for her. I happen to know because he is a specialist I employ frequently myself and he has prior loyalties.'

And you pay him more, Yeadings thought silently.

'There is only one thing Marcia dotes on more than her son, and that is money. You may be sure that if she deserts Dominic's bedside it is for the higher call.'

The old man cackled. 'And wherever Morton had run off to, it was for a quiet moment to breathe in, without her screaming over his shoulder. He has enough to worry him.

'As for Elinor going missing, one should always assume she is with a lover, except that she has never troubled before to cover up the fact. I cannot believe that Elinor, even in a frenzy, could kill her brother, but it must be worth your while to discover just what she was up to.'

Yeadings nodded. 'Doubtless you also know everything about Francine Webster's parentage.'

Now he had made an impression on the old man. There was a brief sparking of some emotion in the eyes, then they were hooded once more. 'So that old question has raised its hoary head? Josh, I assume, couldn't resist making a posthumous claim on her.'

'Which leaves Elinor Godden in a difficult position.'

'Elinor thrives on difficulties. She goes to great lengths to create them. As she did in this case.'

'She has told Francine that she was her adoptive mother.'

The old man's face wrinkled with laughter. He showed long, bared teeth like an ape's. 'My dear Superintendent, I have seen Francine's birth certificate. It states quite clearly that Elinor is her mother, and the father is left blank. How could you, as a good public servant, cast doubt on an official document like that?'

'It could be either a forgery or a false declaration.'

Bascombe's stare mocked him, and Yeadings looked calmly back, letting silence build up between them. Eventually, 'It is neither,' said the old man, barely above a whisper. 'But there is still a possibility which you have overlooked.'

Yeadings smiled. 'That the young lady we all know is not the original Francine Webster at all.'

'Ah!' The sound was one of surprised delight. 'I shall say no more. Elinor will surely take you the rest of the way, if you still so desire. And now I am, quite truthfully, a little tired. Mr Chadwala will see you downstairs.'

'No need,' said Yeadings, rising. He held out his hand. 'I have appreciated meeting you, sir.'

After a slight hesitation Hadrian Bascombe offered his own hand. It lay in the policeman's big one, dry and cold like some shrivelled mummy's.

The call from the Met came sooner than Z expected. 'DI Mott's out on a call,' she said. 'You can give it to me.'

'Bad news, I'm afraid. West End Central are covering a fatality at Oxford Circus Underground last night. Seems it was the man you're looking for.'

'Piers Halliday?'

'No. The Alastair Bartholomew you sent a query about. Lived in Maida Vale and kept a bookshop off Tottenham Court Road. Fell or jumped under an incoming train, according to first reports. But there's a witness says she saw him pushed. Useless description of the other party: back view of a long fawn raincoat and a fisherman's tweed hat, medium height. Not even certain it was a man. It was raining up here at the time and everyone had much the same sort of clothes on.'

'Right, thanks. The inquiry came from his cousin. I guess I get the job of breaking the news to her. He was supposed to be coming to tell her about her missing son, the one I mentioned. I don't suppose he had anything on him which would throw any light?'

'What was the name again?'

'Piers Halliday.'

'Let's see. I've got a list here of the dead man's effects. Piers, yes. There was a letter on him signed Piers. D'you want a copy faxed?'

'We'll need the original eventually. If Bartholomew was

pushed, it fits in with a previous murder we're investigating.'

'Sounds like you've got a multiple killer. I thought you lived in a nice quiet part of the country?'

'Nice for some. Can you see West End Central lets me have the sender's address pdq? It could be that Piers took steps to make sure his whereabouts weren't revealed.'

Angus Mott waited in the kitchen with the housekeeper for Elinor Godden's return.

'It doesn't seem right to worry her any more at such a time,' she said.

'Is she taking it so badly about her husband?'

'She sounded really upset. Of course, he's not been well for days. Some kind of flu, and he kept to his room for fear any of us should catch it. Barely ate anything. And then, straight after, going for a meal where they weren't particular in the kitchens, well, he's bound to go down with it worse.'

But when Elinor arrived, it seemed the restaurant hadn't been to blame. 'Morphine,' she said, almost distraught. 'This morning I've been cooped up for hours in a police interrogation room with a horrible little detective who thinks I tried to poison my husband!'

'How do they know it's morphine?' Mott demanded.

'They made tests at the hospital. I thought they offered me a room just to be near him, but it was to hold me until the police could take over. God, I thought you lot were bad enough, but you're angels in comparison.'

'All the same, I've still got some questions for you, Mrs Godden.'

'Must you?'

'I'll be quick with them. First, your alibi for Tuesday won't wash. You didn't keep your appointment with the masseur.'

'Masseuse, actually. And no, I didn't. I was with a man. He got in touch unexpectedly. We met to say goodbye. I'm not telling you who, because it's all over, and publicity wouldn't do either of us any good. That has to be enough for you. What else?'

'I don't think it will be enough for Superintendent Yeadings. However, we'll move on. It seems Francine doesn't have a father or mother now. Perhaps you can clarify that?'

The language that streamed from her then he couldn't believe she knew. The housekeeper, red-faced and breathing deeply, pushed roughly past him and gathered the woman in her arms. 'There, there,' she comforted. 'Come along to bed, dearie. You need to have a good lie-down, and I'll bring you up a nice hot drink.'

The anodyne clichés, Mott thought gloomily. He waited until the woman came down again and began, 'I said you oughtn't to—'

'Point taken. But I expect you to ring me as soon as she attempts to leave the house. And try to find out where she intends going. It's for her own safety. I've written down my number for you.'

Grim-faced, Mott shrugged on his raincoat and made himself scarce.

TWENTY

AFTER SATURDAY'S DOWNPOUR, SUNDAY HAD been surly. In the afternoon the clouds took on a catarrhal yellow, temperatures dropped, and by midnight the snow had begun again, steady and thick. Monday brought blocked roads, ditched cars and a rash of minor accidents. Throughout Thames Valley, Traffic Division provided the heroes of the hour.

More prosaically, Mike Yeadings came in early to his office, forewarned by Mott that the Met would be in touch on two counts: Elinor as a poisoning suspect, and the death of Alastair Bartholomew. After he had been on the phone at some length, he called his two minions in.

The sender's address given on the letter found in the pocket of the dead man taken off the Bakerloo northbound line had been for a bed and breakfast lodging in Eastbourne. It had been passed to the East Sussex police who phoned back to say that the young man had already moved on. His landlady of six days was co-operative but she'd had no idea of his future plans. She did mention, however, that he had had a young woman with him whom he had referred to as his wife. Her name was Debbie.

'Which can mean owt or nowt,' Yeadings commented.

In view of the letter's mentioning Piers' intention to ring Alastair after the weekend to find out how he had fared in arranging a meeting with his mother, a constable had been installed in the dead man's flat to await a call. Bartholomew's partner Timothy also had instructions how to deal with Piers if he should try to make contact at the bookshop.

'And whether he rings or not, someone will need to ask

him, when found, for an alibi for the time Cousin Alastair was pushed under the incoming train,' said Mott grimly. 'I know that would seem to go against his expressed wish for a meeting to be set up, but if Piers has some serious reason for being in hiding, he may well have chickened out at the last minute and disposed of the man who was to make contact for him.'

'On the score of what's one more killing when he's already being sought for Josh's death?' Z asked. 'Why should he think we've got him in the frame for that?'

'Saturday's *Sun* mentioned that he had failed to turn up in North Africa and his whereabouts were unknown. It came at the end of a paragraph headlined "Mystery Slaying Among Orchids". He could have picked up the implication there. Somebody, even the unfortunate Mrs Halliday, must have let slip the information about Piers when the press were nosing around.'

'More likely it was picked up in London, at Alastair's shop,' Yeadings suggested. 'You can grow long ears lurking behind the bookshelves. I've used 'em myself in my time. Anyway I'm not satisfied that Alastair's killer was Piers. We could be on a wild goose chase there. He says nothing in his letter about keeping the meeting secret. It could be he's not even heard about his Uncle Josh's death. My guess is he's simply eloped, and he's scared of facing up to his mother. Let's leave him out of the Alastair business for the present and take a look at how it could have happened.'

He took a *LONDON A to Z* from the shelf behind his desk. 'Bartholomew asked Edith Halliday to meet his train at her end. He'd have taken it from Paddington Station, to reach which from Tottenham Court Road he'd use the Bakerloo Line, northbound, at Oxford Circus. Since it was raining at the time, he's unlikely to have walked there carrying an overnight bag. If he'd opted for a cab, he'd probably have taken it all the way to Paddington.

'So at Oxford Circus we've got him changing levels from the Central Line to the Bakerloo northbound. This means that apart from anyone who was following him from the shop, he would have run into a whole stream of people going home at that time. If our killer happened by chance to be there (and that Underground serves two mainline stations for our area) he could have acted on the spur of the moment. A jostling crowd moving foward as the train approaches, a good opportunity to knock another name off the tontine list.'

'More alibis to chase,' Mott said tightly.

'The more chances to eliminate the innocent and pinpoint our feller.'

'So who've we got?' Z asked.

'We'll hang on to Piers until proved wrong, then there's the rest of the family, less Edith Halliday if we can believe her story of waiting up for the man who never arrived. But any of them who was in London yesterday afternoon or evening has to be looked at seriously.

'By the way, I've got the gen I asked for on videos. Carradine could well have fiddled his own appearance on to Tuesday's original. Simple really, when you know how. Let me sketch it for you. See, this square is the original video fed to a screen down here, and from there into what they call a Chroma Key. There it's joined by the output from the self-video he's making against a blue background. The mix goes on to a monitor where he can feed himself in, balancing the scale, perspective and lighting exactly to match up with the original. Hey presto! The blue background has disappeared. When the picture's perfect on screen, he records it on the original. No cutting, no splicing. All it requires is know-how, patience and a good eye, all of which our laddo presumably has.'

'But what Carradine was up to on Tuesday is irrelevant, surely,' Z said happily, 'because he couldn't have been the one who killed Alastair. I was interviewing him less than an hour and a half before it happened. And how would he ever have met the man?'

'An hour and a half could be ample for him to get from Pinewood to Oxford Circus,' Mott countered. 'You can work on checking that, first thing. Remember he has a motor-cycle which he could have parked at any intermediate point. And he certainly had the best opportunity of them all to fiddle with Francine's car.'

'Then we have to check on the Goddens who certainly were in town, the Morton Websters and Francine,' Yeadings listed.

Mott tapped his notebook. 'I've already been in touch with the Met about the Goddens. They've questioned Elinor. She drove up from Henley, allowing herself an hour and a quarter before the concert began at the Festival Hall. Just as she was leaving the house she remembers speaking to the gardener who intended packing up for the day because it was starting to rain. He'll remember the time because he's paid by the hour.'

'How about Frank Godden? Coming from consulting rooms in lower Harley Street, he'd have gone to Oxford Circus if he took the Underground. The southbound Bakerloo Line goes direct from there to Waterloo.'

'It was closed instantly along with the northbound. Anyway, the Met have Elinor's unsolicited statement that she saw him arriving by black cab at the Hall's main entrance. He wasn't late for the concert, so it's unlikely he could have disposed of Alastair, got clear, then found a taxi under Saturday's crowded conditions and been driven to the South Bank on time. At the outside he would have had twenty minutes to do the lot.'

'Right; that does seem impossible under the circumstances. Now let's consider the rest of the information we had from the Met: the man's poisoning. The Soho restaurant the Goddens ate at was searched under a warrant and no drugs unearthed apart from cannabis for personal use found on two of the kitchen staff. No heroin at all, nor any other morphine derivatives. So it's unlikely Godden's food could have been contaminated accidentally from that source.

'Tracing back his movements for Saturday, the Met interviewed a Miss Drake, receptionist at his surgery. There were no patients in at all that day, and she was occupied in a separate room with paperwork and phone calls rebooking appointments cancelled during Godden's bout of flu. She believes Godden opened the drugs cupboard himself while he was in his surgery that afternoon. She hadn't checked the contents by the time she was questioned, but she thought that a quantity of morphine had gone missing during the previous week, possibly prior to Godden's absence.

'She left before he did, and it's noted that she twice served him coffee during the time he was there, so she had the opportunity herself to slip him something that would affect him later. Incidentally, the man has no puncture marks whatsoever. If he had a drug habit it was taken by mouth. We have to wait for an analyst's report from the hospital before we can be sure about that.

'Now, that covers the Met end. Back here I want you, Angus, to see the Morton Websters. Z can check on Francine . . .' Yeadings allocated.

He surveyed them with a broad grin. '. . . who may not be Francine Webster at all.' And he gave them the gist of his Sunday interview with Hadrian Bascombe.

'So she was Josh Webster's illegitimate daughter by some unknown woman, who handed her to Elinor, who made a false declaration to the Registrar of Births?' Z assumed.

'That seems to be the outline. Bascombe suggests I get the rest of the story from Elinor herself, but it's hardly a time to distress her further. There must be someone else in the family who remembers what happened all those years ago.'

'Edith Halliday has a taste for scandal,' Z said. 'When eventually we hear directly from Piers, someone will have to inform her. Couldn't we slip the odd question in while she's recovering from the news of Alastair's death, and over the moon about Piers being safe and well?'

'I'll leave you two to toss for the honour,' Yeadings told them. 'For myself, I'm quitting my desk for the day, having quite another fish to fry. You can call my home when there's any movement in the case.'

At a little after eleven a.m. Piers Halliday himself got in touch from a callbox in Bexhill. He had just been speaking to Timothy at the bookship, and was almost incoherent at the news of Alastair's death. The version offered Piers was that he'd lost his balance in the crush on the platform and fallen under the train.

Mott, who took the call, was duly sympathetic.

'It was my fault he was there,' the young man said miserably. 'I'd asked him to go and see my mother about something. I've been away for a while, you see.' He paused and admitted bashfully, 'On my honeymoon, actually.'

Mott gravely congratulated him.

'Apparently Mother's been in a bit of a panic, because she didn't know where I was,' the confession ingenuously continued. 'But she shouldn't have bothered the police. We just went off and did it in private. Got married, I mean. Mother was dead set on me taking more exams and getting established and all that before I took on responsibilities. I guess I shouldn't have pulled the wool over her eyes as I did, but it seemed the only way at the time.'

'I think it might be better,' Mott advised, 'if we met before you went home. Can you come up right away? Have you transport?'

'Yes. Debbie has a little banger. The roads aren't too bad now. The traffic's cleared most of the snow. Where would you like us to meet?'

Mott gave him instructions how to get there, suggested a meeting at three p.m. and opted for a quick visit to Mrs Halliday in the meantime.

He found her still distraught over Alastair's death. 'I had a nice ham salad all ready for him,' she said, 'and his bed aired.'

'Never mind,' Mott consoled her. 'Perhaps that'll do for your son, if he's going to stay over. He should be along to see you in the late afternoon.'

She gaped at him. 'Piers? You're letting him go?'

'We don't have him. He rang in this morning, because he knew we were making inquiries. He's perfectly all right. Nothing for you to worry about, as far as we know.'

'But then why did Alastair—?'

'I think Piers wanted you warned about something: what he's been up to instead of taking up the VSO vacancy. Just so that you'd be used to the idea before you met him – and his wife.'

After that it was hard to get Edith Halliday on to the subject of Elinor. She took off like a hydrogen balloon, but

with such a mixture of relief, astonishment and appre-
hension that she was barely coherent.

'But *who?*' she insisted, once the fact was accepted.

Given the name Debbie, she was no wiser. 'I can't have
met her. Oh, it's too bad of him. He's not even twenty-
one, you know. And all that studying yet to do.'

Eventually it struck her that she too must make a good
first impression. She looked anxiously round the rather
forbidding room. 'I ought to get some flowers. And the
cake tin's empty. I didn't bother for Alastair—'

'Mrs Halliday, if you'd just give me a minute or two and
answer some questions, I'd be on my way and leave you to
get things ready.'

'Oh dear. Yes. Well, what do you want to ask?'

'When did you first see Francine as a little baby?'

It hadn't been a subject she expected. 'You want the date?
I don't know. But she was about ten days old. Elinor had no
shame at all about the – illegitimacy, you know. She insisted
on sending us all cards to announce the birth. And she
wouldn't stay the full recovery period in the nursing home,
although she'd had such a bad time. She was living in Stoke
Poges then, unmarried, of course, and she had Nanny
Burgess come to look after her and the baby. I don't know
how she persuaded her to come. Nanny was very particular
about the cases she took on. But she stayed with Elinor until
she went abroad when Francine was two months old.'

'Where did she have the baby? And is Nanny Burgess still
about?'

'Three Oaks Maternity Hospital. Nanny's retired now,
but she's still quite active. I could find you her address if it's
important.'

She looked out her address book and Mott wrote down
the particulars he wanted.

'I can't think what you need to go so far back for,' she said
reprovingly as she showed him to the door. He grinned,
observing that Mrs Halliday was finally returning to normal.

He found Z had finished calculating times required for
various routes between Pinewood and Oxford Circus by
various means of transport. Motor-cycle, she decided, was

the best bet, but even that was running it fine, the hard part being to find somewhere secure to leave the machine on arrival. And why should Carradine then suddenly plunge into the Underground system? Assuming that Alastair had walked from the bookshop, it was almost certain that Carradine would have arrived there after he'd left.

'Good,' Mott told her. 'I wasn't sold on Carradine for Alastair's killer anyway. It could be that they'd never even heard of each other. Now, while I grab a sandwich, could you contact Three Oaks Maternity Hospital and find out if Elinor gave birth to a live child there at the date on Francine's certificate? They'll have to dive into the archives for that, so while you're waiting for their answer, ring Nanny Burgess at this number. Find out if Elinor was the baby's natural mother, or merely putting on an act.'

Debbie Halliday was small with long, dark hair, soft brown eyes and a tip-tilted nose. Despite Piers' protective air, she impressed Mott as well able to look after herself. After half an hour's question and answer session, it looked to him as if the ingenuous young man had exchanged one organizing woman for another. But his bride had the added virtues of a sense of humour and a modicum of tact. Piers would surely benefit from being under new management.

He was grateful that Mott had broken the ice with his mother and that she was at least partially prepared to welcome the new member of the family.

'There will certainly be questions the Met need to put to you, because of your connection with Alastair Bartholomew,' Mott told the young man. 'But if you're staying over with your mother for a while, I can probably arrange that you needn't go to see them in person.'

He saw the young couple out and returned to see how far Z had gone with checking on the birth of Francine Webster.

'I don't think we need bother with the Maternity Hospital's archives,' she said. 'Nanny Burgess has told all. Elinor had an emergency Caesarean section after partial renal failure, and she was told she'd not be able to have another child. The baby was a "dear little girl, quite perfect". So maybe that one wasn't the Francine we know, if she was really born deformed.'

'Curiouser and curiouser,' quoted Mott. 'We now have not only to match a mother to our Francine, but to find what Elinor did with her own child. Did Nanny happen to say where Elinor went when she took the baby "abroad"?'

'She said Italy, but didn't know what part. Is it too way out to think she might have lost her own baby with some childhood disease and adopted – well, acquired in lieu – some local child not wanted because of her deformity?'

'In which case, Josh doesn't come into it. And he would have named her as his natural daughter merely to ensure she lost less in death duty as his heiress.'

'At risk of branding Elinor with the stigma of incest? I don't think so, Angus.'

'Because he wouldn't rank money above old-fashioned honour? But surely this whole case is about money, and who benefits most from the rest?'

'Well, is it? I get the feeling the Boss is sniffing at quite another track.'

'Now that his nose is getting back to its normal proportions,' said the DI, grinning, 'maybe we ought to take that seriously.'

Godden had been moved from Intensive Therapy to a small room off the Surgical Ward. There were screens round his bed. A young nurse showed Yeadings the way to the waiting-room, where he found Francine sitting with Elinor.

His arrival appeared momentarily to paralyse them, then Francine sprang up. 'Oh no! Not now. Please, not now.'

But Elinor stretched out a hand. 'If not now, then never. And I've a lot on my conscience.'

She looked older, sombre. Her red curls, strained back and tied tightly behind her ears, left exposed the tilting planes and vulnerable hollows of her face. He became aware of the skull beneath the flesh, of beauty's mortality.

'No,' Francine said again, with even greater horror dawning. But she was looking at Elinor. 'Not you! It couldn't have been you!'

TWENTY-ONE

ELINOR GAZED BACK HEAVY-EYED. 'You must hate me if you could think that for a minute. It wasn't I who tampered with your car to make you crash. I certainly never killed Josh. And I didn't put Alastair under any train. But it was my fault just the same. All of it. Francine, I need to speak to Mr Yeadings alone.'

'I'm staying. I have to hear what you say, Elinor. I'm involved. Do you think I didn't see I've been made the scapegoat all along?'

Elinor looked abashed. 'I only want to explain about the false alibi I gave.'

'Oh, that.' Francine took a deep breath. 'You needn't spare my feelings. You see, I know about it. He told me everything last night. We had a sort of cleaning-up session. God, the Augean stables have nothing on my family!'

Yeadings coughed discreetly. 'Perhaps I could be allowed in on this? Mrs Godden has revised her earlier statement to admit she was in the company of an unnamed man. They met to say goodbye to each other.'

'The man was Roddy,' Francine stated defiantly. 'Roddy Carradine. As doubtless you know, we've been lovers for some time. He admitted he'd had sex with Elinor twice while he still believed she was my mother.'

'It was my fault, Francine. All this was my fault. It happened several weeks ago. I was driving home down the M4 and the clutch went soft. I could hardly change gear. I was afraid I'd not get back. You know what a duffer I am about technical things. But I wasn't far from your place and you always know all the answers. I ran off the motorway and rang the flat. You weren't in and Roddy answered. He offered to come and pick me up. We left my

210

car at a nearby garage and he invited me back for a coffee. I was curious about him and . . .'

'And I hadn't declared any interest. I know. At that point I was just using him. I guess you did the same.'

'No! No, it wasn't like that at all. He'd been running some old tapes to re-record them. *La Mer, La Vie en Rose*, all that sweet, innocent stuff from the past. I wanted to hear them. We started dancing.'

'He swept you off your feet?' The sarcasm was there, but tinged with something not unlike sympathy.

'D'you know, he *did*, Francine. I was – vulnerable. I know I'm twice his age, and I'd never set eyes on him before, but – it just happened.'

'So, afterwards, still using my car, he drove you home. It must have been that day I had to go to London for some drawings. I went up by train, and I never noticed afterwards that the car had been used. That was a fortnight before the accident.'

'Shall I suggest what happened next, Mrs Godden?' Yeadings waited, while the two women became aware again of his presence.

'Your husband must have been on his way home when he saw you in the car, witnessed the tender leave-taking.'

'I got out a hundred yards short of our drive. We kissed goodbye.' She shivered. 'Yes, he must have been on the road behind and seen us.'

'And followed the car back afterwards.'

Francine leaned forward, speaking sharply. 'He wouldn't have known it was my car, my flat. I'd kept away so long.'

Yeadings nodded. 'A fortnight before the accident, as you said. Because he needed time to make the tool to cut the brake fluid feed. I imagine he adapted some surgical instrument. He could even have had it done by a hospital technician to his own specifications. There were a number of ways he could have made the car un-roadworthy, but he chose the hardest, a slow leaking of brake fluid through fine perforations in the metal part of the feed. Perhaps he hoped that in any subsequent crash it wouldn't be detected.'

211

'He would have done it the Saturday night before the meeting at Hadrian's,' Elinor said. 'Roddy and I went in my car to the Holiday Inn at Heathrow. Frank must have been appalled when he heard it was Francine and Dominic he'd injured, when he'd meant it to be my lover.'

Woodenly Francine ignored the new mention of Roddy. 'So Frank had picked the garage lock after dark, and fiddled his way into the car to open the bonnet. Did you know you were married to such an accomplished break-in artist?'

'Did I know I was married to a murderer?'

'Oh, sorry, sorry!' Francine rose and moved across the room. She stood, arms folded, looking out at the still, white expanse of the hospital lawn. Even the jasmine bush that framed the window was loaded with snow a half-inch deep, each dark-edged tiny leaf precisely etched, too decorative to seem real.

She remembered standing before at a window at Henley, when the rising gale had whipped fine branches across the panes with an eery screeching. It was the night she had left a note for her mother, who was late coming home to dress for a party. And Frank's car had been coming in as she drove out on to the road. So soon after her own arrival. Coming back with his flu just starting.

Frank, who had surely come up to Elinor's room and found the note left under her hairbrush. Which he would have read. So he knew about Hadrian giving Josh money to place on Tontine. And in his already anguished, disintegrating mind the hideous idea had formed: that if he started killing off the rest of the family, suspicion must fall on the one who'd known that the survivor would take all. And Elinor would be the first to believe that this was Francine.

She closed her eyes, leaning her head against the cool panes. 'You remember the note I left for you – after I'd been up to Josh's the last time?'

'Yes.'

'When you heard he was murdered you must have thought I'd done it.'

'Of course not. You loved Josh. One reason I agreed

with him not to tell you he was your father: you loved him enough without knowing. That way you had both of us. If you'd known, then I'd have had no rights at all . . .'

Elinor shook her head vehemently. 'Besides, if you had killed him, would you have told me you'd been there, that Josh had confided in you about the tontine? No, I never thought for a moment it could be you, even when everything got confused over the photograph Dominic had got hold of.

'That child in the photo wasn't this Francine, you see, Mr Yeadings. That was my own baby, killed in the same car crash that killed this Fran's real mother. I was injured, sitting in the back with the two babies. In the Italian hospital, while I was unconscious, they assumed that the surviving baby was mine. It was Josh's, but all that I had left then, so I said nothing.

'Jill had been Josh's mistress, an ambitious young actress. She wouldn't let him know she was pregnant, but came abroad to me, and I looked after her until Fran was born. It was only a month after that that Jill crashed the car on a mountain road. Her baby's birth was never registered; mine had been, in England, months before. I just did nothing, stayed abroad until the baby was grown enough to pass for mine. Josh was heartbroken after I told him, but we left it this way.'

She raised her head to look fully at Yeadings. 'That photo was all I had to prove to myself the other Fran had ever existed. Somehow Frank must have found it and made the same mistake that Dominic did later. By then we were too far apart for me to be able to talk about it.'

'And sending it in a book to Morton, where Dominic found it, that would be Frank's doing too,' Francine claimed. 'I think it was deliberate, meaning to make sure that eventually it would be shown to me and I'd think that once I'd been quite normal. Like Dominic, he jumped to the conclusion that there'd been some accident which you covered up.'

'Thought I'd been responsible, more than likely. He let it eat away at him; another proof of my deceiving nature. It was all part of his secondary plan – to destroy me by getting at you. And that idea only struck him after he'd wrecked your car, when fate had nearly given him you, instead of my lover as he'd intended.'

Yeadings drew them back to the subject of murder. 'So, on Tuesday, knowing Francine came straight from seeing Josh, Frank Godden drove over to Turville Heath and let himself into the hothouses, perhaps meaning to destroy the valuable plants first. He saw everything still set up after the photographs, and conceived the idea of luring Josh out there where he guessed Francine's recent fingerprints would be.'

He eyed the two women with sympathy. 'We can only guess at this stage how he did it.'

'There's an alarm bell,' Francine muttered. 'It rings in the house when the temperature drops. Leaving the outer door open would be enough to set it off.'

'So if Josh Webster dashed straight out there, Godden wouldn't have had time to lift the duckboards then. He would have started to give some explanation for his presence, waited for the other man to turn his back, and then struck him with some instrument he brought with him. Afterwards, while Josh was unconscious, he arranged the electrocution.'

'Hideous,' said Elinor. 'But you know, don't you, he wasn't in charge of his own mind? He must have been into morphine for some time. It's not unknown for doctors to start taking it when they're dogged by pain. It wasn't flu as he pretended. They've done scans here. It's a brain tumour, quite advanced.'

'Yes, so I understand from the surgeon.'

'What are you going to do?'

'Ask the Met to have one of their men sit by him until we can have a chat.'

'You've no pity, have you?'

Yeadings didn't answer, but started buttoning his raincoat. 'For the present, I'll say goodbye. Mrs Godden, Miss Webster.'

Francine stood at the window until she saw his bulky figure pass below. 'He's gone,' she said dully, then turned on the woman she had so long taken for her mother.

'God, Elinor, why did you marry Frank?'

The older woman spread her hands outwards in a gesture of hopelessness. 'He was wickedly handsome. Or so I thought then.'

She smiled bitterly, censuring her earlier self. 'A dark and brooding presence promising all manner of dangerous excitements. Oberon, the archetypal hunter-lover playing with Titania, determined to have his way. Fascinating, thrilling.

'But it wasn't to be like that.' Her shoulders drooped despondently. She seemed to be seeking inspiration from her fingers tightly latched together in her lap. She took a deep breath, again attempted to explain, as much for herself as for the girl.

'We were drawn physically – fatally – together. Perhaps if we'd only been lovers, not married, if would have flared and been quickly finished. Instead it smouldered uncertainly, never broke into open passion. I think I was too potent a draught for him. I don't mean he was emasculated by my sexuality, just quenched. Imperceptibly he slid into a different rôle. He became part child, part rejected suitor. As though to accept my love wasn't in his gift. I don't know. I've never really understood. Lately I didn't care to.'

She shuddered. 'I suppose that subconsciously I'd recognized something was going very wrong inside his mind. I couldn't stand him near me.'

The established pattern, Francine thought sadly: Elinor craving the dominant master, serving the weak dependant. But on this occasion finding both needs frustratingly centred on the one person.

Finally the ambivalence demanded of her must have become unbearable; and how far had it gone to create the monster Godden turned into, reaping her whirlwind?

No, blaming Elinor was unfair. Accident had brought the two together, a lethal admixture. If not in Elinor, then somewhere else, some other time, he would have met up with the catalyst his strange nature required to complete its disintegration.

Elinor was a victim as surely as she herself had almost

been, although what Godden had felt for his wife was a hopeless love. For herself something totally different.

'It's terrible,' she said in a small voice, 'to know somebody hates you like that. Really hates enough to kill. Why me?'

'Someone had to be blamed for his inadequacy. You were my child, he was my husband. If you wouldn't bond us into a family, you had to be the barrier, the reason that we weren't complete.'

'But he wouldn't have done what he did unless he hated me. He did, and I always knew it, even when I was quite small and he tried to make me like him.'

'Think of it as the counterweight,' Elinor said almost lightly. 'It's only fair, after all, when we all love you so much.'

Francine stared her disbelief.

'Well, of course we do, you idiot,' said the woman she had so long believed her mother. 'Old Hadrian does, Josh did, Roddy does, I damn well know I do.' She gave a little choking laugh. 'And how about your old grizzly of a Detective-Superintendent? If he didn't have such a sense of honour and duty, he'd have swept you off to some desert island long before this.'

'What – utter – bilge!' Francine protested, grinning like a schoolgirl. Then she smiled more gently. All the same she *had* reminded him of his long-lost first love. In all the chill of present disasters, it was a warming thought.

Mike Yeadings made the necessary arrangements with the Met and drove back to Thames Valley, where he found the team assembled because Mott had received a tip-off that 'Fleecy' Lamb (Terminal Greed according to Beaumont) had a big con set up. After the misery of family complexities it seemed a relief to be dealing again with professional criminals.

He was tasking the Intelligence Surveillance Team, when the uniformed Inspector reported a prisoner brought in on a charge of GBH. The victim was an ambulance case, the attacker Janey Hunter's mother. Half the size of the Bowles woman, she'd returned to Holtspur, gone along to her neighbour's house and boiled over. All the respectable, habitual restraint and social conditioning had frayed to bits.

'It wasn't enough for her that the Bowles man should get his just deserts,' said the Inspector. 'She knew his wife had covered up about her own daughter's abuse. Mrs Hunter decided for herself where the guilt lay, and acted on it. So, in the final analysis, who is the victim?'

'Families!' said Yeadings in a despairing way, and prepared to go home to his own.

Two days later, Godden's mental state having stabilized somewhat, and before he was due for surgery, Yeadings went to London again to see him. This time he was shown to the man's bedside and found him alone.

He greeted the detective sardonically. 'I have been expecting you. I'm glad you've come.'

'Sometimes,' Yeadings said heavily, 'criminals make mistakes half-deliberately, to get caught and have it all done with.'

The sick man smiled wanly. 'You were doing so well. I could feel the police getting closer. A matter of time. And you deserved – a little something. Another body. I think, even as I caught sight of Alastair in the crowd, in that confusion of compulsions I could recognize it as a final way out.'

A chill slithered between the policeman's shoulders at the reflective tone, empty of any emotion.

'What finally led you to me? I left you a choice of other suspects.'

'It came together of itself. All I had to ask myself was where you picked up the black cab on the evening you met your wife. A Saturday in January Sales season, you'd have stood little chance of an empty cab anywhere near Oxford Circus. And it's left to the minicabs to pick up at given addresses. So you took the Tube. After you'd chanced to sight Alastair, followed him to the platform for the northbound Bakerloo Line, and dispatched him, causing both directions to be closed, the Victoria Line stayed open. You went four quick stops to Vauxhall Station, and picked up an emptying cab there for the straight southbank trip to the Festival Hall.

'It took us a while to find the right driver, but he remembered you. Your photograph in an old *London Life* helped. He's been in here since and confirmed the identification. You may have taken him for a hospital porter.'

Godden shrugged, smiled, said, 'Although Francine thinks me an utter wimp, it isn't in me to hand you an unsolicited confession. Or would that take more courage than I think I have?'

A look of hopelessness came over his face. 'I don't know. It's a muddle. Don't seem to know anything these days.'

Yeadings sat on. There had to be more.

'Know,' Godden repeated, and seemed to search for some context for the word. 'Know enough – as a surgeon of sorts – to accept that for survival a patient needs the will to live.'

'Are you saying you haven't?'

'Survive for prolonged "recuperation" in prison – shut in with swindlers and thugs and sexual perverts?' His voice was over-fastidious. 'Joe's a clever man with his scalpel, but I'll beat him, poor sod. I'll get away.'

That was his last word, Yeadings knew. He stood, put his chair tidily back against the wall.

In the foyer he ran into a distracted Elinor, coming swiftly in. She stopped and faced up to him passionately. 'You've been harrassing him! Even now. *In here.*'

Yeadings shook his head. 'There were things he needed to talk about. He'd kept silent too long.'

Something seemed to die in her. Even darkened by pain, her eyes were beautiful.

'He didn't do any of it. It wasn't him, Superintendent. That's God's truth.'

Such fervency carried conviction, but he couldn't accept it. He waited.

'Not my Frankie,' she said, her voice breaking at last. 'Not him. It was that thing growing inside him. Killing his brain, killing us all off one after the other.'

*

One thing remained to be done. Next morning Yeadings rang Lynalls and spoke to Mr Chadwala. The nurse brought the news of Frank Godden's guilt along with Hadrian Bascombe's breakfast Bran Flakes.

The old man was dumbfounded. '*He* was the killer? But Frank Godden – he's a non-person. He never counted.'

The Parsee nurse lowered his eyes modestly. 'Exactly,' he said.

Bascombe gave him a startled glance, seemed to see him in a new light, and felt the first stirrings of a personal unease.